THE SNOWDEN AVALANCHE

DEREK SWANNSON

BOOKS BY DEREK SWANNSON

The Snowden Avalanche

Crash Gordon and the Mysteries of Kingsburg

Crash Gordon and the Revelations from Big Sur

Crash Gordon and the Illuminati Underground

New York

THE SNOWDEN AVALANCHE

DEREK SWANNSON

- DICK CHENEY — U.S. VICE PRESIDENT
- GEORGE W. BUSH — 43RD U.S. PRESIDENT
- YASSIN AL-QADI — AL-QAEDA & PTECH FINANCIER
- PTECH
- DONALD RUMSFELD — U.S. SECRETARY OF DEFENSE
- PENTAGON "CANNOT TRACK" $2.3 TRILLION ANNOUNCED ON 9/10/01
- FLORIDA-MACDILL AIR FORCE BASE
- PROJECT FOR A NEW AMERICAN CENTURY
- FTS FLIGHT TERMINATION SYSTEM
- HANI HANJOUR — HIJACKER "PILOT" OF FLIGHT 77 (PENTAGON)
- MOHAMMED ATTA — HIJACKER "PILOT" OF FLIGHT 11 (ONE WTC)

THE SNOWDEN AVALANCHE is a work of fiction. When the names of 'real' places, corporations, institutions, secret societies, and public figures are projected onto *The Snowden Avalanche*'s fictional landscape, they are used fictitiously. All other names, characters, locales, and events are products of the author's imagination or, at best, scribbled missives from the collective unconscious. Any apparent similarity to actual persons, living or dead, is not intended by the author and is purely a matter of the intricate workings of chance and synchronicity, or—as some might call it—fate. (Besides...what harm can come from a little fiction, when the facts are so much more appalling?)

Copyright © 2014 by Three Graces Press, LLC
http://www.threegracespress.com
All rights reserved.

Printed in the United States of America. No part of this book may be used or reproduced in any manner whatsoever without written permission except in the case of brief quotations embodied in critical articles and reviews. For information contact: publisher@threegracespress.com.

Book Design by Darren Westlund
Cover Painting, *The Last Polar Bear*, by Robert Bowen

FIRST EDITION

ISBN-13: 978-0-9981042-1-8

for my three graces

CONTENTS

THE WORLD (REVERSED)
3

THE HIGH PRIESTESS
4

THE HIEROPHANT
8

TEMPERANCE
13

THE HANGED MAN
17

JUSTICE
24

STRENGTH
35

THE EMPEROR
41

THE WHEEL
46

THE LOVERS
49

THE TOWER
53

THE MAGICIAN
66

THE FOOL
71

THE HERMIT
72

THE EMPRESS
89

THE STARS
97

THE CHARIOT
107

DEATH
114

THE DEVIL
135

THE MOON
145

THE SUN
154

JUDGEMENT
174

THE WORLD
181

To be corrupted by totalitarianism one does not have to live in a totalitarian country.

 —George Orwell, *The Prevention of Literature*

The thing about people who are truly and malignantly crazy: their real genius is for making the people around them think they themselves are crazy. In military science this is called Psy-Ops, for your info.

 —David Foster Wallace, *Infinite Jest*

It is no measure of health to be well adjusted to a profoundly sick society.

 —Jiddu Krishnamurti

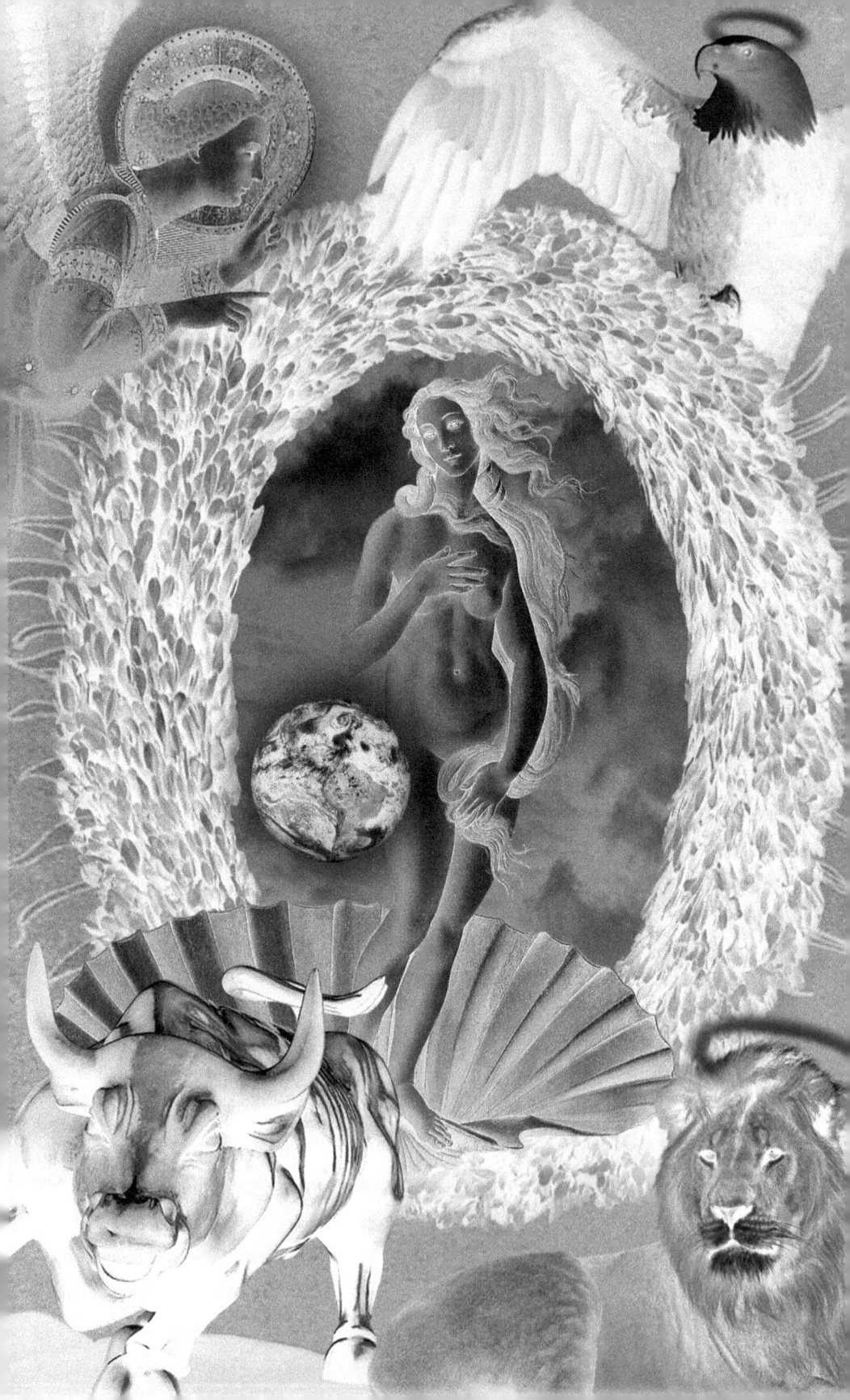

THE WORLD (REVERSED)

No one knows why They did it. Or how.

The keys to the National Security Agency's kingdom were in the top secret documents leaked by Edward Snowden to the *Guardian* and the *Washington Post* in June of 2013. Or so the rumors had it. Somewhere in the 1.7 million documents allegedly snagged by Snowden's web crawler there was an all-access pass to the NSA's vast arsenal of mass surveillance programs—PRISM, X-KEYSCORE, FAIRVIEW, MUSCULAR, BLARNEY, PROJECT BULLRUN, EGOTISTICAL GIRAFFE... all of them. The NSA had been storing and analyzing phone communications, text messages, email, and Internet metadata from almost everyone on the planet without any warrants or oversight since at least 2007. Which was bad enough, but the real blow to our collective sense of privacy came later, during the Snowden Avalanche, when some clever web bot hacked into the NSA's Utah Data Center and started making a mirror site of everything it found there. Suddenly, all that very personal information became searchable and available to anyone for a small fee. MasterCard, Visa, PayPal, or eCoins accepted.

According to the rumors, that was the real reason why Jeff Bezos bought the *Washington Post* for $250 million just two months after Snowden leaked his docs: the secretive Seattle billionaire wanted the Snowden cache so he could get at the NSA intel and commoditize it. But did that really make sense? When Bezos became the *Post*'s owner, his Amazon Web Services was already providing private cloud services to the CIA on a ten-year contract worth around $600 million. He was in too deep with the Deep State in the United States to risk pissing off the NSA. *Unless...*

...unless the NSA and the CIA *wanted* all that data out in the open.

Information wants to be free, right? But some libertarian Noam Chomsky types say we don't live in a free society when we're monitored every second of the day and our every action is subject to public scrutiny and potential legal prosecution. That's a recipe for Orwellian tyranny.

If the rumors are to be believed, we're all royally screwed.

THE HIGH PRIESTESS

Sabina Hrafnsson didn't know what to make of the rumors, but she knew how to capitalize on the Snowden Avalanche. Right after she was laid off from her human resources job at Fordham, she dusted off her old Bachelor of Social Work degree from UC Santa Cruz and started telling people on LinkedIn and Twitter that she was now a professional iAesthetician and eGrief Counselor.

Business was flat-out booming.

As a Manhattan-based iAesthetician, Sabina helps buff up the images of those who got caught in the Snowden Avalanche with their metaphorical pants down (often jacking off in a frenzy, if their marathon YouPorn sessions were any indication…). Alternatively, as an eGrief Counselor, Sabina helps console those snooping souls who paid to find out things about their spouses or loved ones that they really, deep-down, didn't want to know.

On the whole, she tends to like her iAesthetician clients better.

Take Frank McKernan, for example—her first paying customer. She'd met him at a Bikram yoga class near the Whole Foods on West Twenty-Fourth and they'd hit it off. Frank was a sixty-four-year-old former prosecutor for the Criminal Enforcement and Financial Crimes Bureau of the New York State Attorney General's Office. He was now semi-retired, with a lucrative law firm in Montclair, New Jersey and another one, barely turning a profit, in Jamaica, Queens. Frank spent most of his time commuting and writing legal briefs. He had a Bozo frizz of wiry silver hair, a wicked sense of humor, and a strong yen for obese black prostitutes.

"The bigger the booty, the better..." he liked to say. His high-pitched New Jersey accent made him sound like Joe Pesci on helium. Frank was a scrawny little guy—and by his own admission "hung like a hummingbird"—so what he needed with all that bounteous buttcandy remained a mystery.

Prior to the Snowden Avalanche, Frank's sexual proclivities might have remained a mystery, too. But when he made the ill-considered decision to run for mayor of Montclair, it all came out: the selfies on Facebook featuring his lipstick-sized erection; the hi-def video of jovial, jiggly, dark-skinned dominatrixes beating him with rubber iguanas until he jizzed in his tighty whities; his email proclamations of undying love for women named Rashonda, LaQueefa, and Dezsolisha.

"I screwed myself out of a job!" Frank complained to Sabina, although it seemed unlikely he would have won the election even in the absence of such tawdry revelations. He'd come in fifth out of four candidates (a joke write-in campaign to elect Montclair resident Stephen Colbert—the ballsy "Late Show" host—had placed third). Shortly after the polls closed, Frank had hired Sabina to head off his impending divorce.

"What's with all the rubber iguanas, Frank?" she'd asked him while he assumed a Downward Facing Dog pose. Sabina was still months away from renting her own office, so their first business meetings took place in the empty loft after their Bikram yoga class.

"*Ooof,* the iguanas..." Frank huffed, chin nearly touching the mat, his old man butt, in baggy Nike running shorts, hiked high in the air. "It's a re-enactment of my initiation into a fraternal order of lumber merchants," he explained. "The Hoo-Hoo Club, they called it. I was a young man back then, barely out of my teens. I don't know why it still gets to me the way it does. Reminds me of sowing my wild oats, I guess. Those Hoo-Hoos were a depraved bunch."

"The Hoo-Hoos had a thing for voluptuous African American ladies?"

"No. Not that I'm aware of." Frank sat back on his haunches in a shambolic half-lotus. "That's just my personal spin on the initiation ceremony—although if the hoes showed up smelling like lumber, they got a big bonus. The real deal featured a bunch of middle-aged white guys in their underpants. Lots of muttonchop sideburns and aviator shades. The iguanas were called Sacred Jabberwocks. It was the seventies… what can I say?"

"Posting that video on NubianKinks.com might've been a mistake on your part. I guess you can see that now."

"Hey, it was anonymous and encrypted!"

"Yeah, but your face wasn't. With the new multimodal biometric identification systems, nobody's anonymous these days."

"I don't get it," said Frank, feigning guilelessness. "Anthony Weiner hit up all those young gals from Seattle, going around calling himself 'Carlos Danger'—I mean, *c'mon!*—and now look at him. Granted, the man's political career took a nosedive when he had to resign from congress, but six years later he comes roarin' back and blows Bill de Blasio out of the water. Now he's friggin' Mayor of New York!"

"Well, he had that name, Weiner, and—" Sabina had to take a moment to tamp down a hot flame of professional envy. Anthony Weiner's iAesthetician, Shirley Abraxas, had set the benchmark for everyone in her field. She was the person who'd coaxed Weiner into developing a sense of humor after the Snowden Avalanche gave a whole lot of other people cause to feel some sympathy for his former fuck-ups. Her idea to have Weiner campaign from an Oscar Mayer wienermobile had been a stroke of genius. Ditto for her campaign slogan: "You Can't Keep Weiner Down." Anthony Weiner had become the smiling icon of tolerance during a time when ordinary citizens were having their private transgressions revealed in such astonishing numbers that the whole aggrieved nation seemed to be coming to the collective decision that the Puritan prudery of America's first settlers finally, and forever, had to be kicked to the curb.

"So you're thinking your wife should stick by you like Huma stuck by her Weiner Man?" Sabina asked Frank.

"Look," he said, massaging his nuts through his shorts, "my wife hasn't given me so much as a handjob since the twin towers fell. Call it post-traumatic frigidity—or just plain ol' menopause. Doesn't matter. I still love her. I mean, shit, she's the mother of my kids. They're both grown and out of the house now, but who cares? We still have a bond. Besides, who else is she gonna shack up with at her age?"

"Maybe she has plans to take you for all you're worth so she can live out the rest of her life as an independently wealthy single woman." Sabina had some fantasies along similar lines, although she'd never found a rich husband to fleece. Her occasional boyfriends tended to be handsome, creative, charismatic, invariably impoverished—and premature ejaculators to a man. She'd been proposed to at least a dozen times, but she'd never had an orgasm during intercourse (even though she could climax like crazy if the guy was willing to go down on her). Because of that—so she told herself—she was still holding out on the marriage front.

Waiting for Mister Magic Penis.

"Pammy's not like that," Frank admonished her, exhibiting something like chivalry. "She'd be lost out there on her own. I just need to give her a good excuse to take me back."

"Some balm for her wounded pride, huh?" Sabina started to focus on the task at hand. "Then maybe you should play up the helpless diseased sex addict angle. Tell her you thought NubianKinks.com was a hair salon when you first clicked on it. You had no idea it would turn you into a raving sex maniac. Blame it all on the website. Admit you're powerless. Embrace a higher power and all that crap. Promise her you'll go to Gonzo Nubian Goddesses Anonymous."

"Is there really a Gonzo Nubian Goddesses Anonymous?"

"No, but I'll pretend to be your lesbian sponsor. I'll also place a fake ad for GNG Anon in the back pages of the *Village Voice*—and create a website for it on WordPress—so you can show it to her."

"You'd do that for me?"

"Sure—for a small fee."

"You're all right, Sabina. If it wasn't for your skinny little white girl butt, I'd be falling in love with you right now."

"Thanks… I think."

Sabina had been complimented on her ass enough times to know it was one of her best features. Having seen the online pics of Frank's tiny pink mini-erection, she couldn't help but laugh at the absurdity of the old letch thinking he'd ever have a shot with her. Even at thirty-nine, she was way out of his league. Scandinavian genes had blessed her with a heart-shaped face, well-defined cheekbones, a perfect Barbie nose, and a thick mane of toffee-blonde hair that she usually kept in a silky side-braid resting on her left breast, where she tended to flick at it whenever she felt angry or tense. A tranny-chasing friend had once told Sabina she looked like that intrepid Alpine waif, Heidi, all grown up into a high-strung slut wearing see-through yoga pants from Lululemon.

Frank said, "You'll come out to the house sometimes when I get an uncontrollable boner, right?"

More laughter. "Won't Pammy be jealous?"

"I didn't mean it that way. I meant when the jungle fever threatens to overwhelm me. A little play-acting for Pammy's sake."

"Oh. Sure! But it'll cost ya. I don't like commuting."

"I'll pay whatever, if you think it'll do the trick."

"It's worth a shot, you freaky old bastard."

It took a few months, but Sabina's plan eventually worked. Pammy ended up taking Frank back. Their sex life even caught an updraft after Sabina discreetly suggested to Pammy that she might want to put on a little weight, trade in her flannel pajamas for a black crotchless fishnet bodystocking, and start referring to herself in the third person as "Maleeka" after dusk. Frank happily paid Sabina's piratical fees and began recommending her to all his clients in need of, as he called it: "Some PR on the DL."

Now, thanks in a large part to Frank's referrals, Sabina's former salary at Fordham looked like mere subsistence wages. These days she could afford to go out to dinner and shop at Saks pretty much whenever she wanted—even after paying the rent on her insanely expensive street-level apartment with its own private office entrance on the Upper West Side.

Gotta love Frank....

THE HIEROPHANT

Amazon's relentless affinity marketing had suckered her in again, damn them. Sabina was watching a cruddy made-for-web movie called *My Lactation Consultant Was A Lesbian Werewolf* late on a Friday night. The werewolf had just solved a baby's breast-feeding difficulties (by using its sharp claws to perform a near-bloodless lingual frenectomy) when Sabina's iPhone chimed in her Prada backpack. She picked up when she saw it was Frank.

"Hey, Frank. What's up?"

"I got another one for you."

"Another what?"

"Another finance guy. A skittish one this time, but with deep pockets."

Sabina let out an annoyed sigh. Not everyone's post-Avalanche troubles were as easily solved as Frank's. The bankers and other white-collar grifters were having an especially rough time. Vigilante justice was all the rage.

No one seemed to resent J.K. Rowling becoming a billionaire from the Harry Potter franchise. *(She'd put in a lot of hard work, banging out those books, and the kids loved them. Good for her!)* But more than a few people had started to resent all the finance guys getting rich for doing nothing more than feeding off other people's economic misery, for getting taxpayer bailouts when their precious long positions in crap CDOs or LBOs went south, and for thriving on sociopathic behavior that resembled, in toto (as Matt Taibbi famously described Goldman Sachs): "a great vampire squid wrapped around the face of humanity, relentlessly jamming its blood funnel into anything that smells like money."

The Snowden Avalanche had revealed the true extent of the finance guys' crimes, but the Justice Department throughout the Bush and Obama administrations had seemed disinclined to put the thieving assholes in jail to restore the public trust. So someone *(the Mafia? a rogue hackers' collective split-off from the Occupy Wall Street movement? ninja assassins posing as unpaid interns?)* had started offing the worst offenders in a variety of gruesome ways: drive-by shootings, "suicides" that weren't really suicides, and gangland-style executions of not just the number-fudging perpetrators, but often their entire families as well.

For years, the finance guys had behaved as if they had a free pass to steal from the rest of us without any consequences—probably because they believed their own hype that they were "the smartest guys in the room." Now that contemptuous attitude was morphing into something like raw fear. First the zillionaire founder of the Blackstone Group, Steven Schwarzman, had whined that the proposal to repeal the carried-interest tax loophole—from which he and his ilk benefitted—was akin to "when Hitler invaded Poland in 1939." Then the venture capitalist Tom Perkins—another self-appointed spokesman for the supposedly oppressed super-rich—had complained in a letter to the editor of the *Wall Street Journal* that the "rising tide of hatred" against the new crop of cyber-capital robber barons could be compared to the massacres of Kristallnacht.

Oh please. The enormous ingratitude shown to the rest of humanity by the average, exploitative billionaire was already bad enough. Now they had to compound the insult by likening themselves to Nazi-slaughtered Jews?

The finance guys were not among Sabina's favorite clients. A lot of them were pathological liars—and such deadbeats that she'd learned to always get paid up front whenever she had to work with one of them. But they were usually desperate for her services, and that desperation meant she could gouge them on fees, which kind of made her feel like Robin Hood. So screw it… she'd keep taking them on, if only to claw back a little *dinero* for the common people, like herself.

"Is he a hardcore criminal this time, or just another rich fuck with a guilty conscience?" Sabina asked Frank.

"Sabina, sweetie, you should know by now that I only send you guilty cocker spaniels… not real criminals. And hey, what're you doing home on a Friday night, anyway? Shouldn't you be out getting clueless guys to buy you drinks?"

"I can't deal with the dating scene anymore. Tinder and Pinch just make me nuts. I'm thinking I should just freeze my eggs and get a dog."

"I hear Goldendoodles make great pets. And they don't shed."

"Thanks. I'll take that under advisement."

"Boy, you're sure in a sour mood tonight. Wanna come over and watch some old *Soul Train* videos with me and the wife? It might help cheer you up."

"I would if you were closer, but it'd take me at least two hours to get out to Montclair right now."

"Right. And I'll probably have Maleeka bent over the sofa by then."

"I wouldn't want to interrupt your forty-five seconds of conjugal bliss."

Frank laughed. "You're such a pill, Sabina. Be honest with me… what gets you off? Anything?"

"Excuse me?"

"I'm serious! What gets your frosty little Norwegian cooze all hot 'n' bothered?"

"I don't think this is an appropriate conversation for us to be having, Frank."

"Maleeka doesn't mind—if that's what you're worried about. She's right here. She knows you're not my type."

Sabina could hear geriatric Pammy faintly talking trash as "Maleeka" in the background:

"True dat. But you best be gettin' off that phone, boy, or ima sit my fat ass down an' bust a gusher on yo yappy white lawyer face."

Pammy had learned her lessons well.

"I'm not worried about your wife," Sabina said.

"Then don't be so uptight!" Frank implored her. "If you can just unclench long enough to tell me what makes your pussy drool, maybe I can help you out."

"I'm not discussing my sex life with you, McPervin'. Just let it go. Sheesh."

"C'mon! There's nothing prurient about this—or, at least, not very. I just want to help. Like you helped me."

The truth was it had been a few years since she'd gotten laid. When her business had taken off, her sex life had ground to a halt. She hadn't planned it that way—it just happened. Her girlfriends had observed the same phenomenon in their own lives: when their relationships were working out, their careers generally sucked; and when their careers were going great, their relationships were in the dumps. You couldn't have both. That's why Sabina and her friends had concluded that this world had been created by a bad god—some jealous, murderous, patriarchal motherfucker with a long white beard, like Jehovah in the Bible.

A matriarchal goddess would have cut them some slack.

The other thing bumming her out was that the expiration date on her youthful hotness was arriving much sooner than she'd anticipated. Already, Sabina's supple Scandinavian skin was developing a crepey texture around her neck and elbows. It was kind of freaking her out. Sometimes, during her weaker moments, she had desperate thoughts that it was time to snag a man—any man—and pop out some kids. Lockdown her future, before it was too late.

As if thirty-nine wasn't already too late....

Sabina heaved out another annoyed sigh. "Okay, Frank, you really wanna know what turns me on?"

"You bet I do!"

"You ever watch *The Big Lebowski*?"

"Sure. Coen brothers. Great flick."

"Well, you know that scene where Sam Elliott bellies up to the bar next to Lebowski in the bowling alley? You know… with his cowboy hat and his big sexy mustache, sippin' on a sarsaparilla? That scene gets me goin' every time. I guess I like the philosophical cowboy type."

"Jesus, that's kinky!" Frank guffawed.

"Coming from you, that's just an absurd thing to say, Mister Iguana Man."

"Cowboys! Who knew?"

"While you were yanking your little crank to *Soul Train* every Saturday night, I was growing up watching old reruns of *Bonanza*."

"And *Hopalong Cassidy*!"

"That one was a little before my time," Sabina said tartly.

"If you like cowboys so much, what're you doing in New York? You should be out in Montana or Wyoming or someplace."

"I tried that when I was younger, but I just got beat up. Here's the trouble with real cowboys, Frank: most of them are dumb as dirt."

"So you weren't getting the philosophical side of the philosophical cowboy equation."

"Not even close."

"I sympathize with you, Sabina. I really do. A philosophical cowboy isn't something you can just go out and rent by the hour."

"Well, there *is* that one guy who goes around playing guitar for spare change in Times Square while wearing just a pair of cowboy boots and his tighty whities… but I'm pretty sure he's gay."

"I'll ask him about that next time I'm in town, if you're too shy to approach him."

"Don't bother, you crazy fuck."

"Really! He might be the one."

"I'm going to sleep now, Frank."

"Okay. Sweet dreams, Ice Cream Cakes. And hey, that finance guy I was telling you about? His name's Ronald… Ron Geng. He'll be calling you bright and early tomorrow."

"Anything I should know about him?"

"He's not the philosophical cowboy type. In fact, he's the exact opposite—so don't get your hopes up."

TEMPERANCE

Ron Geng turned out to be a freckle-faced, redheaded finance guy in a charcoal gray Brioni suit. He looked like the talk show host, Conan O'Brien—only shorter and with more prominent eyebrows. He met Sabina at her office around noon and said he could only stay for twenty minutes. He was on his lunch break.

"On a Saturday? Where do you work?" Sabina asked him.

"Limelight Research Capital," he said, as if that should mean something to her.

She'd never heard of it. "*Limelight*… wasn't that the name of the old church they turned into a druggy disco lounge over on West Twentieth?" She'd spent a few drink-slurred nights there in her sexually confused youth, but now it was just another yuppified shopping mall—an even worse desecration of the once hallowed grounds, in her opinion.

"That's different. We're a high-frequency trading firm," Ron said, grimacing at the oil painting by Maxine Olson looming above Sabina's desk. It was a five-foot wide hyperrealistic depiction of a cowboy's crotch: a close-up of dusty, hay-flecked Wrangler jeans harboring a huge moose-knuckle bulge crowned by a silver rodeo buckle.

Ron wasn't the first guy to be made uncomfortable by it.

"I'm Limelight's Chief Legal Officer," he added, maybe to reassert his manliness. It didn't help. He had that Wall Street vibe—like a frat boy all grown up, pumped full of testosterone and fast money—but there was something off about him. Guys like Ron usually had a flashy luxury watch on their wrist as a status-asserting fetish object. They also went in for expensive cologne. Ron had the watch—a rose gold Jaeger LeCoultre that was probably worth a six-pack of Rolexes—but he smelled like Pampers and burnt toast.

"What sort of illegal shenanigans have the boys at Limelight been up to recently?" Sabina asked, getting right to the point. "I'm assuming you're not here because you've been doing the Lord's work, helping out the poor and needy."

"No. To be honest, what I've been seeing lately has me thinking I should go in for some plastic surgery and move to South America on a fake passport."

"That doesn't work anymore. You can't just do the Nazi ratline thing and set up your own private torture clinic in the jungles of Argentina. They have ways of finding you now. Quantum compass technology is getting into everything."

"I was afraid of that."

"Limelight's been making some enemies, I take it?"

"That's the understatement of the year."

"Has your name been in the news much?"

"Constantly."

"I see. Well, you caught me off-guard here, Ron. I don't know much about you or your company. I'll have to do some research. But how are you thinking I might help you?"

"I need someone to help deflect the blame from me for what Limelight's about to do. The dookie will be hitting the fan in a big way, and I want my name kept out of it—if that's at all possible."

"First you'll have to tell me what Limelight's planning."

"I can't do that."

"You're buddies with Frank, right? I'm sure he told you I'm trustworthy… and loyal to my clients."

"Of course. But we don't have attorney-client privilege, and that's what I'd need in this situation, if I told you what I know."

"Maybe we can get married," Sabina joked. "Wives can't be forced to testify against their husbands, right?"

Ron wiped a hand across his mouth and mumbled, "I might like that…" with a puppyish look. *Was he blushing?* Hard to tell under all those freckles.

"Well, that ain't happenin', bud. So you either trust me with what you know, or I can't help you. It's your call. I have plenty of other clients to keep me busy."

Sabina was starting to wonder if taking on this Ron character was worth the hassle. What would she do with the extra cash, anyway? Buy some more shares in Google or Apple; get a couple of comfortable, not-too-hideous-looking bras from Natori; maybe eat a few more pork buns than usual at Momofuku?

Seriously, why bother?

"Look," said Ron, "just assume that crimes are about to be committed—crimes against some very powerful people. I need it to seem like I advised against those crimes so the powerful people won't have me killed. Can you help me out, or not?"

"Well, Ron, without knowing the specifics, right now all I can tell you is to quit the company and put some distance between you and your former employers. Then I can use my crack team of hackers and bloggers to help salvage your reputation with a stealth PR campaign on all the major media platforms."

"I can't quit. The money's too good."

"Money's not much use to you if you're dead."

"You don't understand... I have my family to think about. I'm a Mormon."

"So that means—what? You've got, like, fourteen wives?"

"Most Mormons don't have multiple spouses. That's only on TV. The Church of Latter-Day Saints abolished the practice of polygamy in 1890. But our faith encourages large families. My wife, Emma, and I have six great kids. Four boys and two girls."

"That's a lot of Mormon mouths to feed."

"You're not kidding. Plus, figure in the usual expenses on an eight-bedroom Manhattan townhouse and tuition times six for private schools and colleges down the road."

"*Holy Moroni!* It must be expensive to be you."

"That's why I can't quit. Besides, Wes Bramley is my best friend."

"Who's Wes Bramley?"

"Limelight's CEO. We were roommates in college and we've been in business together ever since."

"Yeah, Wes Bramley... I've heard that name somewhere before... but it wasn't connected to Limelight."

"Maybe you're thinking of MegaWire—the peer-to-peer file sharing business we started while Wes was still at Stanford getting his masters in electrical engineering."

"That's it! You guys were making a shit-ton of money until the big media companies took you to court, right?"

Ron nodded. "Millions. All tied up in litigation now. There's a 450 million dollar judgment against us that we're appealing. But that's just a drop in the bucket compared to what Limelight's been hauling in."

Sabina was deeply unimpressed. "I've read some stuff in the *Times* about high-frequency trading. You computer geeks with your sneaky algorithms… you're all just a bunch of high-tech rip-off artists. It's front-running on a scale that's never been seen before. You only make a few pennies on every share, but it adds up quick when you can trade up to a hundred million shares a day, doesn't it?"

"You're misinformed, like most people. The big investment banks and brokerage houses used to take a much larger bite out of investors. They made hundreds of billions, while HFT firms collectively take in only ten or twenty billion a year now."

"That's a psychopath's rationalization. It's like saying Hitler killed six million Jews, so it's okay if we go kill around a million Afghans and Iraqis with the latest high-tech military hardware."

"That's not psychopathic thinking. That was Bush administration foreign policy after 9/11."

"Right. Same fucking thing."

Ron let out an exasperated sigh and blinked his freckled eyelids. "I don't know why people insist on demonizing high-frequency trading. It's not evil. What we're doing is net positive for the world. Trading stock is now cheaper and more efficient than ever, thanks to HFT firms like ours. We provide the market with liquidity. If you have a pension fund and you need to sell some stocks to live on someday, you'll be in trouble if there isn't a buyer on the other side. We make sure there's always a buyer."

"Unless you decide a flash crash is more fun. We've been having a lot of those lately. You and Wes Bramley wouldn't know anything about that, would you?"

"I'm not at liberty to say."

"Fucking computer geeks! You're the same guys who put spy cams in sororities and now you think you run the goddam world."

Sabina decided not to mention that she was a bit of a computer geek herself. She knew HTML6, CSS4, and JavaScript cold, she was learning Python and Clojure just for fun, and she could whip up a cool website in less than a day using Photoshop, InDesign, and either Dreamweaver or the WordPress CMS. Whenever she ran into something she couldn't handle on her own (which didn't happen often), she had a small army of freelance hackers she could call upon to get the job done—young, socially inept geniuses that were loyal to her because she paid top dollar and let them beat off to topless videos of her on SnapChat.

Ron was saying, "Wes thinks someone else is running the world, actually. That's kind of what this is about."

"Oh yeah?" Sabina was ready to show him the door. He was coming across as one of those squirrelly, withholding bastards—another Machiavellian narcissist with nothing but contempt for anyone outside his toxic, über-wealthy tribe. She'd dated enough of those assholes to know she could start to hate him pretty quickly.

Besides, those pork buns at Momofuku were overrated.

"I have some documents on my jump drive here." Ron pulled out his keychain and dangled it in front of Sabina like a hypnotist's pocket watch. She recognized one of the keys as a stainless steel LaCie USB drive. "Wes has sent these around to everyone in the company. I won't be breaching my nondisclosure agreement if I share them with you. He's already published them on a public Internet forum up in Canada called 'Rigorous Intuition.' They make for some strange reading, but they'll give you an approximate idea of who Wes is planning to target."

Intrigued, Sabina took the proffered key drive and plugged it into her MacBook, saying, "There'd better not be any malware on here."

"It's clean," Ron promised her. "Just copy the folder named WesDocs. We'll meet again in a few days, after you've had a chance to look everything over."

"Am I getting paid for this?"

Ron opened his wallet. "How much do you want?"

While walking through her old neighborhood the other day, Sabina had seen some slick-looking speakers in the window of the Bang & Olufsen store on Broadway at Twenty-First.

Maybe she'd get those....

THE HANGED MAN

The WesDocs folder would have to wait. Sabina had a one-thirty appointment at the Union Square Barnes & Noble with a writer named

James Marrsden—another one of Frank's matchmaking gigs. Frank had told her she might want to get there early for Marrsden's reading from noon to one, but the last-minute meeting with Ron had made her late.

By the time she arrived, James Marrsden was already seated at a table signing books for a crowd of well over two hundred people. He looked like someone's lewd Irish uncle: scruffy gray beard, round rimless glasses, a jaunty tweed cap, and the most garish Hawaiian shirt Sabina had ever seen. Flaming toucans dive-bombed cowering, bare-breasted hula girls in a lush forest of fuchsia and chartreuse palm trees, like some hellish tropical vision Gauguin might have painted after dining on the legs of several varieties of psychotropic frogs.

Sabina bought a book and got in line, figuring she'd chat up the celebrated author while he was in his element.

Forty-five minutes later, James looked up at her and said, "And what's your name, pretty lady?" Pen poised above her copy of his latest novel—*The Ouroboros of Amsterdam*—he lowered his gaze until he was practically boring holes in her tits with his boggling eyes, magnified behind the thick lenses of his goofy hippie specs.

"I'm Sabina," she said, sticking out her hand. "Frank McKernan might've mentioned me to you."

"Oh shit! The PR chick!" James flashed her a charming smile enhanced by glittery white porcelain veneers. "Actually, it was Ian who hipped me to you."

"Ian who?"

"Frazier—another author guy, like me. He lives in the same town as Frank."

"Ian Frazier? You mean the guy who wrote *The Cursing Mommy's Book of Days*?"

"You know him?"

"Not personally. But I love that book! It's practically my goddam Bible. For the cursing part, not the mommy part, obviously."

"Yeah, I get that. You don't look like someone who's ever pushed a baby's head out of her vagina."

"Hey, I could be somebody's mommy. You don't know…."

James made a mild farting noise with his lips and started writing something on the flyleaf of her book.

"Oh, fuck you. I could, too," Sabina said.

"Right. Like I could be somebody's daddy."

"You don't have kids?"

"What? Did the shirt give it away?" James closed the book and handed it back to her. "Let's get out of here, Sabina. I've signed enough books for today." He stood up from the table and shrugged on a black silk bomber jacket with puffy white sleeves and a coiling red dragon embroidered on the back.

"You look like a gay Yakuza mobster in that jacket," Sabina informed him.

James laughed. "That's exactly the look I was going for."

Some Barnes & Noble staff members waylaid James before he could get out the door. Sabina opened the book he'd signed for her and read the inscription while James bantered with them:

Sabina!

> *Writing has led me on many adventures. For research purposes, I've flown a helicopter over Hearst Castle, I've gone swimming with whales off the coast of Maui... and I've fellated a polar bear.*
>
> *I'm hoping you can help me with that last one.*
>
> *XOXO, JAMES MARRSDEN*

So he was *that* guy....

It all came rushing back to her: The tabloid headlines and web media mockery, the telegenic hosts of talk shows and *Entertainment Tonight* pretending to be scandalized as they reported the story. At first, it had seemed like someone's sick idea of a joke, too outlandish to be true. Some guy had climbed into the new climate-controlled "Wild Arctic" exhibit at the Central Park Zoo and sucked off one of the polar bears. The man wasn't immediately identified, but within hours a rumor began to circulate—now, a year later, apparently confirmed—that the fearless polar bear cocksucker had been none other than the famed author and occasional movie actor, James Marrsden.

No wonder he needed a little iAesthetician help.

That was the trouble with having a pervert attorney referring clients to you: a lot of the referrals tended to be even worse perverts.

Years ago, Sabina had read a book about Bigfoot *bukkake* fetishists; now she fully expected to have one of those degenerates as a client before Frank was done with her.

It was a mild summer day, so she and James headed east on Fourteenth to Beauty Bar, where the drinks were strong and the walls were lined with vintage beauty salon chairs with the massive, alien-looking industrial hair dryers still attached. The bar, one of Sabina's old favorites, was quiet most afternoons. She thought it would be an ideal place to have a private conversation about what it felt like to give a sloppy blowjob to an Arctic apex predator.

"What kind of lunatic tries to deep-throat a polar bear?" Sabina asked James, point-blank, after they sat down with their drinks. "You could've been killed."

"First off," said James, "I didn't deep-throat him. I have a strong gag reflex. There's no way that could've happened."

"Okay, so you just slobbed his knob. Still… that's all different kinds of crazy. What were you thinking?"

"Honestly? I have no idea. I don't even remember doing it. I'm pretty sure someone spiked my Mocha Frappuccino."

"Oh, sure… a drug turned you into a unstoppable zoophiliac dick licker. Happens all the time."

"*Zoophiliac?* Is that even a real word?"

"It is," Sabina assured him.

"Good one."

"Convenient that you don't remember anything. That's how I would've played it, too. Just like Katherine Hepburn in *The Philadelphia Story*—only with a monster-donged polar bear instead of Jimmy Stewart."

"Okay, look, here's what I remember," said James: "I was in New York to sign a new three-book deal with my publisher. I always get nervous at those meetings, even though my agent handles most of the negotiations and I'm just there for the meet-and-greet, really. So, y'know, to take the edge off, I took a Klonopin a few hours before I was supposed to go in. Actually, I took three Klonopins, which I hardly ever do. So I was feelin' pretty relaxed. On my way to the meeting, I went into a Starbucks near the Flatiron building for my daily Frappuccino and I started up a conversation with these hippie kids who recognized me from my author photos. They said they were fans. Asked me if I wanted to party down with 'em. I said sure, after my meeting.… And then, the next thing I know, two big burly New York City cops are perp-walking me through a shrieking crowd of paparazzis and television crews. I find out I've somehow lost my hat and my glasses and my pants. All I'm wearing is a too-short white tee shirt covered in polar bear splooge with the words 'Let's kill all the penguins' scrawled across it in red Sharpie."

Sabina tried to suppress a laugh. It came out sounding like a seal's bark. She took a slug of her mojito to get a grip. "The penguins are in Antarctica," she told James as the rum did a slow burn down her throat. "I don't think they've ever been seriously threatened by polar bears."

"Just angry rhetoric, I guess. I'm not even sure what I meant by it. Maybe it was a statement about global warming or something."

"How'd that three-book deal work out for you, after you missed the meeting?"

"The whole thing blew up on me. The publisher dropped me like I was a radioactive dildo. My publicist dumped me, too—that cowardly witch. Frankly, this last year has been hell."

"But you got this new book out somehow." Sabina pointed to her autographed copy on the beauty salon chair between them.

"Yeah, at least my agent stuck with me. But we took a major hit on the advance. I got, like, a fifth of what I used to make."

"Maybe you'll make up for it in royalties."

"That's not how the business works with guys like me. We almost never earn out our advances. It's the publishing industry's way of subsidizing their bestselling authors."

"So the rich authors get richer and all the other authors get the shaft, is that it?"

"Pretty much."

"It must suck to find yourself in the 'other authors' category all of a sudden."

"Yeah, my agent, Nick, was super-pissed. But he told me no one wants the publicity that would go along with giving me a big advance. From now on, no matter how many books I sell, I'm always gonna be that guy who blew the polar bear."

"Well, you *did* blow the polar bear."

"Yeah, but I'm not happy about it." James gave her an appraising look, not boob-focused this time. "You wanna know a secret? I'm pretty sure I went in there to fuck a female polar bear. This is just a theory, but it makes a lot of sense to me. I've never been gay, for one thing. And one of my ex-girlfriends was an actress who got raped by a Russian circus bear in a movie called *Stalin Says*—so maybe it was a competitive thing."

"I've *seen* that movie!" said Sabina, recalling it with morbid glee. It was a mind control flick, every bit as weird as anything put out by Stanley Kubrick or the two Davids—Cronenberg and Lynch. Just thinking about that scene with the chainsaw blade made out of human tongues caused her labia to clench all over again.

"So your ex was Rina Rowley?"

"Yup." James downed the remainder of his gin-and-tonic and wiped his lips on the back of his hand.

"Whatever happened to her? She just disappeared back in the nineties, right when she was getting famous."

"Long story. But the gist of it is: I don't know what happened to her. Nobody does. She just took off one day like a bat out of hell. I never really got over her."

"Did you think that having sex with a polar bear might help you get her back? Like maybe, with all the publicity, she'd reach out to you somehow?"

"Like I said, I don't know what I was thinking...."

"You didn't happen to watch a lot of *Mutual of Omaha's Wild Kingdom* when you were growing up, did you?" Sabina was thinking about how *Soul Train* had put the kink in Frank's sexual appetites, and how *Bonanza* might have warped her own unfulfilled desires.

"Marlin Perkins was like a god to me when I was a kid," James confirmed, referring to the show's safari jacketed host. "I learned a lot from him about social dominance among silverback gorillas and shit like that. In fact, ol' Marlin might've been the guy who saved my life down there in that polar bear pit."

"How is that even possible? Is Marlin Perkins still alive?"

"No, but his insights into the wild animal kingdom live on in our collective memory," said James. "Again, this is just a theory, but let's say I was in there doin' a little foreplay, goin' down on some sweet polar bear poontang. It's kind of heroic, when you think about it... my face all up in Pinga's snatch, making her moan and shudder."

"Pinga's a female polar bear?" Sabina asked him.

"Yup. She's the one Augustus likes to hump—his main squeeze. Augustus is the big alpha male…. weighs about three-quarters of a ton and stands, like, over ten feet tall. So here's what I think happened: Pinga's moans of ecstasy woke up ol' Augustus from his afternoon cave nap. So he pads on over to have a look-see at what's causing his lady bear friend to orgasm out loud like that. When he gets hip to what I'm doin' to Pinga with my talented tongue… well, let's just say he doesn't like it. But at the same time it kinda turns him on, in a voyeuristic sort of way."

"Kinky," said Sabina.

"Yeah. But like I said, he was still wildly pissed off. So when Augustus reared up on his hindquarters and, uhm, *presented* to me, I'm guessing it brought back one of the most important lessons Marlin Perkins ever taught me. I realized I was the beta male in that particular situation and if I didn't start acting all submissive… well, that throbbing red polar bear dick would be the last thing I'd ever see. So in my drug-addled state of mind, I must've been like, 'Hey, I better blow this big guy or he's gonna maul the shit out of me.' Literally."

"So you became the alpha polar bear's bitch—"

"—and lived to tell the tale. Other guys who've climbed inside polar bear exhibits haven't been so lucky. Just Google 'Polar Bear Kills Clueless Doofus' and you'll see what I mean. But I had Marlin Perkins on my side."

"Yay Marlin!"

"After Augustus blew his huge sticky polar bear load all over my face, he felt so relaxed that he just let me wade across the moat and climb up out of the exhibit. By then there were cops and reporters all over the place. And you know the rest.…"

"But were you ever officially identified as the crazed polar-bear-cock-gobbler? I thought that was just a rumor."

"We tried to keep it a secret, but that only lasted a few days. Everyone knew for sure after that. I haven't been able to live it down. I'm the Monica Lewinsky of polar bear seducers. Which is why I decided to make this appointment, after Ian told me about you."

Sabina took a meditative sip of her mojito. She was starting to like this guy. He kind of reminded her of Frank in his willingness to talk about his perverse escapades. She decided that she wanted to help him—and she already knew how to go about it.

"I'm not a miracle worker, y'know…" she told James. "I can't just make it go away. But something you said earlier made me think that if you lean into this and really own the experience, you might be able to turn it to your advantage."

"What'd I say earlier? I forget."

"You said, 'Maybe it was a statement about global warming…'."

"How's that supposed to help?"

Sabina laid out her plan for him. If everything went right, he'd wind up looking like a hero. But if it went sideways on them, he'd come off looking like a sad, cum-stained clown. By the end of their conversation, James said he'd be willing to take the risk:

"Let's go for it. I think it was Toni Morrison who said, 'If you wanna fly, first you have to get rid of everything that's weighing you down. And then you have to take a massive shit all over that stuff… y'know, to get rid of the extra ballast.'"

"Toni Morrison said that."

"Yeah, I'm pretty sure."

"Was that before or after she won the Nobel Prize?"

"Before, I think. I boozed it up with her at the Santa Barbara Writers' Conference this one time. Fun lady. Or wait… maybe that was Fannie Flagg."

"The woman who wrote *Fried Green Tomatoes*?"

"Yeah. Forget I even said anything," said James.

JUSTICE

After her meeting with James, Sabina took the subway uptown to the New York Public Library at Bryant Park and rode the elevator to the Rose Main Reading Room on the third floor. She found an empty chair bathed in sunlight slanting through the huge arched windows, opened her MacBook on the golden oak tabletop, put her earbuds in, and spent the rest of the afternoon listening to an iTunes playlist of songs by Cat Power, Nick Cave, and Sharon Van Etten while she read through all the .PDF documents in the WesDocs folder.

The first document was titled "The Coup d'État of 1963: 50th Anniversary of America's Covert Takeover." It was dated November 22nd, 2013—so apparently Wes had been at this for a while. The document kicked off with an epigraph from Gore Vidal:

I'm not a conspiracy theorist, I'm a conspiracy analyst.

What followed was cogent, written with eloquence and verve, but it had a streak of paranoia running through it that was off-putting at first. As Wes explained it, he'd taken an interest in John F. Kennedy's assassination about six years earlier after reading an obscure book called *Crash Gordon and the Mysteries of Kingsburg*. Since that time, he'd read well over 200 books on the subject and had "spent countless hours doing research on the Internet." (Sabina just rolled her eyes at that one, knowing how much sheer bullshit got posted on the Internet every day—some of it courtesy of her own PR campaigns for her transgressive clients). All that due diligence had convinced Wes that a shadowy cabal—or "Dark Brotherhood"—had conspired in JFK's assassination and its subsequent cover-up.

Wes wasn't shy. He was a brainy young billionaire with his own HFT firm disrupting business-as-usual on Wall Street. Why should he be shy? The Skull and Bones crowd already had him in their crosshairs. Mercenaries from BlackRock, Kroll, and Goldman Sachs were likely plotting to take him out, no matter what he said about the web of criminality spanning America's recent history. So Wes named names. He said the conspirators behind JFK's demise were heavy hitters like Allen Dulles, J. Edgar Hoover, and Lyndon B. Johnson, plus a smattering of Texas oil tycoons and some other rich snobs (like the Rockefellers) associated with the Council on Foreign Relations—in short, people at the very highest levels of government, finance, and the military-industrial-intelligence complex.

What saved Wes from looking like just another anarchist rant boy was the exhaustive list of little-known facts that he wove together into a persuasive, logical argument that JFK's assassination absolutely *had* to be a coup d'état. So much of the evidence had been compromised. So many witnesses and potential whistleblowers had been murdered after the fact. A conspiracy was obvious.

But so what? thought Sabina. *That was over fifty years ago. Why did it still matter?*

Wes explained why it mattered in the longer follow-up document: "Evolution of the American Deep State: 55 Years of Total Fuckery."

America had paid an apocalyptic price for failing to bring JFK's killers to justice. The sinister forces behind the 1963 Coup had become emboldened in its aftermath. Their crimes had compounded as the need to silence witnesses to past crimes motivated them to commit even more crimes in a never-ending cycle. As Wes explained it:

> I now have a profound understanding of how the Dark Brotherhood controls the political process in our country. Fifty-five years ago, a network of treasonous criminals hijacked our government. They haven't let go of it since, because to do so would be to risk exposure for a long list of crimes that continue to this day. While I refuse to passively accept living in a country where democracy has been overthrown, I find it hard not to feel helpless against such a powerful, ever-evolving cabal that has been systematically killing its opposition for over half a century.
>
> In my desire to heal our democracy, I've often thought about how the powerless can confront the powerful. The Quakers have a tradition of bearing witness against evil when they've been unable to prevent it, so the evil will at least not pass unnoted. This document is my own humble attempt to bear witness to the Dark Brotherhood's crimes over the last fifty-five years. It was written in the hope that my own small voice can help excise this malignancy from our body politic.

Wes then launched into a secret history of the Dark Brotherhood's Deep State control over American presidents and their policy decisions, from 1963 on up to the present day. Sabina had no idea how much of it was true, but it sure sounded bad:

> Lyndon Baines Johnson was a swaggering psychopath with a Texas-sized ego—the perfect big-dick-swinging frontman for the Dark Brotherhood's power grab. A true believer in the saying "The logical extension of business is murder," LBJ had his own personal hit man on retainer, Malcolm "Mac" Wallace, who'd killed more than half a dozen people since 1951 to cover up LBJ's crimes. Wallace was one of at least

six shooters positioned to blast away at JFK when the presidential motorcade passed through Dealey Plaza. He even might have been the one who blew off the top of Kennedy's head with a dumdum bullet fired from the grassy knoll (or from a storm drain positioned six feet away from JFK's limousine), although there were plenty of other mercenaries to choose from in Dallas that day.

The Dark Brotherhood couldn't have been certain that all their shooters would escape undetected, but the success of the Coup didn't depend on that. Success depended on their ability to control the investigation and the way the story was handled in the media. To that end, J. Edgar Hoover's FBI fingered 24-year-old Lee Harvey Oswald as the "lone gunman" within hours of JFK's death, doing everything in their power to make him fit the crime. Oswald, a CIA contract agent, had been unwittingly set up as a patsy long before JFK arrived in Dallas. So thoroughly had the CIA stage-managed Oswald's prior activities that he could have been made to look like a Soviet spy, a fanatical supporter of Fidel Castro, or a mob-connected contract killer—depending on where the Dark Brotherhood wanted to lay the blame if the lone gunman theory didn't fly with the public.

LBJ assembled the Warren Commission to reaffirm the FBI's trumped-up charges and head off any future Senate investigations. Future President Gerald Ford acted as Hoover's "snitch" on the Commission. John J. McCloy, chairman of the Council on Foreign Relations, quashed all dissent against the Commission's absurd Magic Bullet Theory, which posited that a single bullet had caused seven wounds to both Kennedy and John Connally and then emerged from Connally's thigh, intact, on a hospital gurney. (Similar magic would be invoked nearly forty years later, when Satam al-Suqami's passport reportedly showed up, intact, in the rubble of the World Trade Center towers after 9/11.) Coup leader Allen Dulles became the Commission's most active member—intimidating witnesses, cherry-picking evidence—even though it was widely known that Dulles had become a bitter enemy of the Kennedys after JFK fired him from his position as Director of Central Intelligence in the wake of the CIA's bungled Bay of Pigs Invasion.

(Future President George H.W. Bush had worked with the CIA during the planning stages of that invasion. It was codenamed Operation Zapata in a nod to Bush's oil company, Zapata Off-Shore, which had provided offshore oil-drilling rig platforms to be used as staging grounds for the CIA's anti-Castro shenanigans. FBI memos also placed Bush in Dallas on the day of JFK's assassination. It should be noted that a few months later Bush became a millionaire at the age of forty.)

After the Warren Commission had put their stamp of approval on the way LBJ wanted the assassination to be seen, he was free to move on to other grand deceptions like the Gulf of Tonkin Incident, which became his excuse to escalate the war in Vietnam. Within that context, Vietnam can be seen as a hundred-billion-dollar Thank You gift (paid for by U.S. taxpayers) from LBJ to his incredibly persuasive Deep State friends in the military-industrial-intelligence complex. Other wars to follow (Operation Desert Storm, the invasions of Afghanistan and Iraq, etc.) should be seen in the same light.

The document ran on and on like that, President by President, for over fifty pages. Wes had long lists of detailed facts and links to original sources to back up his every assertion. The guy was fucking relentless.

Next up was Richard M. Nixon, the lying, sweaty stooge of Allen Dulles and Prescott Bush. After many false starts, Dulles and Bush finally managed to get Nixon elected by killing off his strongest Democratic opponent, Robert F. Kennedy (Sirhan Sirhan was another 24-year-old CIA-manipulated patsy). But Nixon started having ideas of his own during his second term in office, annoying hawkish members of the cabal with his agenda of winding down the war in Vietnam and improving relations with the Soviet Union and the People's Republic of China. Watergate was the Dark Brotherhood's solution to that insubordination, a second coup d'état with ties to the JFK assassination. It allowed their old Warren Commission buddy, Gerald Ford, to become the 38th President of the United States without having to bother with an election. Ford—out of gratitude, no doubt—stacked his administration with Dark Brotherhood cronies: George H.W. Bush was put in charge of the CIA, Dick Cheney served as Ford's Chief of Staff, and Donald Rumsfeld became Secretary of Defense.

The fucking Bush family, of course! thought Sabina. *And no surprise goddam Cheney and Rumsfeld were in on it—those ghoulish, profiteering assholes.*

Wes claimed that in the years leading up to the Watergate Coup a vacuum had been created at the top of the Dark Brotherhood's pyramidal power hierarchy by the deaths of Allen Dulles in 1969, J. Edgar Hoover in 1972, and LBJ in early 1973. Three factions within the cabal had been vying for the leadership role: "a network of old boys from the OSS, a group within the Office of Naval Intelligence, and a group within the CIA led by George H.W. Bush." The CIA prevailed and Watergate served to instate Bush as the crown prince of the Dark Brotherhood:

> George Herbert Walker Bush became such a key figure within the Dark Brotherhood because he bridged two worlds: he was deeply involved with the CIA and he came from an elite family with strong ties to the Eastern Establishment. His father, Prescott, had been a U.S. Senator, a close friend of Allen Dulles, and a managing partner at Brown Brothers Harriman—the oldest and largest private bank in America (with a long history of war profiteering and other illicit activities). Bush's grandfather and John D. Rockefeller's brother had been business partners and the two families remained close. Empowered by those dual networks—the CIA and the Republican power elite—Bush was in the ideal position to assume responsibility for maintaining the dirty secrets of the 1963 Coup when Gerald Ford appointed him Director of Central Intelligence.
>
> When Bush took control of the CIA it was under siege. Operation Mockingbird usually kept news agencies in line, but some rogue journalists—not yet on the CIA's payroll and thus still interested in the pursuit of truth—had begun reporting on the massive domestic spying operations being undertaken by U.S. intelligence agencies. (The Citizens' Commission to Investigate the FBI kicked things off in 1971 by burglarizing an FBI field office in Media, Pennsylvania,

where they found evidence of the FBI's COINTELPRO domestic spying and dirty tricks program, which they then distributed to sympathetic members of the press; Seymour Hersh followed up with a December 22nd, 1974 article on the front page of the *New York Times* headlined "Huge C.I.A. Operation Reported in U.S. Against Anti-War Forces.")

Public pressure led to Congressional investigations such as the Church Committee, the Pike Committee, and the U.S. House Select Committee on Assassinations. (The Dark Brotherhood's death squads had to work overtime to sabotage the HSCA hearings: many participants in the 1963 Coup had been subpoenaed by the HSCA, but 21 of them died under mysterious circumstances, often just days before their scheduled testimony.) Those investigations ended up revealing many of the intelligence agencies' dark secrets. Blowback from those revelations and from the Watergate scandal created a political reform movement that seemed unstoppable. Bush was touted as a civilian outsider who could reform the CIA; however, his real task—as the consummate insider—was to staunch the flow of secrets out of the Agency and prevent the exposure of the Dark Brotherhood's coups d'état and other illegal activities.

Bush did his job and he did it well. He initiated the process of moving the Dark Brotherhood's main base of operations out of the CIA and into the private sector, where the Deep State would be able to maintain its control over the American political system without Congressional oversight and interference. (Of course, the CIA still had its uses—specifically, for waging undeclared wars on behalf of corporate interests and securing black budget funding from clueless US taxpayers.) During that public sector transition, while the Dark Brotherhood was in slight disarray, calls for political reform swept Jimmy Carter into office. Wes wrote:

> James Earl "Jimmy" Carter was an anomaly—a relatively honest politician elected during a brief resurgence of American democracy. Within months of taking office, Carter fired Bush as DCI and replaced him with Stansfield

Turner, who cleaned house, eliminating over 800 CIA positions in what became known as the Halloween Massacre. But that was only a temporary setback for the Dark Brotherhood. President Carter wouldn't be getting a second term. Henry Kissinger and David Rockefeller coerced him into reluctantly providing American medical care for the deposed Shah of Iran, Mohammad Rezâ Shâh Pahlavi, and the Iranians retaliated by taking 52 Americans hostage. The hostage crisis lingered like a black cloud over Carter during the 1980 Presidential election. If he'd been able to negotiate an 'October Surprise' release of the American hostages, Carter almost certainly would have been re-elected—but Bush and his intelligence operatives treasonously sabotaged those negotiations, making sure that the hostages stayed put until Reagan and Bush's first day in office.

Ronald Reagan—the Hollywood cowboy grandpa figure that everybody loved. How could he be evil? Sabina wondered. She was sure Wes was about to tell her:

Ronald Wilson Reagan was a President in name only. He more accurately should be thought of as an actor playing his greatest role. George H.W. Bush was the true wielder of Presidential power during the Reagan years. By the time Bush became Vice President, he'd assumed unprecedented control over the national security apparatus, which he intended to use for evil ends. If Reagan had any ideas about reigning in Bush's criminal ambitions, they disappeared after John Hinckley Jr. made an attempt on Reagan's life two months into his Presidency.

There are good reasons to believe Hinckley was part of another Dark Brotherhood sponsored coup d'état. The Bush and Hinckley families were on friendly terms: the day after the assassination attempt, John Hinckley's brother, Scott, had been scheduled to have dinner with Vice President Bush's conniving son, Neil (soon to achieve infamy for his role in the upcoming Savings and Loan Crisis). John Hinckley Sr., the would-be assassin's father, had been a president of World Vision, an international evangelical relief organization and suspected CIA front that had also employed John Lennon's assassin, Mark David Chapman. Coincidentally, both Chapman and John Hinckley Jr. had been reading *The Catcher in the Rye*—written by former counter-intelligence operative J.D. Salinger—just before they put their Manchurian-Candidate-like plans into action.

With Reagan effectively neutered, Bush used his position as Vice President to facilitate a massive criminal undertaking unparalleled in American history. (*At least until that fucker Cheney became Vice President twenty years later...* thought Sabina.) Bush and his cabal pals started running an incredible number of financial scams and shady schemes: the Savings & Loan Crisis, Iran-Contra, CIA and DEA drug trafficking, embezzling from HUD, insider trading, murdering puppies—you name it. Corrupt government officials embedded in enforcement agencies like the FBI, ATF, DEA, and SEC protected most of the congressmen and DC insiders involved—but the beneficiaries of those schemes knew they'd been compromised and could be found out or subjected to blackmail at any time. That was just the way Bush wanted it. Any attempt to expose the multiple waves of criminality coursing through Washington in those days would have resulted in a near wholesale implication of the political class. Those who'd participated in the Dark Brotherhood's crimes had no choice but to cover each other's asses or risk mutually assured destruction. It made political reform all but impossible.

Reaganomics turned out to be the biggest scam of all. It amounted to a wholesale looting of the American middle-class, a massive transfer of wealth to the richest one-tenth-of-one-percent of the population. It came as no surprise to Sabina that many of the famous families in that .1% had attained their wealth by criminal means. The Bush family could have served as their template. As Wes observed:

> Prescott Bush had been cited in 1942 for trafficking with the Nazis under the Trading with the Enemy Act, but his crimes went much deeper than that. Prescott initiated his son into a similar life of crime not just because he knew it could be lucrative, but also because he knew that George would be more likely to protect his family's criminal legacy from exposure if he also had a stake in it. George "Poppy" Bush in

turn—like some amoral, Yale-educated Mafia don—initiated his own sons into the family crime syndicate. Poppy Bush was a criminal mastermind, perhaps the most appallingly successful malevolent in American history, but his sons, with their less wide-ranging intellects, had to specialize: Neil went into real estate fraud; bumbling George W. got by on cushy oil deals with his Saudi pals; Marvin, the youngest, would eventually excel at security services scams; while Jeb hewed closest to his father, with experience in a multitude of frauds involving banking, real estate, gold futures, oil and natural gas contracts, airplane brokerages, and Florida election returns.

But what about Bill Clinton? Sabina had always liked Clinton—probably because he reminded her of her hopeless horndog clients like Frank and James. It took a special kind of perverted genius to come up with the idea of basting Cuban cigars in Monica Lewinsky's vaginal juices for later smoking in the Oval Office as a morale booster. *Go Bill!* She'd rooted for him as a young girl during the slut-shaming impeachment proceedings headed up by that fun-killing old scold, Kenneth Starr. But Wes had some unwelcome news for Sabina:

William Jefferson "Bill" Clinton was attending Oxford in 1968 when he was recruited as a CIA asset by London CIA station chief, Cord Meyer. The Dark Brotherhood is always looking to groom the next generation of compromised politicians and Clinton made an ideal target. He was clever, articulate, dishonest, ambitious, and a compulsive sex addict. That combination of traits made him very easy to control.

Clinton's rapid rise in politics was financed by a network of fast-buck Arkansas profit-takers involved in drug running, money laundering, and illegal gambling operations. After Clinton became the state's young governor in 1979, he was easily steered into supporting the CIA drug trafficking in and out of the Intermountain Regional Airport at Mena, Arkansas—one of the CIA's main hubs for U.S. drug distribution during the eighties and nineties. Legendary cocaine smuggler Barry Seal operated his fleet of planes out of Mena, including *Fat Lady*—the former Air America cargo plane that crashed in the jungles of Nicaragua in 1986 while on an illegal operation to arm and resupply the Contras, which eventually resulted in worldwide headlines about the Iran-Contra scandal. In 1991, the Iran-Contra Special Prosecutor was petitioned by Arkansas Attorney General Winston Bryant to investigate allegations of drug-running out of Mena, but Clinton—still governor and batting for the Bush team—made sure that nothing was ever done about it.

(The Attorney General of Louisiana, William Guste Jr., estimated that Adler Berriman "Barry" Seal "had smuggled between $3 billion and $5 billion of drugs into the United States" before he was machine-gunned to death outside a Salvation Army shelter in Baton Rouge in 1986. Guste was convinced that Seal had been set up. Seal had been testifying as a federal informant in front of grand juries at the time of his murder, yet, inexplicably, he wasn't incarcerated or in the Federal Witness Protection Program. For a good overview of Seal's connections to Mena, Clinton, and the CIA, see "The Crimes of Mena" by Sally Denton and Roger Morris, published in the July 1995 issue of *Penthouse Magazine*.)

As a reward for his corrupt stewardship of Arkansas, the Bush Syndicate used their influence to promote Clinton on the national stage. The Dark Brotherhood is collectively obsessed with controlling all political parties. During the 1992 election they couldn't lose. Their fearless leader, George H.W. Bush, had the Republican nomination, and their main man from Arkansas, Bill "Slick Willie" Clinton, was the Democratic candidate.

Shit! Sabina hadn't wanted to know any of that. She skimmed the remaining Clinton paragraphs, knowing they would contain more of the same, or even worse. And they did: Wes sketched out how Clinton had often tried to do right during his Presidency, but was tragically compromised by his criminal background (Hillary wasn't clean, either, Wes assured his readers). One example, among many, stood out: Clinton had been obliged to keep in place over 1000 Bush appointees who'd been embedded throughout the federal government to cover up the Dark Brotherhood's crimes. For the eight years of the Clinton administration, those appointees just went about their business (getting

Clinton to invade Haiti, bomb the Balkans and Africa and Iraq, repeal key provisions of the Glass-Steagall Act so the big banks could all indulge in high-risk gambling with their depositors' money, and so forth…). Then their cold, greedy little hearts started beating faster in anticipation of the next member of the Bush Syndicate to take office.

Sure enough, George W. Bush stole the 2000 election with a little help from his brother, Jeb, down in Florida and some Dark Brotherhood affiliated Supreme Court justices. From that moment on, the nation was really fuckeroo'd.

Sabina didn't need Wes to tell her about the rest. She'd already lived through it.

STRENGTH

By the time she got to the end of the WesNotes documents, Sabina couldn't decide if Wes Bramley was a total nutcase or just educated enough to understand what was really going on (she was leaning toward the latter…). Wes himself had summed up that conundrum in the last paragraphs of "Wars of the Overworld: The Psychopathic Power Elite's Global Conspiracy Against the Rest of Us"—the third and final document in the folder:

> The Dark Brotherhood is engaged in a secret war on human consciousness. Intuitively, we all know this to be true, but that truth has been devalued and routinely subsumed by disinformation campaigns. We know, and take for granted now, that our politicians are bought and sold by corporate interests, that our daily news has been commoditized, and that wars are started under false pretenses—but the level of crime and corruption in our federal government goes much deeper than that. Hard evidence of the American Deep State's criminal reign has been suppressed in all the major media outlets in this country, but freedom of the press still allows that evidence to be made public in books and on the Internet. While the uninitiated and naïve may dismiss these

essays of mine as the specious by-products of paranoia, the attentive and independent-minded few who care enough to do their own research will find that my fears for our democracy are justified and worthy of the most serious consideration.

If we, as a nation, can't find a way to release the Dark Brotherhood's choking grip—on our minds, our finances, and our political system—then the overwhelming majority of Americans will be doomed to an increasingly controlled and degraded way of life. The pursuit of happiness could soon devolve into a desperate struggle for survival. But it doesn't have to be that way. We have the numbers on our side and the power to improve the human condition for all. First, however, we have to collectively acknowledge that we've been conned by a criminal overclass—which is no easy thing to admit. As Mark Twain allegedly said:

"It's far easier to fool a man than to convince him that he's being fooled."

I'm not at all convinced that Twain actually said that (I haven't been able to find the original source for the quote in any of his books), but it's a true statement, nonetheless.

Unlike so much else we're told these days.

At that point, Sabina couldn't stop yawning. A yawn, she knew, was a silent scream for coffee. She was suffering from information overload and a raging case of cognitive dissonance. Caffeine would make it all better.

Wes had covered a lot of territory, almost too much for her poor, uninitiated brain to process: the Oklahoma City bombing as a government sponsored false flag terrorist attack blamed on the militia movement; 9/11 as a "massive domestic-run black op" funded by Saudi and Pakistani intelligence services with the full consent of the Bush Syndicate (with tactical support provided by Cheney, Rumsfeld, George Tenet, and senior members of the CIA's Alec Station group and the FBI's Radical Fundamentalist Unit, etc.); Barack Obama as a Dark Brotherhood spy working undercover as a liberal Democrat—a reformer manqué, recruited as a CIA asset while still a student at Occidental (no great surprise there, since Obama's mother had been in the orbit of CIA operations from the time he was born); Jeb and Hillary as two sides of the same worthless trick coin; and so on, and so on....

Curious to know what Wes actually looked like, Sabina tapped into the NYPL wireless network and did a Google image search for "Wes Bramley"—but not a single photo with a human face turned up. *Nada.* Zilch. Which was beyond strange. It turned out that Wes Bramley was the J.D. Salinger of Internet entrepreneurs, the Thomas Pynchon of high-frequency trading firm CEOs. Articles had been written about how he wouldn't allow photos to be taken in the offices of Limelight Research Capital. Those same articles also claimed that Wes was a master of disguise who never appeared in public without altering his appearance. And there was something else: unlike the rest of humanity, Wes seemed to have the ability to erase his own images from the Internet.

How was that even possible?

Sabina was thinking about that as she packed up her laptop and left the Rose Main Reading Room to descend the wide staircase leading to the library's lobby. She hardly even noticed where she was going until she found herself standing in the little coffee alcove off to the right of the front entrance. *Coffee!* She bought herself a tall cup and sat down in one of the brushed aluminum chairs they had scattered around. You weren't supposed to go wandering through the rest of the library while you were drinking sweet, hot, life-giving coffee.

"Looks like you're enjoyin' that."

Sabina glanced up from her squint above the coffee's steam. A tall man in jeans and flannel was seated nearby, looking too large for his tiny table and chair. He tilted back his straw Stetson hat as a way of saying hello.

Sabina took another appreciative sip. "Fuckin'-A I'm enjoyin' it."

The big man laughed—a gruff, sexy growl of a laugh. "That's what I like seein'… a woman who knows how t' appreciate what's good in this here world." He had a handsome face with kind, knowing, sea-green eyes set off by a coarse, scruffy mustache and beard.

Outside of her work, Sabina tried to avoid talking to strangers as a rule, but for this guy she'd make an exception. He reminded her of Patti Smith's description of Sam Shepard's character in that play they'd written and performed in together: "A rock-and-roll Jesus with a cowboy mouth." Not that he looked like much of a rock-and-roller…

but a cowboy Jesus? *Definitely.* And how many times had she seen a guy like that in a public library?

Never.

"What're you reading there?" Sabina asked him, nodding at the large book he had splayed open on the tiny round table in front of him. He picked it up and showed her the cover.

Holy fucking shit! It was Sartre's *Being and Nothingness.*

"That ol' Jean-Paul Sartre"—he pronounced it Gene-Paul SarTREE—"he got some right fine ideas 'bout livin'."

"Like how so?" Sabina asked, feeling perky. The caffeine was already starting to kick in. Or maybe it was her libido.

"Welp…" he paused to remove his cowboy hat and rub his forehead with his big thumb for a moment, "fer instance, he says here that we all start from *nothin'*—the big *tabula rasa,* if y'know what I'm sayin'. But we got the free will t' make choices, us *bein'* in the world and all. Them choices though, they rope us in. Make us feel a li'l less free with ev'ry choice we make. But you can't go cryin' about it—or livin' in bad faith, like he calls it. Some folks, they get stuck in their roles like bad actors, kiddin' themselves. But it ain't never too late t' be what you mighta been. Best thing t' do is t' remember you came from *nothin'*— and start over, *bein'* someone else. Make some new choices you might end up likin' better. Find yerself some *gnosis.*"

"Easier said than done sometimes," Sabina said, thinking of her own crummy losing streak with choosing men. She could buy into the concept of existential responsibility, sure—but luck and synchronicity also had to factor into the final outcome of a person's choices in life. She often felt more like the hapless victim of a series of accidents, rather than the indomitable captain of her fate.

"Yeah, welp, the main thing I get from ol' Sartre"—SarTREE— "is you ain't s'posed t' let others define you, or put limits on you, or make yer choices for you. You'll choose yer own destiny better'n anybody, so long as you're willin' t' put in the work."

Sabina related that back to what Wes had written about the Dark Brotherhood. Wasn't that what their global conspiracy was all about: trying to define and limit the choices of everyone else?

"I've never met a cowboy who was into existentialism before," she said. "And believe me, I've been looking."

The man held out a big-knuckled hand for her to shake. "Name's MacDuff."

The big meat of his palm felt warm and strong as he clasped Sabina's tiny hand. "Is that Irish?" she asked him.

"Scottish'd be more like it. Truth is, my momma got it from Shakespeare. 'Macbeth.' Momma was a big reader."

"Isn't that the play with the curse? The one where bad things always happen to the actors?"

"So they say."

"I'm Sabina," she said, finally unclenching from MacDuff's grip. She felt a lush, creamy warmth oozing through her nether regions. Pure, physical lust hadn't spiked in her so hard and fast since she'd been a teenager.

"Well, Sabina, it's a real pleasure. New York's s'posed t' be fulla beautiful women, but I don't think I ever laid eyes on one as purty as you."

"Don't make me blush, MacDuff."

"Just a statement o' fact, darlin'."

"Oh hell…." Sabina could feel the heat rising in her cheeks. She'd probably have to wring out her panties in the sink when she got home.

"You feelin' okay there?"

"Just a little dizzy. Low blood sugar." Her nipples were poking out from under her thin black jersey top like hollow-point bullets. *Jesus!*

"I reckon a fine filly like you must already have a husband. Some big-shot lawyer or coked-up venture capitalist sonofagun."

"Wait, what—"

"Them gol-durned rascally bastards—they always get the best women 'round here."

"Well, they didn't get me." Sabina didn't know whether to be offended or flattered by MacDuff's off-base assumption.

"I'm glad t' hear it. Gives me a shot."

"You're pretty forward for a cowboy."

"Well, not all us cowpokes had the same upbringin'."

"Your book-lovin' mom must've been a big influence."

"Had me readin' Schopenhauer before I was outta short pants. Heidegger and Nietzsche a year later. And Hermann Hesse? *Steppenwolf? Siddhartha?* Oh man, she just loved that dude."

His pronunciation of the German names was much better, Sabina noted. Maybe he just had a problem with the French philosophers. She asked him: "Did you ever read 'The Myth of Sisyphus'?"

"By Albert Camus?" Al-BERT CAM-us. "You bet. 'One must imagine Sisyphus happy.' Right?"

"Bingo!" said Sabina. Okay, so he had a problem with French pronunciation. But he sure knew his philosophers. She thought to herself: *A philosophical cowboy right here in the New York Public Library. How fucking cool is that?* She wondered how long it would take her to get him to ask her out on a date.

"You and me oughta have dinner sometime."

Not long at all.

"Why's that, MacDuff?" she asked, just to toy with him a little.

"Well, the way I see it, if I don't get a chance t' know you better, I'm gonna regret it the whole rest o' my durned life. So I'm askin': Will you go out and eat some grub with me? Nothin' fancy—'less you like that sorta thing. I been told I clean up right nice."

"Why, MacDuff, I hardly know you… but I'm flattered."

"Is that a yes or a no? I can't hardly tell. We got us a Schrödinger's Cat situation here, some kind o' superposition o' states."

"Is the pussy dead or alive? She's both—until you open her box to find out." Sabina barely knew what she was saying.

"What the—?"

"Yes, I'll go out with you!" she said, ending the suspense. "Yes. Even just for pizza. How's this Friday?"

That was weird, about the pussy. Where did that come from?

"Okay. Friday then. *Whew!*" MacDuff removed his hat again. She could see he'd been sweating where the brim met his forehead. He wiped his brow clean with a blue cotton bandanna and put the Stetson back in place. "Lord almighty, you had me goin' there for a sec."

"Sorry. I just didn't want you to think I was easy."

"Never crossed my mind. Ain't nothin' 'bout you seems easy."

"Hey. Watch it there, buster."

THE EMPEROR

The Inuk drove a hard bargain. For a guy who spent most of his time living in igloos and eating whale blubber, he sure was a money-grubber. Maybe he wanted to move someplace warmer, like Santa Fe, and open up an Inuit artisanal cheese store. Sell walrus milk cheddar, reindeer Gouda. Who knows? The Inuk told Sabina it might take a few months before he could deliver the package, so James would just have to chill.

Frank said she was on shaky legal ground, but her DNA hacker buddies out in Bushwick assured her that if push came to shove, they had the technology to cover her yoga-toned ass. And they were willing to face down a Big Media shitstorm, if necessary. In fact, they welcomed it. They needed a new round of financing and Sabina's scheme was sure to spark major VC interest. There was even some loose talk about an IPO.

With all that out of the way, Sabina decided it was time to text Ron Geng and let him know that she'd take him on as a client. She had a hunch about what Wes Bramley was up to, and she wanted to see if she was right. Ron would be her ticket for ringside seats. If her hunch was even close, it promised to be a great show.

They met at the fountain in Central Park—the one with the big angel on top of it, between the lake and the promenade. Ron was on his lunch break again. As soon as he found Sabina, he handed her a five-page nondisclosure agreement and a pen, saying: "You need to sign this." Not even a "Hi," "How are you?" or "You look pretty today." (Sabina was wearing a flouncy new Lilly Pulitzer dress that she'd found on sale at Century 21. It looked fucking great on her. *Last time I dress up for you, Ron...* she thought.) She'd signed a shitload of nondisclosures in the past with other clients, so this one wasn't a big deal to her. Sabina scanned it, signed it, and handed it back to Ron without a word.

"Let's walk," he said.

"Okay...." Sabina just cocked an eyebrow at him as they started walking toward The Boathouse. She still didn't like the guy, but it was a lovely day—a rarity in New York, with climate change making a mess of things—so she decided to focus on her surroundings, rather than on Ron's grating personality. Women walked past them pushing baby strollers, young men with colorful full sleeve tats did their bro handshakes under the shade of the big trees, couples drifted by in rowboats out on the lake. Voices and the distant thunking of oarlocks mingled in the air.

"Did you read the documents?" Ron asked her.

"I did. Boy, that Wes Bramley sure knows his conspiracy theories!" She was making a joke.

Ron frowned. "Wes doesn't deal in theories. What he's written about are conspiracy facts."

"Relax, Ron. You don't have to get all huffy. I think what Wes had to say was pretty cool."

"I'm sorry if I jumped to the wrong conclusions." Ron didn't look sorry—and he still smelled like Pampers and burnt toast. "It's just that the term 'conspiracy theories' has become such a pejorative these days. Which is, of course, deliberate. It's exactly how the real conspirators in America's Deep State want people to think about conspiracies: that anyone who questions what they're told by corporate-controlled news outlets or the federal government must be a paranoid lunatic."

They were coming up on The Boathouse restaurant. Sabina gestured toward it and said, "Should we stop and get some lunch?"

"I'm not hungry. Let's keep walking."

"What if *I'm* hungry?"

"I'm afraid our conversation could be too easily overheard in a restaurant. Wes has authorized me to share some very sensitive information with you."

"Wait... *Wes* is in on this? You talked to him about it?"

"Of course. He's my best friend. We talk about everything. You didn't think I was going behind his back, did you?"

"Yeah, that's exactly what I thought!" Sabina would obviously have to rethink a few things. "And what's the deal with Wes, anyway? I looked him up. He's like the Thomas Pynchon of computer geeks, some crazy master of disguise."

"I know what he looks like."

"You would, wouldn't you?"

"He's just a normal guy. So normal, he could be anyone."

"Great. That helps. A lot."

"Don't get stuck on what Wes looks like," Ron said, acting paternal. "If everything goes right, you'll meet him someday."

"Maybe I already have…" Sabina said cryptically. Two could play this *I've Got a Secret* game.

Ron waggled his big red eyebrows at her. "You're joking, right? How would you even know?"

"Women's intuition," she bluffed. She knew that her intuition—at least when it came to men—absolutely sucked.

"There's no way you've met Wes. I would've known."

"What are you, his CIA handler or something? The guy's life can't completely revolve around you. And by the way, why's the CIA so overrun with Mormons in the first place? I remember reading an article about that back when Mitt Romney was running for President."

Ron deigned to answer her question while looking somewhat peeved: "There's a disproportionate number of Mormons in the CIA because our church expects every young man to spend two years abroad doing missionary work. When they come back, they're usually fluent in a foreign language—Urdu, Swahili, Farsi, or Arabic, for instance. I'm sure you can see how that might prove useful to the intelligence community. Combine that knack for odd languages with our strong sense of morality—Mormons don't drink or have sex outside of marriage—and you have the makings of an incorruptible intelligence agent."

"Except you guys really like money—Mitt Romney being the prime example. And you're not doing too shabby yourself there, I've noticed."

"Money isn't an obsession with us. We tithe ten percent of our income to the church."

"You and your fucking church are so rich it's obscene. Don't talk to me about your lame charities when you're living in an eight-bedroom Manhattan townhouse."

Ron let that pass. "You didn't really meet Wes, did you?" he asked.

"Not yet. But he's on my list," Sabina shot back.

"I think he'll like you. He seems to get a perverse pleasure out of confronting people who have good reasons to hate him."

"Sounds like my kind of guy."

"Have you ever heard of the term 'suicided by cop'?"

"Sure. When someone wants to die and they trick the police into shooting them?"

"Right. That's kind of why I'm here talking to you. I think Wes half-wants to be 'suicided' by the Deep State. It's just my opinion, but I'm convinced that's what these documents are really about."

"You don't think he might just really care about truth, justice, and the rule of law in this country?"

"Oh that, too. *Absolutely*. But most of all, I think he's grown tired of this world and he's looking for a noble way out."

"Doesn't he have any friends? Or family?"

"He was an only child. His parents are long gone. And he almost never dates. Always been married to his work. There's just me and this company we've built up together."

"Maybe you should take him out and get him drunk around some loose women. Get those life-juices flowing again."

"I'm a Mormon, remember? I don't drink."

"Then maybe I should do it. No, wait… Wes isn't a Mormon too, is he?"

Ron laughed out loud. A first. "No, he's definitely not a Mormon. I could see him taking you up on that offer. A beautiful, intelligent woman with no moral inhibitions and a healthy contempt for the rich? You're everything he needs."

"Except, uhm, I might be taken." She was thinking of MacDuff. They hadn't even gone out on their first date yet and she was already thinking of MacDuff. Which was ludicrous. *Insane*. Also typical. It wasn't the first time she'd been clubbed stupid by the careless barbarism of lust.

Sabina felt compelled to add: "That, and I actually *do* have some moral inhibitions, believe it or not."

"Everyone has inhibitions—in public," said Ron. "But in private? Not so much. That's why the Snowden Avalanche was so important."

"How do you mean?"

"Think of it this way: Let's say that when you die you discover, in the afterlife, that your every moment on Earth was recorded on a holographic video feed and tagged with searchable key words. Now try to imagine typing the words 'kinky sex' into your afterlife personal search engine. What would come up?"

"A lot," said Sabina. "Too much."

She was thinking, in particular, of some rather regrettable things she'd done in her adolescence with common household items repurposed for erotic exploration. There was also a cringe-inducing memory of her old college vibrator, a heavy-duty industrial-looking "back massager" that plugged into a wall outlet. It sounded like a 747 taking off when she cranked it to its highest setting—which she did almost nightly during her first year in the dorm, much to her roommate's dismay. *(Note to self: Call Dominique.)* She counted herself lucky that she hadn't completely rubbed off her clit with that goddam thing. She could have ended up looking like a Barbie doll down there.

"It's that way for almost everyone," Ron said, jerking Sabina out of her sleazy reverie, "but we still don't want anyone to know our dirt, do we?"

"Not unless I have the dirt on them, too," said Sabina, always the pragmatist. "I guess that's where the Snowden Avalanche comes in."

"Exactly! The Snowden Avalanche leveled the playing field. Before Snowden, the NSA was gathering almost everything users did on their cellphones and the Internet—but without anyone's knowledge of it. If the NSA wanted to pull a copy of a judge's email or a senator's personal data trails, they could use the X-KEYSCORE program to do just that without any warrants or oversight. Once they had the dirt—and there's always dirt, like we talked about—then it was simply a matter of using that information for purposes of blackmail or character assassination. Because, really, what better way to keep our federal government's system of 'checks and balances' in check than to have the ability to blackmail almost anyone in a key position of leverage?"

"But now that the dirt's already out in the open on everyone, there's no more blackmail, right?"

"In theory, that's how it was supposed to work. In practice, some of the very rich and very corrupt managed to avoid having their privacy compromised—because they saw the Snowden Avalanche coming, or at least anticipated something like it. So the CIA and the rest of the intelligence community has its private data cloud, courtesy of Amazon Web Services, and the big banks have their dark pools, where they can trade huge blocks of shares without going through the major stock exchanges. And while Facebook and Twitter were busy turning exhibitionism into the national pastime, some wealthy people, like Wes, were learning how to *delete* their information from the Internet. I take it you noticed that there aren't any pictures of Wes anywhere on the web?"

"I *did* notice that. I thought it was weird."

"Wes thinks it's weird, too. He doesn't think it's fair that only the rich and the devious have privacy now."

"So wait… are you telling me Wes is the guy behind the Snowden Avalanche?"

"As his attorney, I can neither confirm nor deny that. But what I *can* tell you—what Wes *wants* me to tell you—is this: Limelight Research Capital has been building state-of-the-art server farms that rival the yottabyte capacity of the NSA's gargantuan and highly secretive data storage facility in Bluffdale, Utah—which happens to have been built by a Mormon construction company with which I'm on very friendly terms, if you catch my drift. *However,* Limelight's server farms aren't located here in the US; they're in politically neutral territories all across the world—and in space. So there's not much that US government authorities can do about them, unless they want to send in tactical nukes."

"And those server farms are doing what?" Sabina asked, although she could already anticipate the answer.

"They're in the process of turning private cloud services and the NSA's vast data cache into the ultimate social network. It will be like an obligatory, inescapable Facebook for the psychopathic power elite."

THE WHEEL

"Why me?" Sabina asked Ron.

They were sitting on a Central Park bench in front of a Moorish-looking bridge—the Greywacke Arch, a lime green sign on a lamppost informed them. A brick-lined tunnel under the Greywacke Arch led to the back end of the Metropolitan Museum of Art. Inside the tunnel, a tall, ginger-bearded man in a hipster fedora leaned over a dull brass trumpet, playing an echoing medley of old Chet Baker tunes. Sabina had used the music—melancholy, beautiful—as an excuse to get Ron to stop walking and sit with her for a while.

"What do you mean, why you?" Ron asked her as finches chirped and hopped from branch to branch in the bushes behind them.

"I mean, why do you need me, as your iAesthetician or whatever? Obviously, you guys have more money than God. You could hire anybody—whole teams of anybodys. Why laser in on me?"

"I'm not sure I understand the question. We're hiring you because you're extremely good at what you do. And we already have a working relationship with Frank McKernan, who constantly raves about how great you are at coming up with creative solutions to seemingly insoluble PR problems."

In front of them, through the trees, Sabina could see the Obelisk—the Met's 3,500-year-old gift from Egypt—also known as Cleopatra's Needle. She thought it odd that a phallic symbol of such jutting prominence should be nicknamed after a woman.

Whatever.

"Here's the thing, Ron: you still haven't given me a clear picture of what you expect me to do. At first, I thought I was supposed to be getting your ass clear of the hostilities that are bound to rise up when Wes releases his Twitter for Elite Criminal Shitbirds app. But now I'm not so sure… I mean, do you expect me to somehow *save* Wes, or get him to change his mind about doing this?"

"All of the above, if possible," Ron answered, swatting at a fly. "Or none of it. There's another aspect to this that I haven't told you about yet."

"Oh great."

"You're very good at salvaging the reputations of people who've been caught doing unseemly things. Is that a fair description of your chosen profession?"

"A little reductive, but yeah, sure, that's what I do."

"Wes is looking for someone to do the opposite: someone who can destroy the reputations of those who've been doing horrible things—*monstrous* things—but haven't been caught yet. And who better to do that than someone like you, who knows how the court of public opinion really works?"

"So you're asking me to join Wes in his crazed, Don Quixote quest to take down America's Deep State power structure?"

"In a nutshell, yes."

"Are you fucking insane?"

"I'll admit it's a lot to ask."

"Y'think? Unlike Wes, I don't have a death wish."

"No one would ever have to know you were involved. We can protect your anonymity."

"Sure, that always works…" Sabina said, heavy on the sarcasm.

"I know it seems dangerous. But Wes is afraid that when the truth finally gets out, it will be ignored—because there's such a glut of disinformation being spewed into the world by the big media companies. So he wants to go after the Dark Brotherhood with what might be called anti-PR."

"Like a smear campaign."

"If you can smear someone with the truth of his or her own misdeeds, then yes, like a smear campaign."

"Sure you don't wanna hire Karl Rove? He's the expert in that field."

"He plays for the other side, as you well know."

Ron said something else, but Sabina didn't catch it because at that precise moment a park employee blasted past them on a noisy green machine that looked like what you'd get if an army jeep fucked a golf cart. The noise startled her. Her heart felt like it was trying to escape through her throat.

"Shit!" said Sabina, after the machine had passed. "Can we talk about something else? This whole thing is kind of freaking me out."

"Sure. What should we talk about?"

"Have you read the crazy dedication on this bench?" Sabina ran her finger across the little silver plaque embedded in the top slat of the bench they were sitting on. "It's like bad James Joyce."

The plaque read:

> *Dearest Nora*
> *The rink, zoo and trees behind and the Needle, Ancient and home ahead*
> *Peter and Henry scooting by, with music in the air and popsicles to come*
> *Sit with me awhile to savor our time here in this heart of my heart*
> *Bill*

"I mean, really, what the fuck?" said Sabina. "Some people read *Finnegans Wake* once and they're ruined for life."

"Nora probably thought it was sweet of Bill to do that for her," Ron blandly observed.

"It makes him sound like a sappy schizophrenic."

Some of the things that came out of Sabina's mouth could end up sounding harsh, even to her own ears.

Ron stood up from the bench. "Shall we go get some popsicles?" He held out his hand to her.

"Are you buyin'?"

"Of course."

"All right then." Sabina grabbed Ron's hand and he helped her up. Her butt was feeling a little sore from sitting for so long. As they walked toward the bridge, Ron continued holding hands with her.

Okay, so she was starting to like Wes Bramley's uptight Mormon *consigliere* a little better now.

THE LOVERS

MacDuff's text asked Sabina to meet him in Chinatown around 7 PM at a restaurant called Pulqueria. He sent her the address to pindrop on her iPhone's GPS map, but she still had trouble finding the place because it was located down an unmarked stairwell in a dogleg alley full of Chinese hair salons and dim sum joints. If it hadn't been for the little menu displayed in a glass box out in front, she would have thought she was descending into a basement opium den or a Shanghai-themed brothel. But once she opened the blank blue door and stepped into the subterranean foyer, she was amazed.

It was a different world down there. Off to her right was an elegant candlelit dining room with white tablecloths seemingly afloat like luminous jellyfish in the oceanic darkness. And to her left was what appeared to be a louche tiki lounge: woven grass mats on the beamed ceiling; blue-and-white adobe tiles in a latticework pattern across the floor; and two long, canopied bars lined with wooden stools and backlit glass shelves showcasing scores of rare tequilas and other exotic liqueurs in a range of poisonous colors.

MacDuff waved to her from a stool at the strangely empty bar. "Y'made it!" He tipped back his Stetson and stood up to give her a warm, friendly hug.

He smelled good. Sabina's sensitive nose detected sage, leather, balsam fir, and a hint of musk. There was also a sweet whiff of beer on MacDuff's breath. Glancing past his big shoulder, she saw a nearly empty pint on the bar top. She'd arrived late.

"I felt like I was on a scavenger hunt, trying to find this place," she complained to him with a grin.

"Yeah, sorry 'bout that. I shoulda mentioned the secret passageway." He signaled to the bartender while asking, "What're you havin'?"

She'd come prepared with an answer. After seeing MacDuff's text, she'd done a quick Google search of Pulqueria's reviews, finding raves for the food and booze—and more than a few complaints from self-righteous sorority girls about how they'd had to commit to a $500 bottle fee and slip the bouncer a fifty before they could even get in the door. With that research in mind, she said: "It's a pulqueria, right? So I thought I'd try the pulque."

"Y'might wanna pass on that," said MacDuff. "I heard the authentic version is made with old lady spit—t' get the fermentation goin'."

"*Ick*. I guess I'll have a beer then."

"Dos Equis okay?"

"Fine by me."

"*Dos Dos Equis, mi amigo…*" MacDuff said to the bartender, a buff guy with longish blonde hair who was wearing a dark brown leather vest almost identical to the one MacDuff had on.

"I'll bring them to you in the dining room, sir," said the bartender. "Your table's ready."

The elegant dining room was just as empty as the bar. Candlelit, romantic as all get-out, but empty. *Weird on a Friday night,* thought Sabina, *even for a semi-hidden Mexican speakeasy*. They sat down at a white leather upholstered banquette in the far back corner, facing a rosewood marimba on the other side of the room.

"Where're all the people?" Sabina asked.

"Might be a touch early for all them Chinese-Mexican restaurant patrons 'round these parts."

"How did you even find out about this place?"

"Read about it in *The New Yorker*—like most folks, I'd expect. Thought we should give it a try. They had a couple pulquerias down south o' Santa Fe, where I grew up. I always had a good time in them places."

"So you grew up in New Mexico?"

"Yep. My old man had a ranch down that way. Enough land t' run 'bout thirty thousand head o' cattle."

"Is that a lot?"

"You might say that. There's bigger ranches, but most of 'em are owned by corporations these days."

"So you're a real cowboy, not just some poseur."

"Nah. I ain't roped a steer or rode a horse in a coon's age. But old habits die hard. You stick with what you know, fer the most part."

"So why'd you come to New York?"

"Jus' lookin' t' get rich, I s'pose. I sold the ranch after the old man up n' died. Been here lookin' after my investments ever since."

So he's a trust fund cowboy, thought Sabina. *Oh well....*

"How 'bout you?"

"Me? I just sort of drifted here," she said. "I wasn't looking to get rich, that's for sure. I actually have a degree in social work. Never cared that much about money. I just turned down a date with a billionaire so I could go out with you, I'll have you know."

"Fer real?"

"Well, the truth is I sort of turned down a *potential* date with a billionaire. I'm working for him right now and I didn't think it'd be a great idea to mix business with… whatever."

"Which billionaire was it? I might know the dude."

"I can't tell you. I signed a nondisclosure agreement with his Chief Legal Officer the other day."

"C'mon…" MacDuff cajoled her, "I won't tell nobody."

"No, really, I can't! I take that stuff seriously."

"Welp, it's good t' know you're an honest woman, Sabina."

"Oh, believe me, I'm not *that* honest. I lie like a motherfucker on the Internet. But that's on behalf of my clients."

MacDuff laughed his gruff, sexy laugh again. Then he asked her to explain how she'd become a professional liar, which led to a lengthy discussion of her work as an iAesthetician and eGrief Counselor. Sometime during that discussion, their beers arrived and they ordered dinner from the bartender, who later came back to stand in front of the marimba with three wooden mallets in each hand, which he then used to play a lovely tune that Sabina found hauntingly familiar—although she couldn't remember its name.

"What's that song?" she asked MacDuff. "Do you know?"

"Pretty sure it's 'Where Is My Mind' by the Pixies," MacDuff said in his increasingly familiar laconic drawl.

"The Pixies! MacDuff, you surprise me. I thought you'd be more of a Hank Williams type."

"Sad, whiny songs 'bout drinkin' whiskey and drivin' around in a busted up Ford F-150 after yer wife kicks you outta the trailer park fer fornicatin' with that young slut from the Dairy Queen? No thank you, Ma'am. I'd rather listen t' trip-hop or some o' them local bands they got here, like The Walkmen or The National."

That led to a digression about one of Sabina's favorite singers, Sharon Van Etten, whose breakthrough album, *Tramp*, had been produced by Aaron Dessner from The National. She mentioned that Van Etten had toured with The Walkmen, The National, and Nick Cave.

"Nick Cave! I love that dude," MacDuff enthused. "He's like Elvis Presley, Jim Morrison, and Satan all rolled up in t' one lethal burrito."

"With arsenic guacamole," Sabina added, "and napalm salsa."

"Exactly!" MacDuff said he was particularly fond of Cave's lyrics for "Abattoir Blues." He quoted a few lines from memory:

> *I went t' bed last night and my moral code got jammed.*
> *I woke up this mornin' with a Frappuccino in my hand.*

Which led, of course, to Sabina's retelling of James Marrden's hallucinogenic-Frappuccino-fueled adventures in the Central Park Zoo. By the end of it, she had MacDuff laughing so hard that he splashed beer into his salsa verde enchilada.

There are few things better than hitting it off with someone who gets your sense of humor. Sabina was pretty sure she would be sleeping with MacDuff sometime very soon after that.

Just not on their first date. That would be slutty of her.

THE TOWER

Ron Geng phoned Sabina early the next morning, before she was even out of bed. "Did you decide yet?" he asked her.

For a split-second, Sabina's sleep-addled brain thought Ron was asking her if she'd decided to sleep with MacDuff. *Yes*, she thought, *but not until the third or fourth date, at least. How'd you know?* Then she realized that Ron had to be asking her about something else.

"Decide what?" she asked him.

"Whether you're going to help us."

"Oh… right." Sabina pushed her head deeper into her pillow while she stared up at the ceiling. "I'm still thinking about that."

"I have an excursion in mind that might help you come to a decision."

"An *excursion?* What—are we going on a field trip?"

"You might say that. Are you free around one o'clock?"

"Let me check my schedule." Sabina knew her afternoon schedule was wide open, but she didn't want Ron thinking she was any less busy than he was, so she downloaded her iPhone's overnight emails first before she got back to him. "I can juggle a few things and make one o'clock work."

"I'll send a car for you." Ron hung up without even saying goodbye.

"I guess we're back to being Captain Dickhead," Sabina said to her silenced iPhone.

Five hours later, a black Lincoln Navigator dropped Sabina off on the corner of Eleventh and West Twenty-Fourth. From there, it was just a short walk along the sidewalk to The Vault.

The Vault Gallery was semi-famous for its bulletproof glass windows. As high and wide as a fire department garage door, the windows contained three million dollars in loose twenties and hundreds between their double panes like some ironic art world joke about saving money with insulation. In a sort of perpetual publicity stunt for the gallery and the glass's manufacturers (3M), a written notice at the bottom of the windows declared that any person who broke the windows was entitled to the money contained therein. A flat screen monitor sandwiched between the panes played a continuous loop of all the window-breaking attempts caught on security cameras (usually at night): judo kicks, skateboard slams, hurled cinderblocks, rage-fueled sledgehammer blows, and more than a few blasts from

.44s, gangbanger Glocks, and 12-gauge shotguns. The windows always held. (In the interest of fairness, a permanent reinforced concrete security abutment had been erected along the sidewalk in front of the gallery to prevent anyone from going Mad Max and attempting to drive a battering-ram-equipped monster truck through the glass.)

Someday somebody'll show up with a bazooka and that'll be that, Sabina thought.

Ron stood waiting for her in front of the money-stuffed windows. Above his head, a title in bold red sans-serif font alerted the public to the Vault's current show:

Luna Chicas, Narcocorridas, and the Tarot of 9/11

"I hope this doesn't mean that Mexican lounge singers were the real masterminds behind 9/11," Sabina joked to Ron as they walked in.

"They were not," he said, without even a hint of a smile.

Ron seemed incapable of recognizing when Sabina was just kidding around with him. It made her want to kid him even more—to kid the fucking shit out of him. It was a childish response, she knew, but that wasn't going to stop her.

Before they entered the main gallery, a freestanding white wall confronted them with a ten-foot wide digital C-print of a naked Latina woman in a butter yellow room. She was sprawled sideways across a tacky vinyl recliner, looking into the camera over her round left shoulder with her enormous overripe ass on display, front and center. The painted text on the wall next to the photograph read:

> ***Luna Chicas*** is a complex anthropological tour through the damaged landscape of Nicaraguan prostitutes. Tackling the difficult subject of prostitution with deep scrutiny and sensitivity, Dutch-born photographer and filmmaker Lars von Loon traveled to Nicaraguan brothels to photograph the women and girls who make their livings there. The result is a compassionate portrayal in which von Loon deftly straddles the line between documentary and rigorously staged portraiture, and ultimately restores human value to these marginalized women and children.

"Are you wearing your sacred Mormon underpants today?" Sabina asked Ron.

"Yes, as a matter-of-fact, I am," he answered. "Although we prefer the term *undergarments*."

"Do they help protect you from getting boners in public?"

Ron chose not to answer that right away.

They walked around the end of the wall into the main gallery space, where dozens of large color photographs hung at eye-level—depictions of Nicaraguan prostitutes going about their daily business. A haggard, sooty-eyed blowjob crone lewdly sucked on a red-white-and-blue missile pop. Fat-bottomed girls in pink hot pants and lime green sequined bikini tops cavorted in front of a street mural of poorly drawn Disney characters. A naked, anorexic-looking whore with a wispy black bush lay spread-eagled on a baby blue mattress, her entire rib cage outlined beneath her tawny skin in brutal relief.

That same bare mattress, or one very much like it, had been placed on the concrete floor in the center of the gallery space. Some very authentic-looking fluid stains—*cum, shit, lube, piss*—converged in a shallow, pounded out depression toward the mattress's center.

The photographs were beautifully lit and artfully framed, but the sad tired sleaziness of the subject matter remained palpable.

"I don't find any of this arousing," Ron said to Sabina in a delayed response to her question. "And for your information, Mormon men don't get boners."

Was he joking with her? His face rearranged itself into a tight little smirk. *He was! Ron had made a joke!*

Sabina playfully punched his shoulder. "Your *undergarments* must be tingling with righteous boner-killing holy fire right now. Look at that one with the raccoon. She's cute as hell, but she can't be much older than fifteen."

The photo Sabina was commenting on took up the entire backside of the freestanding wall. A nude Nicaraguan girl with wavy dark hair, budding breasts, and gorgeous doe eyes reclined on a burnt orange bedspread in a shadowy juniper green room. She was propped up on one elbow, caressing a small pet raccoon nestled near her slim little belly. Aside from a grainy tattooed unicorn on her right boob, she was flawless and undeniably sexy, a proud odalisque (or "nymphet"—as a reader of *Lolita* might phrase it—if you were into that sort of thing…).

"I hope she's not a real whore," Sabina thought out loud.

"As I'm given to understand," Ron pontificated, "girls her age and younger are being forced into prostitution on a regular basis. That's one of the reasons why the US Border Patrol has been seeing such an influx of children fleeing from Central America, unaccompanied by adults. They come from Guatemala, Honduras, El Salvador, Nicaragua… places where violent drug cartels have a stranglehold on the local economies and law enforcement agencies are either too helpless or too corrupt to do anything about it. We've been seeing over fifty thousand young migrants a year from those places recently."

"Christ…" said Sabina. She felt an impulse to adopt the girl in the photo—and her raccoon, too—if she could. But then she noticed the photograph's date next to Lars von Loon's signature in the lower right-hand corner: *2001*. The raccoon girl would be in her twenties or early thirties by now, if she'd survived.

And that baby raccoon was probably long gone.

"The worst thing," said Ron, "is that most of those needy children are quickly turned away from our borders and sent back to their home countries, where they'll be condemned to lives of prostitution or drug-running if they don't want to die. It's shameful. America's immigration system is a dysfunctional quagmire—thanks, in a large part, to the jingoist Tea Party Republicans in Congress. We have a moral imperative to do better."

"Yeah, but how? Congress doesn't seem like it's up for fixing much of anything these days."

"There are other solutions we can talk about later," Ron said. "But everything will make more sense if you'll let me walk you through the rest of the exhibit first."

To that end, Ron guided Sabina toward a second exhibit in the next room over. Another freestanding wall confronted them at the entrance. This one displayed a moody portrait of a young man with a shaven head, full sultry lips, and pale, striking blue eyes.

It was a glamorized mug shot, heavy on the gang ink. An elaborate tattoo of a dark blue Tibetan demon with a gaping fanged mouth, three round bulging eyes, and a crown of rotting skulls stared out from the center of the young man's muscular torso. A large, stylized "18" was tattooed around the Adam's apple on his veiny neck and a faded prison ink teardrop was etched just below the far left corner of his eye. Sabina was finding it hard to look away from those pale blue eyes. Whether they were soulful or empty, it was hard to tell, but they had a mesmerizing pull—about that, she was absolutely certain.

The wall text beside the portrait read:

Narcocorridas is the final body of work to be completed by the Los Angeles based social documentary photographer, Javier Pendejos de Amores, pictured here in a self-portrait.

From an early age, de Amores had been a member of the Malditos, a multiracial Orange County subset of the 18th Street gang—long thought to be the largest transnational criminal organization operating in Los Angeles. Because of de Amores' reputation with the Malditos, he was allowed to document 18th Street gang activity in the U.S., Mexico, and Central America with almost complete freedom, first with a stolen Leica M6, and later with a Toyo-View 8X10 field camera. His chromogenic prints on Alu-Dibond celebrate Mexican color palettes and Aztec kitsch (flowers, sacrifice, idol worship) while focusing a remorseless documentary lens on the martial culture of street gangs and drug cartels—and the violence strewn in their wake.

In July 2016, while traveling in Mexico, de Amores was slain by members of Los Zetas, a drug cartel known for carrying out multiple massacres against civilians and rival cartels. In a sickening twist of fate, de Amores' severed head was photographed on his own camera equipment. That film and equipment was later delivered to this gallery by a Los Zetas courier, for reasons unexplained.

As they walked around to the other side of the wall, Ron and Sabina were met with the sight of a red Jeep Cherokee blasted full of bullet holes. It was parked in the center of the gallery space, surrounded by glossy chromogenic prints on all four walls. A bloodied mannequin's hand hung from the Jeep's window in the driver's side door. The mannequin within, seen through the bullet-riddled windshield, seemed amazingly life-like. Or make that *death-like*… the side of its waxen, forensically accurate head had been blown off, with fake brain tissue spattered all over the Jeep's interior. A police outline of an absent dead body had been traced in red-white-and-green-dyed carnations off to the right of the Jeep's flat front tire. Gold-plated machine gun bullet casings littered the concrete surrounding it.

The photographs were equally vivid and grim. In the one on the back of the freestanding wall, a naked man was laid out on a city street, handcuffed and gagged with a white jock strap bound tight through his mouth. His lidless eyes stared up at the sky in a rictus of bewildered terror. Dozens of cheap kitchen knives had been hammered into his face, his neck, his chest, his crotch, and his thighs. He looked like one of those African nail fetish dolls that Sabina had seen at the Met. Worst of all, a group of young girls had gathered in the street behind him like they were lining up for a One Direction concert. Seen only from the waist down in the photograph's crop, all those bare female legs and bicycle wheels just seemed to add to the image's banal horror.

"Who would want to hang this crap on their walls?" Sabina asked Ron. "I mean, I'm sorry this Pendejo kid died and everything, but this is just beyond ugly."

"There's a long tradition of ugliness in the art world," Ron said, "from Goya's Black Paintings on up through Cindy Sherman's recent ooze and vomit photos. I'm sure you can think up a few examples of your own. But a gallery like this one doesn't have to sell anything it exhibits. Most of the deals are done over the phone or in back rooms, with works of art that the public rarely sees. It's the art dealer that makes the gallery, not what's on the walls."

"But still, why put up stuff that's so… *yucky?*"

"Because it has a point to make?" It sounded more like a question than an answer. "Or maybe because—to paraphrase Oscar Wilde—the art that the world calls immoral is the art that shows the world its own shame." He pointed to a string of grey painted words running above the photographs on the far white wall:

No one pays attention to these killings, but the secret of the world is hidden in them. — Roberto Bolaño, *2666*

"I read that book," Sabina said. "It was about the hundreds of young girls who were getting murdered while they worked in the *maquiladoras* around Juárez. But this is just drug dealers killing other drug dealers—like a self-cleaning oven. It's less evil and mysterious than the Juárez thing."

"I would say they're very much all of a piece. If these young men had better opportunities—and above all, better educations—they wouldn't be so easily lured into working for the drug cartels."

"You think they'd all be working for Apple or Google instead?"

"Wouldn't that be better?" Ron asked her.

"I suppose. At least Steve Jobs never hammered a knife into some guy's eyeball—I mean, not that I know of.... *Oh sick!* That must be Javier!"

Sabina put a hand up to cover her mouth. Without thinking too much about it, she'd gravitated toward the back wall of the exhibit, where the line of photographs ended. The last photo showed the bloody severed head of Javier Pendejos de Amores. His pale blue eyes and full sultry lips had been crudely sewn shut with festive red-white-and-green ribbons, but the distinctive faded green teardrop tattoo and the sawn-through number 18 on his neck were unmistakable.

Poor Javier's head was cradled in the lap of a guffawing Mexican child wearing an oversized black sombrero with fuzzy little orange balls dangling from strings along its brim. The boy couldn't have been much older than ten or eleven. He was missing a few front teeth and his right eye was drawn up into a hideous bruised squint. He sat cross-legged in a patch of heat-cracked dry mud with a half-empty tequila bottle raised at a tilt in his right fist. In his left, he held up a battered AK-47 with a scorch-marked bayonet and an improvised buttstock made from a hacked off shovel handle.

The kid looked like he was having the time of his life.

"I need to get out of here…" Sabina said to Ron. She felt like she might start puking if she stayed in that room a minute longer.

"Understood," Ron said.

They fled to the last room at the back of the gallery. There was no image on the freestanding wall in this exhibit. Instead, they found two tall steel-grey columns of wall text. Sabina started to read, hoping it would quell the nausea rising in her:

> **The Tarot of 9/11: For Mark Lombardi** was created over the course of seven years (2001 - 2008) by the neo-conceptual artist known as Démerder…

She stopped reading when a big white dog appeared at the wall's right edge and padded out to greet them.

At first Sabina thought *White Labrador. Or Standard Poodle*…. But then she knew he had to be a Goldendoodle—one of those dogs that Frank had mentioned to her. He was carrying a fluffy raccoon plush toy in his mouth with the self-contented air of a happy toddler. He came right over to Sabina and dropped the raccoon at her feet. It was kind of chewed up and slobbery, but still very cute. Then the big dog sat on his haunches and looked up at her with his big brown eyes, as if he expected her to pet him. He seemed to be smiling. Sabina crouched down and stroked his neck with both hands just beneath his silky white ears. The dog tilted his head back and started panting with his long pink tongue lolling out of his mouth in a kind of doggy rapture.

And just like that, Sabina's nausea vanished.

"Ohh, you're such a sweet pupperoo," she said to the dog as his flopping wet tongue grazed her wrist. "*So nice!* What's your name?"

There was a silver tag in the shape of a cartoon dog bone on the dog's leather collar. The name **GUY** was inscribed on it, along with a phone number and an address on West Fortieth, near Bryant Park.

"Guy? Is that your name? Guy?"

The dog just batted his long blonde eyelashes and panted even harder. He really seemed to enjoy having Sabina's hands on him.

"That's Guy de Bored," Ron said, pronouncing the Guy with a long *E*, like the French Situationist, Guy Debord. "It's Démerder's dog. He must be somewhere in the gallery, talking to Laylon."

"Who's Laylon?"

"His dealer. This is her gallery. She's the only person who really knows him. He won't speak to anyone else."

"Seriously?" Sabina stood up, but Guy de Bored patted the air in front of her knees with his big fuzzy paw, demanding further strokes, so she crouched back down and patted him some more.

"Démerder never does interviews," Ron elaborated. "He's rarely seen in public and he seems to have no close friends—aside from Laylon. I've heard he's very monk-like."

"He sounds a lot like Wes." *Could Démerder and Wes Bramley be the same person?* she wondered.

Quietly, Ron said, "There's a whisper going around that he's autistic. Sort of an idiot savant."

"Really."

"That's just what I've heard. No one aside from Laylon actually knows—and she's not talking."

Sabina stood up again to read the wall text with the dog standing beside her, leaning his surprisingly heavy body up against her right leg for further pats:

The Tarot of 9/11: For Mark Lombardi was created over the course of seven years (2001 - 2008) by the neo-conceptual artist known as Démerder. It is an hommage to the pioneering work of Mark Lombardi, the American artist whose elegant pencil diagrams documented the financial and political frauds perpetrated by a global criminal overclass. A short list of the scandals that Lombardi's work examined would include: Iran-Contra, BCCI, Harken Energy, Nugan Hand Ltd., the P2 Lodge, the Savings and Loan Crisis, and the Reagan-era arming of Saddam Hussein. Lombardi almost certainly would have addressed the September 11 attacks in his work if he hadn't hanged himself (or died from a covert lynching) at his apartment in Williamsburg, Brooklyn on March 22, 2000.

While remaining true to Lombardi's original vision, Démerder expands upon the artist's work both in scale and by taking it to its natural destination: the Internet. *The Tarot of 911* exists in the digital realm as processable data structures (sociograms, tree charts, hyperlinked texts, photographs, scans of original newspaper and magazine sources, etc.) that are now accessible to everyone. The 22 cards from the Tarot's Major Arcana have been incorporated into the artwork as wireless entry nodes. Log into Démerder.com and point the camera lens on your Bluetooth-enabled mobile device at any card and it will link to the data that card represents.

Lombardi's work—and now Démerder's—has been studied by the FBI, the CIA, and consultants to the Department of Homeland Security for insights into how they might better organize their own vast data caches. However, most of the elite global powerbrokers clearly implicated in those crimes against humanity remain free.

• • •

A Black Box For Humanity's Redacted History, also by Démerder, is a 33" X 33" cube constructed of 6 panels precision milled from a large iron meteorite discovered in the sands of Rub' al Khali ("The Empty Quarter") in the Arabian Desert in 1999. It contains a sophisticated, custom-programmed computer that wirelessly connects to the Internet and auctions itself on eBay every six weeks in perpetuity. A contract between the artist and collector stipulates that the work must be connected to the Internet at all times so it can attempt to resell itself during the prescribed period and maintain contact with the artist, who receives a 6% commission from each sale. The minimum auction bid is automatically set 9% higher than the previous sales price (after taking into account shipping, handling, and transaction fees); if that minimum bid is not met, the work remains in the collector's possession—at least until the next auction, six weeks later.

The last recorded sales price for *A Black Box For Humanity's Redacted History* was $17 million.

"Seventeen million dollars!" Sabina exclaimed. "For something you can't even own? That's crazy."

"It's no crazier than someone paying fifty-eight million dollars for one of Jeff Koons' Balloon Dog sculptures," said Ron. "In fact, I'd argue that it's a much safer investment. The *Black Box* has a long history of making people money. No one's lost a dime on it yet."

"So it's like an art world Ponzi scheme."

"That's a cynical way of putting it, but you're essentially correct. Only this particular Ponzi scheme is legal and it has the added benefit of supporting an artist who's doing important work."

"What's the six percent commission on seventeen million?" Sabina asked Ron. She was too flustered to do the math in her head.

"It comes to just over a million dollars," he told her.

"*Jesus!* And he can get that every six weeks? For doing nothing? That guy's no idiot... he's a fucking genius!"

They walked around the freestanding wall to view the work. "You must have the best dog bed..." Sabina said to Guy as he followed along behind them. *"Oh. My. God."*

The metallic black cube stood on a concrete pillar in the center of the large room. It was beautiful in its polished darkness, but also somehow ominous. Like the monolith in Stanley Kubrick's *2001,* it seemed to open onto infinity.

The cube was impressive enough all by itself, but beyond it was an absolutely monumental drawing of the World Trade Center towers in mid-collapse, taking up the entire three-story back wall. The drawing was almost frightening in its intensity. The debris clouds had been rendered in swirling swipes and slashes of charcoal. Within them, monstrous grimacing faces seemed to be emerging through the smoke and ruin: George H.W. Bush, Dick Cheney, Donald Rumsfeld, W., some Arab-looking guys that Sabina didn't recognize (definitely not Osama bin Laden...). The remaining steel and glass yet to undergo dustification had been sketched out in graphite and colored pencil. But as Sabina drew closer, what she found amazing was that each pencil line connected in some meaningful way to a circle—a node of influence—with the name of a person or corporation written inside it, along with a brief explanation of why that name mattered.

It was mind-blowing when you contemplated the sheer amount of man-hours it must have taken to plot everything out. Démerder had encoded a detailed narrative structure of the 9/11 terrorist conspiracy right into a drawing of that conspiracy's wicked culmination. It was like something out of a dream that spoke in images merged with language, conveying knowledge in an instant intuitive thought-ball of... *what was the word?*

Oh hell... there was a word for it—*MacDuff had used it the other day at the library*—but she couldn't think of it right at that moment. Maybe it would come to her later.

A legend on the wall to the left of the drawing explained what the various lines meant in relation to the circular nodes. A solid black line indicated some type of influence or control between businesses or individuals. A jagged cyan blue lightning bolt line indicated the sale or transfer of an asset. A spiraling grey line that looked like an old-fashioned telephone cord indicated a spin-off or front company. A green line showed the flow of money, loans, or credit—with an arrow at one end or the other indicating its direction. A red line indicated bankruptcy, a court judgment, criminal conviction, or death. And finally, the use of a dotted line, color-coded as above, indicated a speculative transaction or line of influence that couldn't be proven (yet) in a court of law; while two vertical slashes near the end of that dotted line indicated a blocked or incomplete transaction—or in the case of a vanished person or asset, an unknown outcome.

"It's a lot to get your head around," said Ron, indicating the legend, "but once you become familiar with it, you'll be amazed at how it helps you visually understand these complex networks of 'Elite Criminal Shitbirds'—as you so glibly referred to them. Wes loved that, by the way. He now owns the web domain for Shitbirds.com."

"Glad I could be of service," said Sabina. She bent down to pet Guy again. "Your dog dad is one smart cookie," she told him.

"That's an understatement," said Ron. "When Wes and I first started trying to organize the data on the hidden crimes we were discovering, we soon ran into a wall. The plots we saw unfolding were too complex for the average person to comprehend. Mormons are pretty good organizers, as our genealogy library will attest, but I just couldn't see my way through the thicket. Only the most dogged and educated could even begin to penetrate it. You had to know so many esoteric facts about how the Deep State operates—not to mention the sheer number of names, dates, and places that you had to keep straight in order to make sense of what was going on. It seemed almost impossible to describe in a linear narrative without cognitive dissonance setting in. At a certain point, the brain rebels. It doesn't *want* to understand this information. It's too much… too horrible to contemplate. But Lombardi and Démerder have gone a long way toward simplifying that mountain of cerebrally-stultifying data by organizing it into shapes and colors that lead the mind to meaning."

"And Wes wants to do the same thing for every psycho shitbird power player on the Internet, is that it?"

"You're beginning to get the picture."

To the left of the legend, a pair of quotations in grey paint dominated the remaining space on the huge white wall. Sabina rose from petting Guy and took a few steps back so she could read them:

The majority of politicians, on the evidence available to us, are not interested in truth but in power and in the maintenance of that power. To maintain that power it is essential that people remain in ignorance, that they live in ignorance of the truth, even the truth of their own lives. What surrounds us therefore is a vast tapestry of lies, upon which we feed.   — Harold Pinter, Nobel Lecture, 2005

Authority has always attracted the lowest elements in the human race. All through history mankind has been bullied by scum.   — P.J. O'Rourke, *Parliament of Whores*

"There's something you're not telling me…" Sabina said to Ron. "Is Démerder Wes?"

"No. They're two different people. But Wes has been helping Démerder financially, without him even being aware of it. When Démerder first showed *A Black Box for Humanity's Redacted History* here in this gallery back in 2007, Wes saw the show and was so impressed that he immediately created two shell companies with the sole purpose of purchasing the *Black Box* on eBay. In the beginning, there were no other bidders, so the two shell companies traded off ownership every few months. Wes saw it as a way to secretly become Démerder's patron, to make sure that Démerder had the time and money to complete his work on *The Tarot of 9/11* and his other projects, like *The Fed and the Vampire Squid*. But then a funny thing happened. Other bidders started competing for the *Black Box*. Major bidders."

"Like who? Do you know?"

"Hedge fund managers, art savvy CEOs, private investor groups… you name it. Some of the very same people that Démerder was implicating in his other work ended up buying the *Black Box* and turning a profit on it. You can see the irony in that, I'm sure."

"More for them than for Démerder," Sabina observed. "It's almost like they're colluding in their own doom."

"They're doomed only if Démerder's work becomes widely disseminated and understood. So far, that hasn't happened. But Wes is doing everything he can to change that. That's why he's so intent on hiring you."

"I'm just one person. There's not that much I can do…."

"Don't sell yourself short," said Ron. "Radical cultural change can be accomplished with as few as four key people, if Kurt Vonnegut is to be believed."

"I never thought of Kurt Vonnegut as any particular expert on social engineering or whatever," Sabina said. "I liked his books when I was in high school, though."

"You may not know this, but Vonnegut's doctoral thesis examined the Ghost Dance—which inspired a peaceable Indian tribe to fight the US Army at Wounded Knee. It then compared that movement's leaders to the leaders of the Cubist movement, to see what they had in common. Vonnegut found that they shared three key elements which, when combined, could produce a major cultural shift."

Ron ticked off the three elements on his fingers:

"Number one, you need a gifted, visionary leader who describes cultural changes that should be made. That'd be Démerder in this case.

"Number two, you need at least two or more respected citizens who will testify that the visionary leader is not a madman, but is, instead, worthy of serious consideration. That'd be Wes and myself—and hopefully others soon to follow.

"And finally, number three, you need a glib, personable explainer. Someone who can tell the general public what the leader is up to, and why it matters, day after day after day. That'd be you."

Ron looked at Sabina expectantly. She had a sneaking suspicion that he'd had that little speech memorized.

"Well, I'm flattered," she said, crouching to scratch behind Guy's silky ears again. "No one's ever called me a glib, personable explainer before. But I'm still not convinced I should put my life on the line for the sake of some crazy artist like Démerder."

"He's not crazy," said Ron, getting defensive. "Artists like Démerder are the natural antagonists of the world's covert dictators. Both want to transform human consciousness: the dictators by controlling what other people think, and the artists by providing the people with liberating knowledge, or *gnosis*."

Gnosis! That was the word MacDuff had used in the library the other day. Synapses started firing in Sabina's brain like a string of firecrackers going off, making connections she'd been too blind to see until that very moment.

Sabina stood up and said to Ron: "Take me to see Wes Bramley right fucking now. Otherwise the deal's off."

THE MAGICIAN

MacDuff was kicking back, sipping a Mocha Frappuccino with the worn heels of his boots propped up on Wes Bramley's executive desk, when Sabina burst into his office. His sea-green eyes boggled beneath his Stetson and his reflexes caused him to crush the plastic Starbuck's cup in his fist as Sabina shouted at him:

"Goddam you, MacDuff, you snooping cowboy fuck! You had Ron put spyware on my fucking laptop!"

"Well hello there, darlin'…" said MacDuff, as laconic as ever, despite the Frappuccino goo dripping down his wrist onto the desk.

Ron came through the door at a dead run behind Sabina. He didn't stop until he hit the edge of Wes's desk. "I tried calling to warn you, but she took my phone," he panted, tie askew, suit soaked with sweat.

"Ron, you puss… you coulda fought her fer it."

Ron bent over with his hands on his knees. "You have no idea how fast she is…" he gasped.

"Here's your phone, asshole," Sabina said, bouncing it off the top of Ron's sweaty red head.

She wheeled back around on MacDuff. "So what's your real name?" she demanded to know. "Is it Wes? MacDuff? Or Baron Dipshit Von Tinycock?"

"See, Ron? I told ya she could cuss the stink off a buzzard."

"I think I have to go throw up now." Ron lurched and quickly exited the office, slamming the door behind him.

"That sonofagun don't get enough exercise," said MacDuff with a grin through his beard. "It's good t' see you, Sabina. What brings you t' this here neck o' the woods?"

"You know why I'm here, shithead. You fucking lied to me."

"More like a tiny omission o' the truth, the way I see it."

"Oh, it's a whole lot more than that. You goddam set me up. Those documents on Ron's key drive must've had some EFI malware that opened a backdoor on my laptop, so you could track me. That's how you knew to find me at the library that day."

"Now now... t'weren't nothin' the NSA don't already do. They been sniffin' 'round yer backdoor fer years with their durned God Mode malware."

"So this whole cowboy act of yours, the philosophy... was it all just a way to sucker me in? Stuff you found out about me on my computer?"

"T'weren't that way at all, darlin'. Truth is, ol' Frank McKernan was the one who said you might be susceptible t' my cowboy charm, such as it is."

"Frank's in on this, too? Oh *great!* That's just fucking great! Even my supposed friends have been screwing me over on this deal."

"Now don't go gettin' mad at Frank. He just thought you and me might make a cute couple. Everything else that happened—welp, that's my fault. You gotta trust me on that."

"How can I ever trust *anything* that comes out of your lying cowboy mouth after this?" Sabina felt like she was on the verge of tears, but she was too pissed off to let MacDuff see her cry. She'd hold it in. "*Christ!* I'll bet you don't even *like* Nick Cave."

"Aw, now that ain't true at all." MacDuff picked up a remote from his desktop and pointed it at a jukebox on the other side of the room. "Have a listen... I got him right here."

Cave's brooding love song, "Into My Arms," began playing from speakers hidden throughout the room:

I don't believe in an interventionist God
But I know, darling, that you do....

God, I love that man's voice, Sabina thought, stifling a sob.

"That there's a work o' modern art, by the way," said MacDuff. "It's called *A Jukebox o' People Tryin' t' Change the World.* Came from an artist by the name o' Ruth Ewan. She's been stuffin' it fulla protest songs since around 2003, but I had her put in a couple o' my favorites, too—like ol' Nick here."

For all Sabina knew, it was just another prop for his crappy con artist act. "Goddamnit, MacDuff, or Wes—or whoever the fuck you are…" she said, "if you don't come clean with me right now, I'm walking through that door and out of your life forever."

"I'm willin' t' come clean, but I gotta ask you somethin' first: How'd you figure it out so fast? I got the best durned coders in the world workin' here. That spyware shoulda been downright invisible."

"Ron used a word I'd heard you use earlier, at the library. *Gnosis.* It's a word most people don't hear every day—or ever, really. It made me think you two had to know each other."

"Good ol' human fallibility…" MacDuff chuckled to himself. "Yeah, Gnosticism's kinda the rulin' philosophy 'round these parts. Me and Ron started out as existentialists at Stanford, but Gnosticism's where we ended up."

Sabina wasn't in the mood to hear about MacDuff and Ron's bong-fueled metaphysical circle jerks at Stanford right at that moment. "So what's your real goddam name?" she asked him.

"My real name's MacDuff, like I been sayin' all along. Wes Bramley's jus' my business name—sorta like a shell company. It's easier t' fly under the radar when yer name don't have a history."

"So the ranch in New Mexico, the mom who loved books—that's all true?"

"Scout's honor."

"Then why'd you spy on me?"

"Welp, consider it from my end, Angel Tits. I been trustin' you with secrets that could land me in a whole heap o' trouble—or even get me killed. I had t' know what kinda person you were before I went in whole hog with ya."

"Those secrets could land my ass in hot water, too. So from now on, if you want me around, you have to be honest with me. No more sneaky shit. And don't call me Angel Tits, by the way… at least not in public. It's disrespectful."

"But Baron Dipshit Von Tinycock—that's downright honorific."

"Okay, well, I was mad at you when I said that. I don't actually know how big your frank-and-beans are when you heat 'em up around the campfire. And fuck you, by the way. I'm still mad."

Not really... she realized.

"I reckon you got a right," said MacDuff. He tilted back his Stetson and scratched at his brow with his dry right hand. "And I'm sorry, Sabina. I truly am. It was ungentlemanly o' me t' go lookin' at yer backdoor like that. Although the way you wear them yoga pants, well, who could blame a man?"

"You can't just make this whole thing go away by flirting with me again."

"Flirtin' ain't the half o' it. I want you t' marry me."

"What?"

MacDuff stood up from behind his desk. He pulled open a drawer and took out something shiny.

"A six-shooter, MacDuff? Are you fucking kidding me?"

"I'm dead serious 'bout this marriage proposal, darlin'. Ron told me a wife can't testify against her husband in a court o' law. It's the only way fer us, goin' forward."

"What if I say no? Are you gonna shoot me?"

"Nah. It ain't loaded." MacDuff set the gun down on his desk, acting somewhat chagrined. "But it coulda been. You'd do right t' see it as a symbol o' my devotion t' becomin' yer lovin' husband. No pre-nups, neither. You'll be my equal partner, worth more'n half-a-billion, soon as you say 'I do'."

On a strictly cash basis the offer was certainly tempting, but under the circumstances it came across as batshit crazy. "I'm not marrying you, MacDuff," Sabina said. "So you can just get that idiotic idea right out of your skull."

She turned and started walking toward the door, self-consciously aware of MacDuff staring at her ass on the way out. With a flick at her blonde braid, she said to him over her shoulder:

"But if I ever decide to forgive you, you *might* get a shot at a second date."

Did she hear a *Yee-haw!* as she slammed the door behind her?

She did.

THE FOOL

Everyone is a Fool at the start of his or her journey.

Each of us is born wordless and innocent. The first things we learn about our new world come to us through sensual observation: the warmth of our mother's breast, the shrill cry of a seagull, the wafting green spark of a firefly on a summer night, the smell of newly mown grass on a basset hound puppy's fur. Soon we start to make basic connections: cry out in hunger and milk might arrive, that tall man who's around in the evenings responds with a smile when called Dada, teething pain can be somewhat alleviated by chewing on a finger. Then our formal education begins. For most, that education amounts to one long humiliation. There's so much to learn, so much we'll never know, so much we're taught imperfectly.

Our brains, we discover, are less than ideal repositories for knowledge. We tend to forget some lessons and deliberately ignore others, especially when those lessons are too complex or disturbing to easily comprehend. Certain people always seem to know more than we do. They're richer, more connected, better educated. Some of those same people make it their business to exploit the rest of us. Call them psychopathic personalities, intraspecies predators—or simply, greedy fucks.

It can take years—even a lifetime—to understand how we've been exploited, but that understanding is crucial. The intraspecies predators operate as though incomprehension is a form of consent. So they tend to make their exploitative schemes as complicated, opaque, and intimidating as possible.

The Tarot of 9/11: For Mark Lombardi is one Fool's attempt to make sense of a day that nearly everyone is aware of, but almost no one fully understands. The September 11 attacks were used by the Bush administration to justify the passage of the USA PATRIOT Act and wage illegitimate wars in Afghanistan and Iraq. Americans became significantly less free because of those acts, which had been planned far in advance. The official story of 9/11, as handed down by the White House, is riddled with omissions and distortions—even former members of the 9/11 Commission will tell you that. *The Tarot of 9/11* is designed to uncover the true story behind the official story.

It's a crash course in false flag terrorism, as it turns out....

THE HERMIT

Sabina had been skipping around in Démerder's *The Tarot of 9/11* website for days. The interface was slow and clunky. Either Démerder needed a web hosting upgrade from his ISP or someone was trying to sabotage his site with a distributed denial of service attack—but the information was still there to be had if you were patient. Sabina now knew more about the September 11 attacks than she ever would have imagined.

Much of that newly acquired knowledge was appalling.

The one thing that really stood out for her was Transportation Secretary Norman Mineta's testimony to the 9/11 Commission about Dick Cheney's odd behavior just before American Airlines Flight 77 hit the Pentagon. Mineta had been in the Presidential Emergency Operations Center with the Vice President on 9/11 because he had two sons who were pilots for United Airlines and he didn't know where they were that day. American Airlines Flight 11 and United Airlines Flight 175 had already crashed into the North and South towers of the World Trade Center. The committee asked Mineta if he'd been present when the order was given to shoot down American Airlines Flight 77. He answered (on a video of the testimony that Démerder linked to):

"No, I was not. I was made aware of it, uh, during the time that the airplane coming in to the Pentagon, uh, there was a young man who would come in and say to the Vice President, 'The plane is fifty miles out…' 'The plane is thirty miles out…' And when it got down to: 'The plane is ten miles out…' uhm, the young man also said to the Vice President, 'Do the orders still stand?' And the Vice President turned and whipped his neck around and said, 'Of course the orders still stand. Have you heard anything to the contrary?' Well, at the time I didn't know what all that meant. And (…) then later I heard of the fact that the airplanes had been scrambled from Langley to come up to DC, but those planes were still about ten minutes away."

Okay, so it was no smoking gun, but add it to all the other weird circumstantial evidence and it made Sabina think this: Cheney knew the Air Force jets from Langley were still too far away (deliberately, because of NORAD games) to intercept Flight 77. Cheney also knew that the Pentagon had on-site anti-aircraft defenses capable of taking down a hijacked plane. Given that two hijacked commercial airliners had just been used as weapons to destroy the World Trade Center, shooting down the hijacked plane approaching the Pentagon would have been the most logical course of action to take. But the young man was clearly anxious to hear Cheney *change* his standing orders, which meant that Cheney's orders must have been to leave the Pentagon undefended—orders so contrary to common sense that it made the young man dare to ask the snarling Vice President if he was having second thoughts. *(You would think an observation like that might be important—and that investigators might have wanted to follow up on it—but Mineta's testimony wasn't included in the 9/11 Commission's final report.)*

The success of the September 11 attacks depended not only on gaining control of commercial airliners and having a reliable means of guiding them to their targets. *(Computer-guided remote control, anyone? Hani Hanjour, the alleged pilot of Flight 77, couldn't even land a Cessna 172 without looking like a dangerous fucking idiot, yet he somehow managed to fly a 767 at excessive speed into a tight, spiraling 330-degree descent and then level out just a few feet above the ground before ramming into the first floor of the Pentagon on the only side that was virtually empty and had been recently hardened to withstand a terrorist attack.)* Just as essential to the plan's success as controlling the airliners, nothing could be allowed to interfere with them hitting their intended targets.

In that regard, Secretary of Defense Donald Rumsfeld's behavior was just as suspect as Cheney's that day. Like Cheney, Rumsfeld didn't order Flight 77 to be shot down as it was approaching the Pentagon, even after going to all the trouble of having the standing order that covered the downing of hijacked aircraft altered on June 1, 2001, so that discretion was taken away from field commanders and placed solely under his control, as Secretary of Defense. Then, right before Flight 77 crashed, Rumsfeld abandoned his post and couldn't be contacted—not even by National Security Advisor Condoleezza Rice—even though at least one hijacked plane (United Airlines Flight 93) was still in the air.

Démerder pointed out that Rumsfeld's direct subordinate, US Air Force General Roger Eberhart—the commander of NORAD—had been in charge of the multiple war games and simulations that had disrupted the nation's air defense response on 9/11, leaving the nation's citizens "completely undefended... for 109 minutes" according to Senator Mark Dayton in a 2004 US Senate hearing. NORAD's representatives, including Eberhart, testified that NORAD wasn't even notified that three out of the four planes had been hijacked until after they had hit their targets. FAA air traffic controllers say that simply wasn't true—NORAD was, and still is, immediately notified of all hijackings. *(But nobody wants to listen to a bunch of whiny, stressed-out air traffic controllers: as reported in the* New York Times, *at least six air traffic controllers who dealt with two of the hijacked planes on 9/11 made a tape recording that same day describing what they'd witnessed, but when they gave the tape to their FAA supervisor, he "crushed the cassette in his hand, shredded the tape and dropped the pieces into different trash cans around the building.")*

There was more—much more: About the Project for a New American Century's perverse longing for "a new Pearl Harbor." About Presidential brother Marvin Bush's connection to the Kuwaiti-owned company that provided electronic security to the World Trade Center, Dulles International Airport, and United Airlines—which all experienced security breaches on 9/11. About Presidential uncle Jonathan Bush's connection to Riggs Bank, which was found guilty of laundering terrorist funds and fined a then-record $25 million in 2004. About stymied whistleblowers like FBI agent Colleen Rowley, former lead counsel for the House David Schippers, FBI informant Randy Glass, FBI Special Investigator Robert Wright, and FBI translator Sibel Edmonds. About Larry Silverstein's cleverly worded insurance policy and his instructions for firefighters to "pull it" just before the third tower, WTC Building 7, collapsed in a neat footprint at virtually free-fall speed, looking for all the world like a prime example of controlled demolition—but no, it was just the failure of one crucial support column due to "thermal expansion" that brought the whole 47-story skyscraper tumbling down, according to the National Institute of Standards and Technology's hotly contested 2008 report.

And then there were all the weird Saudi connections and the payoffs to the hijackers facilitated by Pakistani intelligence agents.

What a clusterfuck... Sabina thought. *Time to call Frank and give him hell for tangling me up in this shit.*

Frank didn't pick up, so she left him a snarky voice message. Fifteen minutes later, he texted her to say he could meet her for lunch at Bryant Park, promising he'd bring sandwiches and explain everything to her then. She didn't believe that—the part about explaining everything (the sandwiches she was sure he could deliver)—but it was another nice day, so why not?

Sure. What time? she texted.

12:30 south side of park on 40th. What kind of sandwich?

She told him a tuna salad would be fine.

Frank was wearing an elegant light grey summer suit when Sabina spotted him from across the park. *He must be having one of his days in court,* she thought. Sometimes she almost forgot that he was still a working attorney who had once been a formidable prosecutor for the New York Attorney General's Office. She walked toward him past all the other New Yorkers sitting in their little chairs having lunch at the round metal tables scattered around the terraces overlooking the big central rectangle of green lawn behind the library. Bryant Park was one of her favorite places in the whole city. She felt happy and safe there, always.

"What the hell did you get me into, Frank?" Sabina asked him in lieu of saying hello.

Frank just smiled at her and spread his arms wide for a hug. His wiry silver hair was glinting, angelic, in the sunlight streaming down through the park's tall trees. Somehow, he knew she wasn't really mad at him, despite the act.

"I introduce you to a billionaire cowboy with a big cock and this is how you thank me?" he asked.

"The big cock has yet to be confirmed," Sabina said, hugging him.

"He's big everywhere else, so I just assumed you'd—"

"Yeah, well, we only had time for one date before I found out he was spying on me."

"Right. I heard you threw quite a snit...." Frank guided Sabina over to a small forest green table near the sidewalk, where two paper bags from Pret A Manger sat, reserving their seats. "Ron says he still has a lump from where you bopped him with his cellphone. Are you over it yet?"

"I'm not sure. He violated my laptop."

"Sounds kinky—especially for a Mormon. But you can understand why they needed to know more about you, right?"

"I guess...." Sabina recognized that she sounded like a sullen child. Her lower lip was even extended in a pout. She pulled it back in. "How much do you know about these guys, anyway?" she asked as they sat down. "I mean, are they even safe to be around?"

"With what they're up to, no, I wouldn't say they're safe. But I think they're worth the risk." Frank unwrapped his sandwich. He was having something labeled Posh Cheddar & Pickle on Artisan. "I wouldn't have introduced you to them if I didn't think the potential good to come out of this far outweighs the danger."

"You could've warned me about it first." Sabina unwrapped her own sandwich—tuna and cucumber on a slender baguette.

"It was too complicated to explain, as I'm sure you must realize by now. But there's still time for you to back out. I'm willing to bet you won't though."

"Why the hell shouldn't I?"

"Because you're a good person, Sabina. One of the best I know. Sure, you swear like a sailor on shore leave, and your relaxed sense of morality isn't always PC, but you care about people—and you don't like seeing them exploited. That hunger for justice is deep inside you, just like it was for me when I started out as a major-crimes prosecutor."

"That's not true, Frank," Sabina said, licking tuna off her fingers. "I've helped a lot of semi-skuzzy people get off the hot seat." She was thinking of her clients in finance, for the most part—although she'd also polished up the dubious reputations of other assorted liars, cheats, and perverts, just to make a buck.

"I'm not talking about the victimless crimes and human foibles that you help smooth over—although from a personal standpoint I've found your almost saintly generosity in that area to be one of your most endearing qualities. What I'm talking about, instead, is that other side of you. The side that wants to see real criminals punished. Criminals who get away with crimes that leave victims in their wake—that doesn't sit right with you, does it?"

"Does it with anybody?"

"More people are okay with it than you might think—especially when the criminals come from the upper crust. The priesthoods and the kingly classes have been getting away with murder for 10,000 years, just because the majority of people don't think there's anything that can be done to stop them."

"But isn't that your job? Isn't that why we have the rule of law and a criminal justice system in this country?" Sabina was leaning a little heavily on the sarcasm there.

"Ha!" said Frank through a mouthful of cheese. "You know as well as I do that the law gets bent or broken for the kind of people we're talking about. When I was with the Financial Crimes Bureau, I had to choose my battles carefully. I'm sure you've read about movie directors who say that each film project takes a few years out of their life, so they don't want to shoot just any old script—they only want to work on films that matter to them."

"Sure." Sabina was thinking of Stanley Kubrick obsessively filming take after take for *Eyes Wide Shut* and David Lynch putting in five or six years to complete *Eraserhead*.

"Well, it's kind of the same for a criminal prosecutor," Frank explained. "Some trials can take years. If you decide to indict one of those Wall Street pricks who've ripped off a ton of people—like a Jon Corzine or a Stevie Cohen—and you want to put the greedy bastard in jail, where he belongs, instead of just letting him off the hook with a fine that he'll have no trouble paying with all his stolen loot—well, all I can say is 'Good luck with that.' You can kiss half-a-dozen years of your life goodbye… and then there's a good chance you won't even win in the end. The greedy bastard's attorneys will harass the living shit out of you with all kinds of frivolous crap. What do they care, when they're billing by the hour?"

"So you're saying that's why no one goes to jail for white-collar crimes anymore?"

"Not if the crimes are big enough. When it comes to reigning in the criminal rich, our justice system is broken."

"So how do we fix it?"

"We can't—at least not as things stand now. First, we have to get a whole lot of people to start caring."

"And you think Shitbirds.com will make people care? Dream on, Frank."

"It's a start, isn't it?"

"It's a website. For your info, WikiLeaks already did that—and so did Démerder, in his way—but it hasn't changed a goddam thing."

"You don't know that. And besides, Shitbirds.com, as you call it, isn't *just* a website. It's a whole truth-telling network that the big media companies and the US government won't be able to touch."

"I don't think you know enough about how the Internet really works, Frank. Remember the Stuxnet worm that targeted the Iranian nuke program and set them back by about ten years? If Shitbirds.com is anywhere near as rabble-rousing as you think it'll be, you can bet that a Shitbirds-destroying worm or a massive DDoS attack will hit it at the speed-of-fucking-light. DARPA's Plan X cyberwarfare program and the NSA's MonsterMind are both set up for exactly that."

"MacDuff says he's ready for a cyberwar."

"MacDuff...." Sabina just rolled her eyes. "Where do you know him from, anyway?"

"We go way back. He consulted me for the first time when he was getting sued in my jurisdiction over MegaWire. That's one of the ways the big boys get to you: they sue you in multiple jurisdictions, tie you up and wear you down with multiple lawsuits until you either run out of money or give them what they want. Ron really made his bones in those days. MacDuff came to me and asked if they had a chance of pulling through."

"Did they?"

"Fuck no. The MegaWire platform was like an early version of what Apple ended up doing with iTunes. Even better, maybe. It could've made them a fortune, but they didn't have anywhere near enough clout to get everyone to agree to the terms. So I told MacDuff that Ron was doing a great job of putting out fires, but the big media companies would just keep outspending them until they were totally screwed. I think he appreciated my honesty. I've been sort of informally on retainer with them ever since. That's why I'm so rich."

"I didn't know you were rich, Frank," Sabina said. She'd been out to his house in Montclair. It was certainly nice, but it didn't strike her as ostentatious—at least not for the neighborhood it was in.

"Well, I don't flaunt it, but I actually have a goofy amount of money." Frank grinned and wiped some pickle juice off his chin. "MacDuff likes to take care of the people who are on his side, because there are so few of them. You heard about what he did for Démerder, didn't you?"

"With the shell companies and that big black cube? Yeah, I thought that was pretty cool. Kind of genius on Démerder's part—although I guess without MacDuff it might not have worked."

"Every visionary needs some serious cash behind him if he's going to change the world."

"I think Jesus might disagree with you there," Sabina ribbed him. "Remember that shit he pulled with the moneylenders?"

"Sure, but the Catholic Church has been backing Jesus since at least the Fourth Century, and you know how rich they are…."

"Okay, point taken—although I don't know how thrilled Christ would be with everything that the Catholic Church has done in his name. Nazi ratlines, pedophile priests, repressing women… they have a lot to answer for."

"I'll grant you that."

"Do you know Démerder personally?"

Frank laughed. "No one knows Démerder on a personal level. I think he's outgrown the need for human companionship. He just has his dog and his crazy obsession with trying to figure out how the world really works. You've met the dog, right?"

"Guy de Bored. He's a sweetie."

"Yeah, he's Démerder's goodwill ambassador to the world. He walks that dog right past here every afternoon around one o'clock."

Sabina's synapses did a mini-version of their string-of-firecrackers routine, making a dozen connections instantaneously. "Oh shit," she said. "Is that why we're here?"

"It is," Frank confirmed, tilting back his head to drain the last few drops from his can of ginger beer. "MacDuff wants to mirror Démerder's websites on the network he's building, where they'll be safe. He also wants to hire him as a consultant. He's been trying to set up a meeting with Démerder for years, but it's never happened."

"He probably just doesn't want to be spied on, like me."

"He's a lot worse than you in that regard. Démerder has some serious trust issues—especially around men. My guess'd be that something happened to him as a kid, some kind of trauma that put him permanently on edge. But he'll talk to women. He seems to trust Laylon, his dealer… although he doesn't share his feelings with her, if he has any."

"And you think he'll talk to me?"

"What man wouldn't? Have you looked in the mirror lately? He'll probably think you're a honeytrap at first, but once he gets to know you—and maybe even trust you a little—you might be able to convince him that MacDuff is on the side of the angels."

"I'm not entirely convinced of that myself yet."

"Well, just see what you can do. Chat him up. Be his friend, if he'll let you. Think of it as a service to humanity."

"Does that mean I'm not getting paid?"

"I'd pay you myself to do this, but I'm sure MacDuff will be willing to come through with a much more generous offer."

"You rich guys just think you can buy anything…" Sabina griped facetiously.

"Here he comes." Frank pointed toward the sidewalk about midway down the block, where a man had appeared walking Guy de Bored on a leash. "I better scoot."

Frank snatched the crumpled Pret A Manger bags off the table and left Sabina with a peck on the cheek before he headed off into the park, blending in with the crowd.

Half a minute later, Guy de Bored came right up to Sabina, leash taut, tail wagging, his big furry paws laying down some muscular, sidewalk-scratching traction to drag his owner along behind him. There wasn't any question that the dog remembered her. He sat right down in front of her and immediately started in with his paw-waving trick, demanding to be petted.

The man at the other end of Guy's leash laughed and said "Guy!" pronouncing it in the American way. "I'm sorry," he apologized to Sabina, "but he's acting like he knows you."

"He does," she answered, massaging Guy's neck beneath his ears. His big pink tongue lolled out, right on cue. "We met at your gallery a few days ago. You must be Démerder."

If Démerder was taken aback, he covered it well. He was a lean, tall, Nordic-looking man—mid-forties, maybe—with unruly blonde hair and dark raccoonish eyes that put Sabina in mind of a tired Viking, or a fair-haired Luis Buñuel. He was wearing black loafers (no socks), faded jeans, and a crisp black linen shirt with the cuffs rolled up. He didn't strike her as autistic or strange in any way.

"You must be Sabina Hrafnsson," he said, surprising her.

Okay, so he was a little strange. How did he know that?

"You probably didn't notice, but Laylon's gallery is watched over by several cameras that feed images into a computer with the very latest in biometric surveillance software," Démerder explained. "I've been testing it out to see how well it works."

"I guess it works pretty fucking great, huh?" She was getting spied on from all sides these days. *Crap!*

"It identified you in just a few minutes. Laylon and I were watching when you walked in with Ron Geng."

"You know Ron?" she asked.

"Only by reputation. But I appreciate what he and Mister Everton have done for me. I'm just not much of a team player. You can tell them that."

"Who's Mister Everton?" Sabina asked before she had a chance to think it through.

"MacDuff Everton?"

Jesus! Only then did she realize that she hadn't known MacDuff's last name.

"Oh, right! MacDuff! Sorry." She didn't want to look like a total idiot while she was making her first impression, but that seemed to be the way things were going. She invited Démerder to sit down, adding, "It looks like Guy wants to stay here for a while."

Guy was now resting his two front paws on Sabina's knees so she could have full access to pet the rest of his panting doggy body.

"He's not supposed to put his paws up like that," Démerder said, still standing. "Guy, get down. *Now.*"

Guy didn't move. He just looked over his shoulder at Démerder with his big brown eyes and his flopping pink tongue as if to say, *Don't you see how great this is? You should try it!*

"It's okay," Sabina said. "I like the attention."

"I'm sure he does, too."

Was he flirting with her, just a little? Hard to tell.

"Speaking of attention…" Sabina said, "how did you and Laylon happen to tap into the national image database? Passport photos, driver's licenses, mug shots—that stuff isn't available to just anyone."

"We didn't have to go that route," Démerder said, finally sitting down beside her. "You were on Facebook."

"But I deleted my Facebook account years ago!" Right when she'd decided to become an iAesthetician, as a matter of fact. She'd had too many self-incriminating photos in her timeline, so she'd made the decision to shitcan the whole thing and reinvent herself as a professional businesswoman.

"Doesn't matter. *You* may not have an account, but your friends still do. And they post pictures of you—and very helpfully tag those same pictures."

"So wait… your image database is the whole goddam Internet? How much crazy fucking computing power does that take?"

"Not as much as you might think. The software is very smart. It constantly refines its parameters to narrow the image field at lightning speed. But it helped that you live here in New York and you're still on Twitter and LinkedIn. If you'd been from out of town, it would have taken a lot longer. Maybe fifteen or twenty minutes."

"*Jesus….*" Sabina was thinking through all the implications. The whole concept of anonymity for the average person was basically null and void.

"It's funny, but I knew one of your friends a long time ago. I doubt she'd remember me though. Dominique Luccardi?"

"My old college roommate! How'd you know Dominique?"

Démerder apparently got around a lot more than Frank thought.

"When I moved from Seattle to New York back in 1999, Tonino Luccardi gave me my first job here," Démerder said. "He hired me as a photo retoucher at Pier 69 Studios. Tonino was dating Dominique at the time, so he was always shooting pictures of her. And I was always retouching those pictures before they went out into the world. Dominique used to sit with me sometimes during the retouching sessions. I actually learned a lot from her about, uhm… how should I put this?… *female vanity*, I guess you could call it."

Sabina started cracking up. "Female vanity! That's Dominique, for sure."

"Don't tell her I said that. I actually liked her a lot… when she wasn't snorting coke."

Démerder knew her, all right. Dominique had acquired a near-Stevie-Nicks-level coke habit right out of college, around the turn of the new millennium. She claimed it had helped kick her modeling career into high gear. She easily could have ended up with a Teflon septum, but she got her addiction under control a few years later after Tonino promised to marry her if she would check herself into rehab. Rehab, in her case, had actually worked. Dominique had been clean ever since—at least so far as Sabina knew. And Tonino had made good on his promise. They'd married in 2004. Sabina had been Dominique's maid of honor.

The fact that Dominique and Tonino were *still* married was something of a miracle, considering their personalities. Sabina sometimes dreaded having dinner with them. When they were happy, they both could be charming and generous. But when they were angry at each other—which happened often—their arguments could be fierce. They seemed to have no problem with insulting each other in front of their guests. Somehow, they always made up later. Dominique said it was the sex, but Sabina suspected they both knew that no one else could put up with them, so they had to keep putting up with each other.

"How'd you get along with Tonino?" Sabina asked. It was a loaded question and they both knew it.

"I liked Tonino just fine until he fired me," Démerder answered. "Actually, I still like him, from a distance. I didn't know it at the time, but getting fired by Tonino was one of the best things that ever happened to me."

Tonino came from Italian royalty. Sabina still wasn't exactly sure how it all worked, but Tonino was supposed to be an Italian prince. He certainly acted like one of the most entitled people she'd ever met. And he was, beyond any doubt, filthy-rich. Pier 69 was the largest and most successful photo studio complex in all of Manhattan. Catalogs for Victoria's Secret, double-page spreads for *Vanity Fair*, publicity stills for just about any actress or singer or leading man you could name—they'd all been shot there, at one time or another.

"It was Dominique who convinced me to move out here from California," Sabina said. "Why'd that asshole husband of hers fire you?" she asked.

Démerder sidestepped that question. "You're from California? Me, too. Which part?"

"I grew up in the Bay Area and then went to college at UC Santa Cruz."

"Did you ever make it down the coast to San Simeon or Big Sur?"

"Plenty of times. I love Big Sur!"

Démerder smiled as if recalling happier times. "I spent five years in a resident scholar program at the Esalen Institute. Then I moved down the coast to live for a while in a little town called Cambria, near San Simeon and Hearst Castle."

Sabina put her hand on Démerder's knee and squeezed it. He flinched a little, but he didn't swat it away. "Omigod! I've been to Cambria!" she exclaimed. "I lost my virginity there."

"Not to me, I hope," Démerder joked.

"I wish…" Sabina joked right back. "But no. It was with my sophomore English professor from UCSC. God, I was such a clueless ditz back then. I used to flounce around everywhere in this camelhair cape. I don't know why, but I thought it looked really good on me. And I had no interest in dating boys my own age. So I let this sexy gray-haired professor take me on a weekend trip down the coast in his vintage ragtop Porsche."

Démerder just widened his eyes.

Okay, so it made her sound like she had daddy issues, but fuck it, that's what really happened. "Yeah, he was one of *those* guys…" Sabina continued. "I was clueless, like I said. I thought he was in love with me. So when we got to Cambria and he checked us into a motel by the beach called the Moonstone Inn, I let him deflower me right there on the tacky polyester bedspread."

Démerder burst out laughing. "I used to live right down the street from the Moonstone Inn."

"That's too weird! Small world, huh?"

"And getting smaller all the time. You can find anyone you want now, anywhere on the planet, if you know what you're doing. Just like you and Frank McKernan found me today."

The grim set of Démerder's jaw told her that he saw her as a honeytrap—a slutty espionage agent—just as Frank had predicted.

"What do you want from me, Sabina?" he asked, more curious than angry.

"Nothing! I swear!" Sabina knew that whatever she said next would sound like a lie to him, but she wanted to tell the truth, anyway.

"I didn't even know I'd be seeing you today. Frank set it up without telling me."

"Then what does Frank want?"

"The same thing MacDuff wants. They just want to have a meeting with you, but you keep blowing them off. At this point they think you're autistic, or so paranoid from some weird childhood trauma that you've become a total headache—but that's obviously not true. So why won't you meet them?"

"Why should I? I don't need any new friends."

"MacDuff wants to hire you as a consultant and host your websites on this new network he's building. He'll pay you a lot of money."

"Money's not an issue for me anymore."

"Yeah—thanks to MacDuff." Cheap shot, but in Sabina's line of work she'd found it impossible to always be tactful.

Démerder looked up at the sky and sighed. "I didn't ask MacDuff to buy the cube, Sabina. And just so you know, he doesn't own it right now—which means he's turned a profit on it. I don't know how much he's made from flipping it over the years, but it could be more than I've made. So let's not get too self-righteous about MacDuff just handing me money. People like him don't operate that way. They always expect to see a return on their investment."

"That sounds pretty cynical. He was doing you a favor."

"I don't know *what* he was doing, and you don't know, either—regardless of what he may have told you. What I *do* know is that MacDuff wants something from me right now. But I don't want anything from him."

"He just wants more of the world to see your work."

"It's my work. Shouldn't I be the one to decide how much of the world gets to see it?"

Sabina thought about that for a moment. Then she said: "There's a song by Wilco that I like, where Jeff Tweedy sings about how once your paintings get hung they belong to everyone."

"And I always defer to the superior wisdom of Jeff Tweedy whenever I'm facing a life-or-death decision."

"I just thought I'd mention it. Sheesh. You don't have to get so snippy. You don't *really* think you'll die if you break out of your little art world shell, do you?" Sabina was being a little too sarcastic, maybe, but she was getting the impression that Démerder liked a little sarcasm sprinkled on his honeytraps.

"No, I probably won't die. But you know what happened to Mark Lombardi."

"Okay, but maybe he was just depressed and really hung himself. You have to admit that's a possibility."

"It's possible, but unlikely, considering that his art career was just starting to take off in a big way. He also told friends that he was being followed."

"But a lot of other people have written books and made movies about 9/11 and the bank scandals and the Bush family, or whatever—and most of them are still alive. I mean, look at Michael Moore. He's obviously still eating hamburgers. So why not go mainstream?"

"Because going mainstream can have unintended consequences. Have you ever heard of the term 'human-flesh search'?"

"Is that a zombie movie I somehow missed out on?"

"It's an Internet phenomenon that started out in China. There was a video getting passed around back in 2006 on the Chinese equivalent of YouTube, I guess. It showed a woman in a leopard-print dress standing on the bank of a river holding a little white kitten. Smiling, acting nice. But then she put the kitten on the ground and stomped it to death with the spikes of her high heel shoes."

"*What?!* Omigod, that's sick!"

Taken aback by Sabina's sudden outburst, Guy sat down flat on his haunches, perfectly upright, while holding up his front paws in a prayerful position, so that to Sabina's eye he resembled an overgrown penguin. He had really good balance for such a big dog, she noted.

"A lot of people felt the same way as you," Démerder said. "They started writing things in online forums like, 'This is not human' or 'Let's find her and kick her to death like she did to the kitten.' Then they started figuring out ways to discover the woman's identity and hunt her down. They organized into the first iteration of *renrou sousuo yinqing*—human-flesh search engines."

"You wouldn't do that to a kitten, would you, Guy?" Sabina asked the dog, taking his paws in her hands.

Guy licked his smiley black-lipped chops, as if to say: *Stomped kittens! Yum!*

"So did they find her?" she asked Démerder.

"They did. It was a great example of crowd-sourced detective work. The video was being distributed from a website called *crushworld.net*. Someone traced that site to a server in Hangzhou. Then they asked if anyone from Hangzhou could identify the background in the video. No one could. But someone from a town further north said she recognized the woman, writing, 'God, she's a nurse! That's all I can say.' That was enough. Six days after the video went viral, they had the woman's name, phone number, and the address of the place where she worked. They got the cameraman, too. Hounded them both right out of town. The two of them lost their government jobs and had to assume new identities."

"So let that be a lesson," Sabina said to Guy, who still sat weirdly erect with his paws now resting in her palms: "No more kitty snuff porn for you."

Guy just yawned, exposing pearly white fangs.

"Wow! It looks like Guy's been doing a really good job of flossing!"

"He uses a Waterpik," Démerder deadpanned.

"So I don't see what the problem is…" said Sabina, thinking out loud. "This human-flesh search deal sounds great! Imagine if we could get it working on all the people who pulled off 9/11, or all the bankers whose systemic crimes wiped out 40 percent of the world's wealth in 2008, or whoever it was that shot down that Malaysian Airlines jet over Ukrainian airspace and started the US-Russian Cold War, Version 2.0."

"That's what I thought at first, too," said Démerder, "but it doesn't work that way, unfortunately. What happened in China is that the human-flesh search engines started going after more and more people who were just like the clients you represent as an iAesthetician—did I say that right?—people who were basically decent but had made some bad decisions. A guy who got horny and cheated on his suicidal wife, a girl who admitted online that she got turned on by earthquakes…. For the most part, the human-flesh search engines weren't interested in going after the real criminals—the relatively small number of psychopathic personalities that try to exploit the rest of us. Instead, they were turning into an angry, self-policing mob—a mob that might very easily be persuaded to go after someone like Frank McKernan, for instance… or me."

"Oh no… don't tell me you have a thing for gonzo Nubian goddesses, too."

A wry smile flashed across Démerder's face. "No. That's just Frank," he said. "Strict Slovenian schoolmarms are more my type. But you're familiar with my work, right? Think how easy it would be for Fox News to portray me as a crazed conspiracy theorist that should be locked up, or shot on sight, because of my anti-American slandering of blameless, God-fearing patriots like Donald Rumsfeld and Dick Cheney."

"They wouldn't do that. This is America. You still have the right to free speech."

"I do. And I can say whatever I want with my work. But if that work becomes too widely known, and starts to seem like a credible threat to the psychopaths-in-charge, then someone might decide that I've said enough—like they did for Mark Lombardi."

"Which would suck," Sabina appended.

"Well, who knows? Maybe this world is some other planet's hell, like Aldous Huxley used to say. And maybe death launches us like a rocket to a far, far better place. But like most people, I'm in no hurry to find out."

"Me either," Sabina concurred.

"A long time ago," Démerder continued, "right around when Tonino fired me from Pier 69, I decided I might as well document hell while I'm here. Leave behind a few road maps for my fellow travelers. So that's what I've been doing, at my own pace, in the venues where I feel comfortable."

"And you don't think you can do that with MacDuff?"

"With MacDuff, I think things would get very complicated, very fast. That's just how he does business. He's like Tonino that way. They both thrive on chaos."

"MacDuff is nothing like Tonino," Sabina said. "Believe me, I should know."

"I believe you know Tonino. With him, what you see is what you get. He keeps his Italian emotions right there on the surface. But some of the American princes like to put on a folksy show. Think about George W. Bush, President Reagan.... I can't say for sure, but I think MacDuff is one of those. I'm not saying he's evil. Just that there's another side to him that you probably haven't seen."

Maybe Démerder really was paranoid....

"How do you know so much about MacDuff?" Sabina asked him. "Or at least *think* you know so much about him?"

Démerder calmly explained: "I make it my business to learn about my so-called patrons. I'm documenting hell, remember?"

"Well, I think you're wrong about him."

"Okay, so maybe I am."

"You are for sure. I can tell. Women's intuition."

While she was saying that it occurred to Sabina—not for the first time—that her intuition when it came to men wasn't worth a bucket of warm spit.

"Has he pulled a gun on you yet?" Démerder asked, point-blank.

"Yes, as a matter-of-fact, he has," Sabina sniffed, really annoyed now that Démerder seemed to have the upper hand. "But it wasn't loaded."

"Next time it might be. MacDuff has a history of brandishing firearms when he wants to close a deal—although he hasn't shot anyone yet, at least that I'm aware of. Just be careful, Sabina. In my experience, if you know half-a-dozen extremely wealthy people, you'll find that at least one of them got that way by behaving like a completely amoral psychopath. Rich people are dangerous—to themselves and to those around them."

"I guess you could include yourself in that category, Mister 'I-make-a million-bucks-every-six-weeks-for-doing-absolutely-nothing'."

Démerder grinned and said, "Yeah, I guess you could."

THE EMPRESS

The cheerful Polish doorman at Sabina's building had called and left a message, saying there were several large packages waiting for her in the lobby. After her semi-successful ambushing of Démerder, Sabina went home to pick them up.

It turned out that MacDuff had sent her some high-end audio gear as his way of apologizing: a super-expensive matching pre-amp and amplifier set from McIntosh, a space-age-looking Oracle Delphi turntable, and a pair of those great-looking Bose speakers she'd been eyeing in the store window just a week ago. Sabina wondered how

MacDuff had known about the speakers, but then she remembered that she'd made a note to herself about them on her iPhone. And the iPhone was synced to her laptop. And…

…*maybe it was time to buy a new laptop.*

MacDuff had also sent along a complete collection of Nick Cave's albums on vinyl, which must have been hard to track down. Too bad she'd never had much love for those old Birthday Party albums. They sounded like discordant punk noise to her ears (although she always got a smile on her face whenever she heard Cave singing "Nick the Stripper"). MacDuff had also included a card with a note that read:

> DEAR SABINA,
>
> I'VE BEEN A DAMN FOOL. I HOPE YOU'LL FORGIVE ME.
>
> WITH LOVE AND RESPECT,
> MACDUFF

She'd have to think about that….

She decided it was time to have a chat with her old friend, Dominique, who knew more about dealing with a rich man's errant ways than she ever would. Besides, she also wanted Dominique's take on Démerder. Sabina thought it might be helpful to know what he had been like when the two of them had worked together.

Dominique answered on the first ring. Sabina hardly had time to say hello before Dominique said she was heading out the door to meet Tonino for a late lunch at Pier 69. She invited Sabina to join them, promising they'd have a chance to go off by themselves and talk in private later. The Pier 69 photo studio complex had a fantastic Italian restaurant on-site. Sabina felt like she could do with a second lunch—Franks's tuna sandwich hadn't satisfied her—so she told Dominique she'd show up just as fast as a taxi could get her there.

The restaurant—more of a café, really—was just beyond Pier 69's front desk. It was bustling and loud, as usual, with dozens of animated conversations echoing off the smooth concrete floors and walls.

"*Hey, Sabina! Ciao bella!*" said Tonino, rising from the table where he was seated with Dominique. Behind them, tall glass windows framed a view of the pier jutting out over the sun-sparkling Hudson.

Tonino kissed Sabina's cheeks in the exuberant European fashion. He was dressed all in black—black silk shirt, black leather pants. The only accents of color were the two vertical red stripes on the heels of his Prada boots and the turquoise-and-silver concho belt around his skinny waist. Years ago, Tonino's wavy shoulder-length hair had been black like the rest of his outfit, but now it was turning gray and going thin on top, which Sabina couldn't help but notice since she stood a good six inches taller than him. He was short, sort of toad-faced, and twenty-five years older than Sabina and Dominique. But if anyone had ever been driven to achieve photography-related greatness by a Napoleon complex, surely it was the charming and charismatic Tonino Luccardi.

Tonino pulled out a chair for Sabina and slid it in behind her as she sat down. "Some prosecco?" he asked her, already reaching for the bottle in its silver ice bucket.

"Hell yes!" Sabina answered. Having lunch at Pier 69 was always a treat—made even better by knowing that she wouldn't have to pay for any of it.

Dominique looked gorgeous, as usual. She was a French-Lebanese redhead with luminous, unblemished skin. Even in college she'd been one of those girls that made the boys go stupid when she walked into a room. Most of them couldn't even find words to say to her. They just stared as if they wanted to gnaw off her clothes. That was one of the things Dominique appreciated most about Tonino—he always had something to say to her. Maybe the things he said weren't always kind, but at least he was never tongue-tied. The man loved to talk.

Dominique smelled of jasmine today, Sabina noted. Or maybe a bouquet of jasmine was somewhere in the room. She did a quick scan for celebrities. Among the lunchtime crowd she saw: the singer and former Disney Channel actress, Miley Cyrus, in a fluffy white bathrobe; the notorious flannel-wearing photographer, Terry Richardson, with his endearing muttonchop sideburns, widow's peak, and thick-framed glasses; the aging lead singer-songwriter from Pink Floyd, Roger Waters, looking somewhat uncomfortable in a dark pink velvet suit with leopard-print loafers; the former lead singer of the Talking Heads, David Byrne, in an oversized cream-colored zoot suit; the eccentric Icelandic singer, Bjork, in another fluffy white robe, with her hair in curlers; and the artist, Matthew Barney, shooting Bjork a dirty look.

There were probably other celebrities in the room that Sabina didn't recognize. She'd stopped reading fan magazines and watching "Entertainment Tonight" a long time ago. With such a preponderance of singers in the room, though, she suspected some magazine was doing a music-related nostalgia shoot.

"So what's been going on with you?" Dominique asked, placing her hand on top of Sabina's from across the table. "We haven't heard from you in a while."

It had been months, actually. Sabina had been laying low after witnessing Dominique and Tonino's last marital meltdown during dinner at their floor-through loft in SoHo. Tonino had called his lovely wife "a washed-up Victoria's Secret skank" and Dominique had responded in kind, telling him he was "a smarmy little Italian shitweasel" who was becoming less virile and more incontinent all the time. But it appeared that all had been forgiven. Again.

"I thought I'd give you guys some breathing room after that last round of pasta *vaffanculo*," Sabina said, deploying the Italian slang for *fuck off*. Tonino had familiarized her with that term's usage on many festive occasions.

"See? She's learning to speak Italian!" Tonino was delighted.

"You know we don't really mean all those things we say to each other when we're angry," said Dominique.

"Yeah, I didn't actually believe that Tonino had 'fucked a whole pimped-out platoon of gonorrhea-dripping Dominican whores'."

"Dominique loves to exaggerate!" Tonino rhapsodically beamed at his wife.

Around the time of their last dinner together, Tonino had been named in a sexual harassment suit brought against Pier 69 Studios by a pretty young Dominican receptionist who had formerly worked at the studio complex's front desk. The lawsuit had made the Page Six column in the *New York Post* after the columnist had called up Tonino to ask for his rebuttal to the accusations. His whole defense? "That woman is insane. She's too ugly for me to make love to. Have you seen my wife?"

It was kind of romantic in a backhanded way—but still, Dominique had been super-pissed.

"Hey, I've got a question for you two," Sabina said, changing the subject. "Do either of you remember a guy named Démerder who used to work here a long time ago?"

"Démerder?" Dominique smiled. "That's not a name. It's French for getting yourself out of the shit. I hear Parisian photographers use it all the time when I'm there."

Sabina felt kind of dumb—she should have known that. "Well, whatever his name was…" she persevered, "he used to be a retoucher here. Back around 1999, when you two first got together."

"Who did we have working for us then?" Tonino asked Dominique. "Do you remember? Giuseppe? Shin? Vince?"

"He's a tall blonde guy," Sabina prodded them.

"Oh, I remember!" Dominique said happily. "Gordon!"

"The quiet one," Tonino recalled. "A good retoucher, but he'd go for days without saying two words."

"I think he was shy," said Dominique, "but he would talk to me."

"Did you know he's a famous artist now?"

"No, really?" Tonino seemed to find that hard to believe.

"Well, I don't know how famous…" Sabina said, "but he's gotten rich from selling his art. He calls himself Démerder now."

"De-Shitter," Dominique translated for her.

"I guess…" Sabina said. Then, recalling the lesson Démerder had taught her about Mister Everton, she asked, "Do either of you remember his last name?"

"Swannson," Tonino said without hesitating.

"Gordon Swannson," Dominique agreed. "A nice guy, but shy."

"It's the quiet ones you have to watch out for," said Sabina.

Later—after a lunch of beef carpaccio, veal cannelloni alla piemontese, risotto alla primavera, and crepes alla crema, with plenty of white wine, grappa, and espresso shots knocked back throughout—Sabina and Dominique staggered from Pier 69 to the Vault Gallery so they could have a private conversation and take a long look at Démerder's work. They were both feeling rather elegantly wasted, but the gallery wasn't far—just a few blocks north. Sabina was hoping they'd run into Démerder and his dog while they were there, but no such luck.

"Seventeen million dollars!" Dominique exclaimed when she saw the black cube. "And he gets how much every time it sells?"

"A million and change from here on out."

"Every six weeks?" Dominique sadly shook her head. "I bet on the wrong horse."

"What do you mean?" Sabina asked her.

"Gordon. I could have made him mine. I'm sure of it."

"Are you saying you guys had a thing for each other?"

"No. But the chemistry was there. I felt it. And he was closer to my age than Tonino. And kinder. But you know Tonino... he had such power and charisma in those days. Still does. And Gordon was such a long shot."

"Excuse me for saying this," said Sabina, playing the oldest and closest friend trump card, "but you were a coked-up narcissistic slut back then. I don't think he would have liked you that much."

"Oh fuck you. He did too like me."

"Actually, he told me he liked you," Sabina admitted. "I just didn't get the impression he was lusting after you."

"He would have if I'd wanted him to. You know how that works."

She sure did. Dominique was referring to the brief lesbian affair they'd had while they were roommates during their freshman year at UC Santa Cruz.

It was Sabina's noisy old vibrator—the one that sounded like a 747 taking off—that had started it. Dominique had complained that it was keeping her awake at night. But Sabina was addicted to it and couldn't sleep herself unless she used it to grind out a few orgasms under the covers. Finally, one night after they'd both had too much to drink, Dominique—in a fit of exasperation—had thrown a pillow across the room at Sabina in the dark and yelled, "I'll lick your cunt myself if you'll just turn that damned thing off!"

Sabina didn't think she was serious, but she yanked the plug on the vibrator, anyway—mostly out of embarrassment. A few moments later, she felt Dominique lifting the covers to climb into bed with her. Sabina had never really thought of herself as a lesbian, or even bisexual, but her pussy flooded with pure lust as soon as Dominique bent down to give her a kiss. It was a French kiss, of course, done with style and finesse. Sabina raised her hands to feel Dominique's breasts. They were bigger and a bit softer than hers, but still round and firm. And her nipples... *God*, her nipples were hard! Just like hers. When Dominique moved lower and took Sabina's left nipple in her mouth, she almost came right then and there.

To this day no one—absolutely no one—has ever licked her clit as expertly as Dominique did that night. Sabina lost track of the number of orgasms she had. In the morning, when she woke as if falling from a lust-crazed dream, Dominique was still there behind her, spooning. And from that moment until the first day of school their sophomore year, they'd been in love.

Or at least Sabina had been in love. She'd never been quite sure if her feelings were reciprocated. Dominique had been parsimonious with clues. Regardless, they'd shared hundreds of orgasms together. And then they'd split up (Dominique had met a boy over summer break that she thought might be *the one*—although he turned out to be just one of many…). Their friendship had survived that episode and remained intact over the years because, deep down, Sabina knew she wasn't much of a lesbian at all. She just really liked Dominique. When faced with the prospect of losing her entirely, Sabina quickly came to the conclusion that having Dominique as a friend was much more important to her than satisfying her pseudo-lesbian lust. She could easily get her clit licked somewhere else—which is why Sabina spent her next summer break in Livingston, Montana, learning to ride cowboys.

"That reminds me…" Sabina said to Dominique, "I wanted to get your opinion about this billionaire cowboy I've been seeing."

"A billionaire? Really?" Dominique cocked an eyebrow at Sabina. "Billionaires are dangerous."

"That's exactly what Démerder said!" she blurted out.

"Gordon. Call him Gordon," said Dominique. "I just keep hearing De-Shitter when you call him by that other name. It's vulgar."

"Hey, he picked it, not me."

"He's obviously not French. So tell me about the cowboy."

Sabina ran through the whole story: how MacDuff had met her at the library, their incredibly successful first date in the Chinatown pulqueria, her sudden intuition while talking to Ron in the Vault Gallery—almost right where they were standing—and the subsequent showdown in MacDuff's office.

Dominique was smirking by the end of it. "Typical rich guy," she said. "He sounds just like Tonino. They might wear different hats, but they're the same underneath."

"Oh, they are not…" Sabina scoffed.

"Tonino spies on me all the time. He thinks I don't know, but I do."

"Tonino spies on you? How? I mean, aside from his cameras, I've always thought of him as technologically-challenged. Isn't that why he hires people to do his retouching?"

"He hires people to do Photoshop because it's *boring*. It takes patience that he just doesn't have. But you're right—he doesn't spy on me with computers. He pays stylists and studio assistants to follow me around and report back to him. Some have told me. Others, I just knew...."

"After all these years he still doesn't trust you?"

That remark could have been inflammatory, but Dominique took it with a shrug. "Rich men, they need control," she said. "But they can't stand anyone having control over them."

"Not even when they're married to you?"

"Especially then. That's why we fight so much." Dominique gave Sabina an unexpected hug. "Look, this billionaire cowboy of yours might really want to marry you. I hope it works out."

"He seemed pretty serious," said Sabina, having neglected to mention anything about the gun. "And now that I've cooled off, I'm seriously considering him."

"Just know that as soon as he's made you his wife, he'll start fucking around on you. Going behind your back, having stupid little affairs, trying to convince himself that he's still in charge."

"*Jesus*. Are you kidding me? Does Tonino do that?"

"Constantly."

"You never told me."

"Because it's not important. Tonino and I have an understanding. He screwed up recently with that Dominican girl, but I've already forgiven him for that. He'll be more careful in the future."

"Dominique... that sucks."

"No, it doesn't. I married Tonino with my eyes wide open, knowing that sort of thing would happen from time to time. A famous photographer who's around beautiful young models all the time... how could it not happen?"

"And you don't care?"

"I care, but not as much as you might think. European culture is much more relaxed about the whole concept of mistresses than we are over here. And Tonino's mistresses are never around for long. There's a high turnover rate. But we have a bond that lasts."

"How many mistresses are we talking about?"

"I don't even try to count. How many tissues do you use when you have a cold?"

"*Dominique!*"

"Oh, don't act so scandalized. You know the kind of life I've had. It's been pure hedonism: exotic trips, fabulous meals, famous friends."

Sabina knew *exactly* what Dominique was talking about. She had been invited along on some of those exotic trips, had eaten some of those fabulous meals with Dominique and Tonino, and had met some of their famous friends. Sabrina had always been a little jealous of her BFF's posh lifestyle, but maybe everything hadn't been quite so rosy as she'd imagined.

"You don't get all that without making some sacrifices," Dominique said with a defiant look.

Putting her arm around her friend's waist, Sabina said, "That sounds a little sad to me, but if you're okay with it…."

Dominique waved her hand in the air as if dismissing a trivial irritant—a fly, or a philandering husband. "I wouldn't have even brought it up if you hadn't said you were serious about this billionaire. I just want you to know what to expect. Your moral compass hasn't always swung in the same direction as mine."

"I didn't say I was *serious* serious…" Sabina backpedaled.

"You're serious enough. It's in your eyes."

"Oh hell…" Sabina looked up at *The Tarot of 9/11: For Mark Lombardi* without really seeing it, "I guess you're right."

THE STARS

Right after Sabina got home from the gallery, she hooked up her new stereo system, put *Nick Cave and the Bad Seeds Live from KCRW* on the turntable, and started Googling images for "Gordon Swanson." A bunch of random Gordon Swansons filled her laptop's screen: sporty Gordons holding up big fish, porcine Gordons with oily foreheads and sleazy cop mustaches, drunken Gordons downing tequila shots, suit-and-tie Gordons smiling wide on square LinkedIn headshots like their careers actually meant the world to them. None of them were Sabina and Dominique's Gordon.

Weird how I feel possessive of him now that I know his real name and we've exchanged email addresses... she thought.

Trying to come up with a way to refine her search, Sabina switched out of images to a general web search and typed in "Gordon Swanson Cambria Esalen Big Sur."

Bingo.

She'd been spelling his last name wrong. There was a Gordon *Swannson* associated with Cambria and Big Sur. Following those links, she hit the mother lode. An author named Derek Swannson *(somehow related?)* had written about Gordon Swannson in two novels published by Three Graces Press: *Crash Gordon and the Mysteries of Kingsburg* and *Crash Gordon and the Revelations from Big Sur.*

The title of the first book rang a bell. And then Sabina remembered where she'd seen it: MacDuff, writing as Wes Bramley, had mentioned *Crash Gordon and the Mysteries of Kingsburg* as an influence at the beginning of his spyware-sneaking essay on her laptop: "The Coup d'État of 1963: 50th Anniversary of America's Covert Takeover."

That had to be more than a coincidence. Sabina ordered both eBooks from Amazon and had them uploaded on her Kindle two minutes later.

She was about to sit down and start reading when MacDuff called. Seeing his name light up on her vibrating iPhone, Sabina's first impulse was to let him leave a voice message. But she was still buzzed from lunch, feeling woozily adrift and non-specifically horny, so she decided to pick up.

"MacDuff. You've got some nerve, foisting expensive stereo equipment on me like that."

"So them packages turned up okay?"

"Can't you hear Nick Cave crooning to me in the background?" Sabina held the iPhone closer to the Bose speakers, which were pumping out a melancholy live version of "People Ain't No Good."

"Sounds great, doesn't it?" she asked as she put the phone back to her ear.

"Hard t' judge the fidelity from where I'm sittin'," said MacDuff. "Maybe I should come over t' get a better listen."

"Oh, you'd like that, wouldn't you?"

"I was gonna volunteer my services as an expert stereo hooker-upper, but I guess you done beat me to it."

"I'm a pretty good hooker-upper myself."

"I don't doubt that fer a second."

"You should see me in action."

"I got no fonder wish."

MacDuff's subtle flirting was getting to her. "Oh, fuck it…" said Sabina, caving in under the influence of loneliness and residual Italian alcohol. "Why don't you just come on over? Maybe we can go out to dinner. Or watch a movie."

"Really? Y'mean it?"

"Sure. You know my address, right? If you don't, you can just open the backdoor on my laptop and track me here."

"Darlin', I won't be doin' that no more," said MacDuff, exultant. "I done learnt my lesson."

Maybe it wasn't the right move, letting MacDuff come to her place, but it was too late to back down now. Sabina said, "Just give me an hour, so I can clean up a little." She still had open shipping boxes and packing materials scattered everywhere. The place was a mess.

"I'll be there at eight o'clock, on the dot."

That gave Sabina an hour and thirteen minutes. "Okay. See you then," she said. She hung up before he could prolong the conversation.

Jesus W. Christ. What the hell did I just do? she asked herself.

MacDuff had spied on her. Pulled a gun on her. And just a few hours ago, her best friend had warned her that he'd likely fuck around on her. Why on earth was she inviting a guy like that over to her apartment?

Because he turns me on, Sabina's clitoris answered for her. *Plus, he's rich, which never hurts.*

That's not what Dominique and Démerder said, Sabina reminded her snarky clit. *Rich people can be dangerous.*

They can also buy you things. That's good.

Despite its more than 8,000 sensory nerve endings, her clitoris was obviously operating on a much lower order of intelligence than her brain. She'd heard guys complain that their penises were the same way—cocky blunderers that often got them into serious trouble. You shouldn't let your sex organs make your decisions for you. But that's exactly what Sabina had done.

As promised, MacDuff showed up right at eight, wearing spiffy new cowboy duds and a pristine black wool Stetson. He entered carrying a picnic basket. It was stuffed full of great things from Zabar's: fresh baguettes, St. Andre and Le Cornilly cheeses, duck foie gras, truffled mousse pâté, dried figs, fresh grapes, Serrano ham, smoked salmon, herb-marinated olives, a jar of cornichons, and some other things that Sabina couldn't make out right away. He was also carrying two bottles of champagne.

When Sabina gave him a quizzical look, MacDuff said: "We can either eat here or go out. I jus' wanted you t' have the option."

"I didn't think cowboys shopped at Zabar's," was all she could think to say.

MacDuff set everything down on the counter in Sabina's cramped apartment kitchen, which opened onto the main living area. He put one of the champagne bottles in the refrigerator and set to opening the other one. "You got any glasses?" he asked.

"Cupboard on your right."

He sure was quick about making himself at home....

"Nice place you got here," MacDuff said as he popped the cork and filled two of Sabina's champagne glasses. "Doin' all right fer a girl on her own."

"I get by…" Sabina said, sitting down on her comfy old leather couch in the living room, "but I've got nowhere near your income, of course."

"Welp, I got a headstart. My daddy's ranch set me up purty good." MacDuff walked the two champagne glasses over to the couch and presented one of them to her.

"Cheers," he said, clinking glasses.

"*Cin cin*," Sabina replied, still in Italian drinking mode. She wasn't sure what that phrase meant. Judging by the way Tonino relied on it during his drinking jags, it could be a cheery exhortation to liver damage.

MacDuff sat down next to her on the couch. "What about your folks?" he asked. "Still alive and kickin'?"

Sore subject. But what the hell, she'd tell him anyway, since they were supposedly being honest with each other from here on out.

"My folks," Sabina said, "died when I was six. Car crash, coming home late from a party. They were both drunk… like me right now."

Putting a big hand on her knee, MacDuff said, "I'm sorry, darlin'. That ain't fair at all. Who ended up raisin' you?"

"My mom's spinster aunt in Marin County. She had a nice house in San Rafael. Made good money as a real estate agent. But she was totally unequipped to raise a child. I mean, I appreciate what she did for me, but emotionally, she just wasn't there at all. Took care of my physical needs, and that's about it. I grew up feeling like an unwelcome guest. She died around ten years ago. Left all her money to a breast cancer research group. I'm sure you can guess what killed her."

"Sounds like you had a tough row t' hoe."

"Yeah, well, plenty of other people have had it worse. At least I wasn't raped by my stepdad, like my friend Dominique."

"It's a messed up world we live in," MacDuff sighed. "That's fer sure."

Sabina let out a low, rueful laugh. "I was talking to Démerder today and he said our world might be some other planet's hell."

MacDuff tilted back his black hat to telegraph his astonishment. "Hold on there, Sunshine… you talked t' Démerder?"

With a clench, Sabina realized she'd forgotten to call Frank to tell him how their Démerder ambush had played out.

"We actually talked for quite a while," she told MacDuff. "He's nice. Not weird at all, despite what you guys think."

"We been tryin' t' set up a meetin' with that hombre fer years. Dude won't have nothin' t' do with us. So how'd you get him t' be so durned chatty all o' a sudden?"

"Female persuasion, I guess. Plus, he knew my best friend."

"Dominique?"

"Yeah, how'd you know?"

"You just mentioned her. And since we're bein' honest, I read some o' your emails."

Sabina slugged MacDuff in the chest, harder than she'd really meant to. "You flaming asshole! That's supposed to be private!"

MacDuff spilled a dollop of champagne on his jeans and coughed out some stale air from deep inside his lungs. "Man, you pack a wallop," he said when he could breathe semi-regularly again. "I think you mighta broke a rib."

"Serves you right, you nosy bastard."

"Like I said, I done learnt my lesson. I won't be doin' that no more. Promise."

"You better not."

"Is that Dominique up there on the wall?" MacDuff indicated the framed color photograph hanging above her new stereo system on the opposite side of the room. It was a larger-than-life close-up of Dominique caught in the act of applying lewd red lipstick to her slack mouth while checking her reflection in the distorting polished mirror of a well-hung cowboy's silver rodeo buckle. Terry Richardson had shot it in his usual full-frontal-flash style for a vodka ad campaign several years earlier. Dominique claimed she'd gotten the idea from the cowboy crotch painting by Maxine Olson in Sabina's office, and had suggested the tableau to Terry. The client had loved the image and featured it on billboards and subway posters all over the world. Terry had made a large digital C-print and signed it as a way of thanking Sabina for the inspiration. He could be generous that way....

"That's Dominique all right," Sabina confirmed. "She's had a pretty good run as a model. Terry Richardson shot that."

"Ain't that the dude who got in all kinds o' trouble fer havin' models give him handjobs?"

"That's Uncle Terry...." Sabina smiled. "I wish I could've helped him through that mess, but most of it went down before I started my PR business."

"Did Dominique...?"

"Gladly. She thought it was hilarious."

"Ain't she married though?"

"To Tonino. Believe me, he's got no right to complain. Besides," said Sabina, "everyone in the photography business knows that Terry's not out to steal anyone's wife. He's a good guy. Just super-horny. Dominique told me it was about as romantic as letting a big friendly dog hump her leg."

MacDuff got up from the couch and went to retrieve the bottle of champagne in the kitchen. "Artists... I don't pretend t' know why they do half the stuff they do, but I sure do like some o' the stuff they put out there. They've gone and turned this sorry world into one big ol' Easter egg hunt."

"I'm not sure I'm following you," Sabina said as MacDuff refilled her glass.

"I mean, like, thanks to artists, there's little nuggets o' beauty t' pick up wherever you go lookin'. Like the first time I heard Erik Satie's piano pieces—that was somethin' special. Like listenin' to a nightingale with a toothache, as he put it. Or the first time I saw a painting by Max Ernst, or a movie directed by Francis Ford Coppola, or read a book by Haruki Murakami…." MacDuff sat back down on the couch and refilled his own glass. "I mean, nature's great and all, but it don't make champagne all by itself. Artists, they teach us new ways o' experiencin' things. Makes life richer. That's what I like about Démerder: he taught me how t' see the world in a way I never woulda come up with on my own."

"But he teaches you to see this world as some other planet's hell," Sabina protested—not that she really wanted to rag on Démerder (*or Gordon*, she reminded herself).

"Welp, maybe it is, or maybe it ain't," MacDuff equivocated. "But the Gnostics are on Démerder's side, just so's you know. They think this here material universe is a trap for souls. 'The nest o' the Unspeakable,' Thomas Merton called it. But I know fer durned sure we ain't got no chance o' makin' this place any better without facin' up t' what's wrong with it. Just like you can't break outta the hoosegow without first knowin' you're *in* the hoosegow."

"Gurdjieff," Sabina said.

" 'Scuse me?"

"Gurdjieff said that—about first having to know you're in prison before you can break out of it. I thought you liked reading philosophy books."

"I do. Guess I'm just a lil' rusty on Gurdjieff and Ouspensky."

At least he knows who Ouspensky is… and Thomas Merton, Sabina thought to herself. *The philosophical part of his philosophical cowboy act might not be a total sham, after all.*

She said to MacDuff: "It's one thing to look at Démerder's work for a fresh perspective on the world. But to act on it—like you're doing with Shitbirds.com—that's another thing altogether. Why do it? I mean, you're already rich. You could just kick back and have fun for the rest of your life. It just seems like you're inviting a whole lot of trouble your way."

"Some people *like* trouble, darlin'. Merton said that when we get t' be more deeply human, the wellspring o' compassion moves us t' confront the Unspeakable—what's harsh and remorseless in this here world… systemic evil—even though by confrontin' the Unspeakable you might get yer ass whupped."

"You really think you can handle the full wrath of the US intelligence community coming down on your ten-gallon hat?"

"Them boys been hasslin' me fer years. It ain't like we ain't already acquainted. But here's the real question: Who's gonna bully the bullies?"

"Who's *what*—?"

"Who's gonna stand up fer the little guy when the big guy in the red-white-and-blue top hat turns corrupt? You know things're rotten in the good ol' US o' A, but who's gonna stand up and give Uncle Sam a swift boot t' the nuts?"

"I guess that'd be you, huh?"

"I'm just one man. There's only so much I can do. But if the truth can be put out there in a way that everybody understands, it'll be believed."

"Y'think?"

"I'm bettin' my life on it, Sugar Buns."

"Sugar Buns? Really MacDuff?" Hoisting her empty champagne glass, Sabina said, "Pour."

"I been on the side o' the shit-disturbers ever since I was a young'un," MacDuff said as he filled Sabina's glass again. "I grew up readin' my daddy's nudie magazines."

"Oh, I can believe that, all right…."

"I meant fer the articles." MacDuff pretended to take umbrage at Sabina's sleazy assumptions.

She gulped down the full glass of champagne in a single go. "Again," she rasped, pinching her eyes shut as the bubbles tickled her nostrils. She held up the glass for a refill. Her clitoris had a plan.

As he poured, MacDuff rambled on: "Not that I minded them sultry pictures none. But some o' them articles… man, they was a revelation t' me. You couldn't get news like that nowhere else. This was back in the glory days o' investigative porn: Abbie Hoffman breakin' the Iran-Contra story in *Penthouse*, Sally Denton and Roger Morris publishin' 'The Crimes o' Mena' there, too, after the *Washington Post* tried t' spike it—and let's not forget ol' Larry Flynt over at *Hustler*, offerin' a million bucks t' anyone who'd help him nail JFK's real killers, and then goin' all the way t' the Supreme Court t' fight fer our First

Amendment rights, so's we can make fun o' public figures without getting' sued."

"Oh, those adventurous pornographers!" Sabina fluttered her eyelashes and sighed. "Didn't Larry Flynt end up in a gold-plated wheelchair because of his crusading horndog ways?" She recalled Ron telling her of his concern that MacDuff was trying to get himself 'suicided' by the Deep State. "Is that what you want?" she asked him. "To get shot?"

"All I'm lookin' t' do is create a lil' information parity. Them boys in the intelligence community know that ain't worth shootin' me over. They already got X-KEYSCORE and their ICREACH surveillance engine, which can look up just about anythin' on anybody. It's only fair that the rest o' us'll have Shitbirds.com."

"I think they've probably shot people for a lot less."

"You might be right about that," MacDuff said, unconcerned. "But by the time we launch, it'll be too late fer them t' stop it, anyway. So at most, they'll maybe seize my computers on some bullshit technicality. Try t' put me outta business."

"And you're okay with that?"

"I'm willin' t' chance it. But they got a surprise comin' if they think they can wipe Shitbirds.com off the 'net. Once it's up, it's gonna *stay* up, fer good. Hey, that reminds me… you mind if I make a quick call?"

"Sure. Go right ahead. I'll just change into something more comfortable. I'm thinking we should stay in tonight."

"Fine by me…" MacDuff said with a leer.

Sabina got up and walked down the short hallway to her bedroom. Just as she was about to close the bedroom door, she overheard MacDuff talking to Ron on his cellphone. She paused to listen in:

"Yeah, Ron, hey… there's one more thing I almost forgot. The auction fer Démerder's cube ends tomorrow at midnight. Let's get it back. I'm itchin' t' see it in my livin' room again—as a morale booster fer when we launch. What…? No. No limit. Just make sure we get it…. Welp, put ol' Sergei on it then. Have him find the fastest fiber route t' eBay's servers. Tell him t' put a computer right up next t' theirs, just like we do with them stock exchange matchin' engines. I'm sure Pierre won't mind, now that we're both helpin' out our good friends Glenn and Ed…. Yeah…. Let's just make sure we don't get outbid at the last microsecond, like last time…. Okay. Thanks. And tell

Emma t' get her honey-do list ready. You'll be gettin' a few weeks off after this last big push."

So it sounds like Shitbirds.com will be launching sometime in the next six weeks... Sabina deduced. *And Glenn and Ed were likely Glenn Greenwald and Edward Snowden. So did that mean that Pierre Omidyar, eBay's billionaire founder, was secretly in on Shitbirds.com, too?*

Sabina knew that Pierre Omidyar had already pledged $250 million to finance his own independent journalism project, First Look Media, with heavy hitters like Glenn Greenwald, Jeremy Scahill, Laura Poitras, and Matt Taibbi already working for him. *Was Shitbirds.com just an offshoot of that project, or something else entirely?* She wouldn't be able to ask MacDuff about that without admitting that she'd been listening to his conversation—*spying* on him—which she didn't want to do. So she just quickly changed into her beloved black velour tracksuit from Juicy Couture (with her sexiest silk camisole underneath it—*and no panties...*). Then she went back down the hall to rejoin MacDuff on the couch.

"All taken care of?" she asked MacDuff as she sat down next to him. She tucked a bare foot high up under her thigh, leaning up against him as she did so.

"Done," said MacDuff. "Seems like it's gettin' warm in here." He removed his hat and stroked Sabina's forearm. "I like this here fuzzy outfit you got on. Feels nice and soft."

"You should feel the rest of me," she taunted him.

"Is that an invite?"

"Take it however you want."

MacDuff leaned over and nuzzled her neck. "You smell real good, too," he murmured.

Sabina started to squirm. "Your beard's kind of tickly," she giggled. "Stop!"

Like a true gentleman, MacDuff leaned back on the couch and didn't press any further.

Feeling a boozy sincerity welling up within her, Sabina took MacDuff's big hand in her own and asked him: "Do you really believe one man can change the world? Because in my experience, it's the world that changes us—not the other way around."

"Are we havin' us a *Bull Durham* moment here?"

"A what?" For a split-second, Sabina thought MacDuff might be using some obscure rodeo term as a metaphor.

"Y'know… that baseball movie with Kevin Costner where Susan Sarandon asks him what he believes in and he says—"

"Oh! Right! *Bull Durham*… I should've known that."

"Welp, since you're askin', here's what I believe…." MacDuff paused to run his hands through his hair as if preparing for a leap off a high diving board, or some other semi-dangerous endeavor. "I believe that, yeah, Shitbirds.com can fly and help change the world fer the better. But it'll take a whole lotta people t' make that happen—not just one. I also believe in gnosis: the daimon, the Eternal Twin, and the True God waitin' t' ambush us with total consciousness once we're good 'n' ready fer it. I believe in a tall cold *cerveza* with a slice o' lime on a hot summer day while eatin' nachos with cunty fingers. I believe Lee Harvey Oswald and Sirhan Sirhan were mind-controlled decoys fer the real assassins. And I think there oughta be a constitutional amendment outlawin' lobbyists, super PACs, the CIA, and the plumb crazy notion that corporations get the same rights as people. I believe in the G-spot and slo-mo lady squirt porn and only goin' t' church on Easter Sunday so's t' ponder what that false god, the Demiurge, let them *culeros* do t' Jesus. I believe in the power and the glory o' perky tits, them two dimples high up on a curvy woman's ass, and long, slow, soft, wet pussy lickin' that goes on fer days. You got any questions?"

"Just one…" said Sabina: "Can you demonstrate the pussy lickin' part?"

"Be my pleasure, darlin'."

THE CHARIOT

Sabina woke up the next morning feeling poisoned and exuberant. The poison was from all the alcohol boiling off in her system, making her feel dehydrated and pukey. The exuberance was a lingering aftereffect of her first coital orgasm, which she'd experienced while riding cowgirl with her new best friend, MacDuff. It turned out Frank was right about him being big all over. He also had the stamina of a plow horse.

She'd finally met her Mister Magic Penis.

Already dressed in full cowboy regalia, MacDuff walked into the bedroom carrying two steaming mugs from her kitchen. "You're a coffee drinker, right?" he asked her.

"I am this morning. Damn, that smells good."

"Zabar's own special blend. I came prepared."

"Yeah, that box of Longhorn condoms was a nice touch," Sabina said with affectionate snark as MacDuff handed her a mug.

"The Boy Scouts taught me that."

"What? To be prepared?"

"'I' always bring condoms on a second date. Or maybe that was somethin' I learnt from my old man's stroke books.... Don't matter. It's a solid piece o' advice."

"Works for me," Sabina said, sipping and contemplating. "I hope you don't think I'm a slut."

"Nah. Just frisky is all."

"It's actually been a few years."

"A few years since what?"

"Since I got laid."

MacDuff sat down on the bed next to her, striking a gentlemanly pose. "It didn't seem like you was outta practice," he said, fondling her left boob.

Sabina's loins started churning again like a cement mixer. What was it with this guy, that he had such a powerful erotic hold on her?

"Do y'think you could do me again before you go to work?" she asked, trying to disguise the naked lust in her voice.

"I reckon I could..." said MacDuff, taking off his black hat.

Three hours later, Sabina and MacDuff took a limousine downtown to his place. MacDuff had a seven-level penthouse with an outdoor observatory in the same tall skyscraper that housed his offices in the Financial District. He even had his own special key for the elevator, which opened directly into his living room.

"Jesus, it looks like an overgrown hobbit lives here," Sabina said as the elevator's doors closed behind them. "Who did your interior decorating—Peter Jackson?"

"You don't like it?" asked MacDuff, hanging his Stetson on an elaborately carved hat rack.

"No, don't get me wrong. I think it's incredibly cool," said Sabina, trying to take it all in. "It's just so... *woodsy* for Manhattan."

There wasn't a straight edge in the entire place. The walls were made of cedar logs. Or maybe they were redwood. Sabina wasn't a goddam lumberjack, so she couldn't say for sure. But what she did know, without a doubt, was that a team of master carpenters had spent a good chunk of their lives in that apartment, making sure that everything fit together without a single flaw. What she saw in front of her wasn't a typical Manhattan construction crew hack job. It was a work of art.

The double-height living room had two enormous atrium windows facing north and south from sixty or seventy floors up. They gave Sabina the vertiginous sensation of flying high above the city in a Jules Vernesian wood-lined steampunk submarine. But everything else about the place was warm and cozy: a huge riverstone fireplace, deep pile Turkish rugs, comfy-looking leather couches and club chairs, potted orchids and bonsai trees everywhere, and lots of lovely old brass lamps glowing against all that rich, warm, beautiful woodwork. It was like one of those shipshape houses that rich old sea captains built for themselves when they wanted to retire—only better.

God only knew how many millions the place was worth....

"I got somethin' I wanted t' show you..." MacDuff said, leading Sabina by the hand into a side room that turned out to be one of the world's greatest home offices.

The room was dominated by tall, curving bookcases made from some exotic honey-colored wood with a beautiful grain. The shelves were lined with art books, philosophy books, and hardcover fiction. She saw the complete works of James Joyce in one section, in what appeared to be the original first edition dust jackets. Also well represented in that same bookcase were Jorge Luis Borges, Julio Cortázar, Don DeLillo, Philip K. Dick, Umberto Eco, Jonathan Franzen, Erich Fromm, William Gibson, Barry Hannah, Jim Harrison, Hermann Hesse, Aldous Huxley, Denis Johnson, Franz Kafka, Jonathan Lethem, Sam Lipsyte, Thomas McGuane, Thomas Merton, Lorrie Moore, Haruki Murakami, Vladimir Nabokov, Flannery O'Connor, George Orwell, Charles Portis, and Thomas Pynchon. MacDuff's books were alphabetized. A leather-padded Stickley reading chair sat next to a mica-shaded floor lamp held up by two very realistic-looking black bear cubs cast in bronze.

Cute, in a kitschy Adirondacks kind of way... Sabina thought.

"I love the bears," she said to be kind.

"I got a thirty million dollar Kandinsky up on the wall over there, and you like the bears…" MacDuff griped. "Just goes t' show, art is a sucker's game."

"Oh, I love the Kandinsky too!" Sabina said, noticing it only then, hanging above an impressive burlwood desk against the far wall. "But jeez, shouldn't that be in a museum?"

"It will be, after I go boots up," said MacDuff. "Meanwhile, I lend it out wherever I can get a good tax break."

"You trust fund cowboys and your goddam tax breaks… you sound like an anal-retentive CPA. Is that what you wanted to show me? Your high-priced trophy art?"

"Nope. I know better than t' try and impress you with the stuff I bought. I was just hopin' you'd take a gander at the Shitbirds site."

"Is that up already?" Sabina wondered if she'd misunderstood the implications of MacDuff's call to Ron last night.

"It ain't launched yet, but we got us an in-house prototype." MacDuff pressed a concealed button under the lip of the desk. Hidden computer monitors started rising up out of the deceptively smooth burlwood desktop. "I got my own personal spy-proof fiber-optic line up here that runs straight down t' Limelight's main servers, so I can show you everythin' while the kinks are still bein' worked out. We're mostly down t' figurin' out how t' make things look good. The code behind it's solid."

A keyboard also appeared on the desktop with the slow rolling flip of a burlwood plank. MacDuff sat down in a polished nickel Aeron chair and called up a web browser that Sabina had never seen before. He typed Shitbirds.com into the web address box.

"What the hell is that?" she asked as the homepage loaded. It looked like the Internet-equivalent of projectile vomiting: lame-ass banners all over the place, cruddy photos and ugly fonts. "What're you trying to be, the *Huffington Post* here?"

"I know. Too durned busy, right?" MacDuff turned to Sabina with a look of exasperation. "I told them boys t' keep it simple, but they're programmers, not artists. Which is why I was hopin' we'd get Démerder t' help us out."

"New York has plenty of great web designers," Sabina said. "I even have a few on my payroll."

"Yeah, but how many could really get what we're tryin' t' do here? Plus, there's the security risk."

"You could've asked me. I would've given you some great referrals."

"I *did* ask you."

"Oh. Right." Sabina realized that her qualms about working with Ron and MacDuff were now officially over. Without having said as much, she already considered herself part of the team.

"Let me see this…." She leaned over beside MacDuff and grabbed the wireless mouse out of his hand. She started clicking and scrolling through the website. The navigation made sense to her—and the damning formerly private info on the rich and the powerful was definitely there to be seen. *(HolyFuckingChrist! A convicted child porn peddler was a cybersecurity director of the US Department of Health and Human Services? How Orwellian could this shit get?)*

Aesthetically, however, Shitbirds.com was an embarrassment. No one was going to trust the information they found there because it looked like a team of sixth graders had uploaded it after going off their meds for ADHD.

"How can you expect to change the world if you don't even have a decent logo?" Sabina asked MacDuff.

"We got one right there," he said, pointing to the upper left corner of the screen, where Shitbirds had been written out in a multi-colored font that looked like Frutiger.

"You can't just rip-off the Google logo," Sabina told him. "Besides, it sends the wrong message. Google's the company that started out with the motto 'Don't be evil'—and then it got into bed with the intelligence agencies and the US military. If you parody anything, it should be Twitter."

"Why Twitter? We're not doin' the hundred-and-forty word thing here."

"No, but Twitter's more democratic and people-driven, right? I've actually been giving this some thought. What if your logo had a simplified bird icon on it, sort of like the Twitter icon, only more like a buzzard—or a turd with wings?"

MacDuff grinned. "I like it."

"Do you have Adobe's Creative Suite on this computer?"

"No, but I'll buy it for you right now, if you want."

"It's like sixty bucks a month. Sure you can afford it?"

"It'll be a tax write-off."

About two hours later, Sabina had a scalable vector-based icon that she liked well enough to show MacDuff. It split the difference between cartoon buzzard and flying turd—and could be read as either from a distance. Beneath the icon, she'd written:

"When's your launch date?" Sabina asked.

"September Eleventh," MacDuff answered. "We figured that'd be a good day t' kick-off. Sort of a yin-yang thing goin' on there with… well, you know… I don't have t' explain it, do I?"

"No. I get it." Sabina typed in **9/11** under the Shitbirds slogan. "There's your first all-purpose ad," she said, feeling satisfied with her handiwork.

"Well I'll be…" MacDuff breathed.

"Do you have a media plan?"

"A what?"

"A media plan. To let people know when the site goes live?"

"Hadn't thought that far ahead, actually. I mean, we'll be doin' ads on the Internet, o' course… 'bout half-a-mil's worth o' paid search engine marketing, more or less."

"No out of home campaign?"

"T' be honest, I don't even know what that means."

"Billboards, subway posters, bus wraps, taxi tops… you know—things people see when they're outside their homes."

"Oh! Yeah, that'd be great."

"You should probably do New York, Chicago, and L.A., at least. Maybe San Francisco and Seattle, too. You could start with billboards on Sunset Boulevard and the Santa Monica Freeway, airport posters at O'Hare, station dominations here under the World Trade Center—to get the tourists—and at Fourteenth and Eighth, right by the Google building."

"What the heck're station dominations?"

"Multiple posters that take over an entire subway station. You should also put the same ads on trains."

"Why do we wanna be so in-yer-face with Google?" MacDuff asked. He seemed genuinely interested, but somewhat out of his depth.

"They've been hiring the best and brightest for a while now—aside from your guys, of course. You want people like that to know about Shitbirds.com and help spread the word. Besides, if Google doesn't link to your site, the majority of Internet users won't even know you exist."

"Okay. Makes sense."

Sabina wasn't done yet: "You should also probably do some big banner displays at Comic Con this October—to get more of the cool nerds contingent. And you'll want to start telling your story on all the social media sites: Facebook, Twitter, YouTube, blogs…. I have people who could help you there. I can get them all to sign nondisclosure agreements, if you need that. They've all worked with me before."

"How much money we talkin'?"

"Overall? Around five or ten million should get us off to a good start."

"Done." MacDuff stood up from the desk. "That's just a good week o' tradin' fer us. I'll have Ron set you up with a business account and you can start hirin' whoever you want."

"Just like that?"

"Just like that."

"You realize, of course, that once I release the mechanicals to GSG for printing, this whole thing won't be a secret anymore."

"That's a risk we'll just have t' take. The whole world's gonna know about it soon enough, anyway."

"Sure you don't want to launch first and then advertise?"

"Nah. I wanna come at 'em all at once," said MacDuff. "Give them bastards a taste o' their own medicine. Shock and Awe, darlin'. Shock and Awe…."

"You sound very studly when you say that," Sabina teased him. "Kind of reminds me of George W. Bush when he landed on that aircraft carrier with his flight suit bulging at the crotch."

"Shoot. Don't go comparin' me to that *My-Pet-Goat*-readin' jackass." MacDuff leaned over and gently kissed the back of Sabina's neck. "I been away too long. I gotta get downstairs t' check on a few things. You can stay here if you want. I'll take you out t' dinner when I get back."

"Deal."

As MacDuff was leaving the room, he said, "Just get me some good web designers and make sure them ads'll be up by the eleventh." He patted the front of his pearl-buttoned shirt, took out a phone from the left pocket—an old Blackberry—and tossed it to Sabina.

"Almost forgot… don't use your own cell phone," he cautioned her. "The NSA can track it by GPS and even turn it into a listenin' device by remote activation. It's like ol' Tom Pynchon said: 'The Grid is wide open, all messages can be overheard.' This here's a burner phone with a couple o' tweaks from my lab guys. Use it fer now and we'll just toss it at the end o' the project. From now on, you'll check yer iPhone at the front desk before you come up here. Ernesto there'll run you through the drill."

"Hey," Sabina said sharply, "just because you're ponying up ten million bucks, that doesn't mean you can boss me around."

MacDuff turned in the doorway and tipped the brim of his Stetson at her as he replied: "I got the distinct feelin' that from here on out, if anyone's the boss, it'd be you."

Sabina smiled and flipped open the burner phone. She had a shit-ton of calls to get through.

DEATH

The next month went by in a blur of work and rodeo-style fornication. Sabina essentially moved in with MacDuff at his penthouse so she could supervise the aesthetic revamping of Shitbirds.com. A team of her most trusted web designers, bloggers, and production artists joined her there, using their own laptops to wirelessly connect with MacDuff's desktop computer (which, in turn, was connected to Limelight's main servers). At the end of each long day, they all met with Limelight's chief programmer—an introverted Russian physicist named Sergei with a bristly buzzcut and a constipated eagle's face—who personally saw to it that their laptops were digitally scrubbed clean before they left the building, so that nothing Shitbirds-related could be carried into the wider world. (On their way out, they retrieved their personal phones, wallets, and watches from a security guard named Ernesto, who kept those items in a Faraday-caged locker room behind the front desk in the lobby.)

It was weird, hermetic existence. There was so much to do that Sabina and MacDuff rarely went out. Most of their meals were delivered. Démerder's *A Black Box for Humanity's Redacted History* was also delivered three days into Sabina's stay, making things even weirder. During their evening interactions with Sergei—with the stars and city lights glittering outside the big bay windows and the ominous Kubrickian cube in the center of the living room, sucking up the reflections of everything around it like a square peg in a black hole—it almost felt like they were suspended on a US-Soviet space station.

Their only respite from work came late at night, when Sabina and MacDuff took time out to screw themselves delirious and then relax by watching their favorite old hippie detective movies on Netflix: *The Big Lebowski, Inherent Vice, Serpico, Cutter's Way, The Parallax View, The Long Goodbye*…. Already knowing how those movies ended, they usually fell asleep before the final credits. Then, after a few blissful hours of spooning, they got up and went back to work. The pace only quickened as the launch date neared. Weekends were no different.

On top of all that, the Inuk had finally gotten back to Sabina. He'd secured the package, but his tundra buggy could only get it as far as Churchill, Manitoba. No roads led out of Churchill to the rest of Canada, so Sabina started looking into other transportation options. None of them were great. When she complained to MacDuff about it early one morning over coffee, he told he'd send in his helicopter.

"You have your own private helicopter?" Sabina asked him, appalled, yet also secretly thinking, *How convenient!*

"I always wanted a chopper when I was growin' up," said MacDuff. "It was that scene in *Apocalypse Now* that got t' me. You know… the one where they're blastin' 'Ride o' the Valkyries' and they napalm that beach so Robert Duvall and them guys can go surfin'?"

"Billionaire boys and their toys, huh?"

MacDuff just grinned. "I got me a decommissioned Sikorsky Super Stallion. It used t' fly Marines around, but I had it retrofitted fer civilian use. Mostly I use it t' get out t' my beach house in Montauk… beats sittin' in traffic… but it'll handle a trip to Canada and back. *No problema.*"

Sabina said, "I'll get James to pay for your gas."

"Nah. No need fer that."

"Oh, believe me, he can afford it. After this press conference I'm setting up for him, the pop in his book sales will more than make up for whatever money he spends up front. He's gonna be famous."

"It was my understandin' he already was…."

"I mean more famous—but in a good way. Not just as America's Number One Polar Bear Fluffer."

"Welp, how 'bout if Shitbirds.com sponsors this lil' shindig then? Get us some publicity in exchange fer the chopper service. We could give away T-shirts, hang up a few posters—stuff like that…."

"I was trying to get Greenpeace to sponsor it. Are you sure you're up for that?"

"Don't see how it could hurt. You already sent the mechanicals to GSG, right?"

"We're proofing everything this week," Sabina confirmed.

"So Schrödinger's Wildcat is already out o' the box."

"I suppose it is."

"So is that pussy dead or alive?" MacDuff asked, referencing Sabina's Freudian slip from their first conversation in the library, when he'd asked her out on a date.

"It's alive…" Sabina purred, climbing onto MacDuff's lap, "thanks to you, you big dog."

After taking time out for an early morning quickie on the living room couch, watched over by Démerder's cube, they both headed off to work: MacDuff downstairs to Limelight's corporate headquarters, where he would dispatch his helicopter to Manitoba with detailed instructions for the pickup; and Sabina uptown to Graphic Systems Group on East Seventeenth, at the northern edge of Union Square (directly above the same Barnes & Noble bookstore in which she'd met James), where she would be looking at proofs of the subway posters, bus wraps, and billboards that would be going up all over the country next week.

When she got off the N train at Union Square, Sabina made a mental note to call Frank about hosting the press conference at one of the city's zoos. The Central Park Zoo had already turned them down flat, wanting nothing more to do with James Marrsden and his degenerate polar bear shenanigans, but the Bronx Zoo had expressed some cautious interest. Now that the package was due to arrive soon, maybe Frank could seal the deal. He still had plenty of pull around the city from his days with the New York Attorney General's Office—especially with cops, schoolteachers, firemen, social workers, honest politicians, and (so he'd told Sabina...) *zookeepers.*

Up in the sunlight again, Sabina strolled through the Union Square Greenmarket, deliberately slowing down to let her senses take in her surroundings. Like Bryant Park, visiting the Greenmarket always made her feel happy. She usually made a point of going there to stock up on fresh, healthy, farm-to-table food at the end of a long work binge. Sometimes, when she got super-busy, she felt like she couldn't take the time to buy groceries and cook real food, so she just drank Soylent for days on end (which tasted like fish granola water, but at least it halfway took care of her hunger and gave her body the nutrients it needed). When she finally got some free time again, she indulged herself by buying whatever looked good at the Greenmarket's tented booths: rustic breads, pasture raised meats, farmhouse cheeses, free range brown eggs, tree ripened fruit, local honey, jams, and chutney…. If MacDuff's penthouse hadn't been consistently stocked with great things to eat—thanks to pricey delivery services—she would have been due for another Greenmarket run right about now.

Sabina's vague but persistent love of humanity was brought into sharper focus as she passed among the many people buying, browsing, and selling at the Greenmarket. She saw a wrinkled but perky old Asian lady wearing red cat eye glasses in front of the Maple Avenue Farm booth ("Can't Beat Our Meat") negotiating over the price of a steak with a pale, skinny, bearded dude with dirty blond dreads piled high on his head into a kind of bird's nest. A younger and much sexier Asian woman with dyed platinum blonde hair going black at the roots walked in front of Sabina wearing low-slung suede boots and a micromini, showing off great legs. She was on the arm of a freakishly tall and handsome Nigerian-looking boyfriend, talking to him in such a low, mannish voice that Sabina wondered if she was transgender. Across from them, an older man in a shabby herringbone suit and a porkpie hat was selling ostrich eggs and Berkshire pork. In the booth next to his, an artsy girl with mauve curls and a silver nose ring tried to interest passers-by in free samples of Holy Schmitt's Homemade Horseradish. To the right of her booth, two smiling Latinas stood behind a Plexiglas case full of delicious-looking bread loaves from the She Wolf Bakery. Then there was a great-smelling booth selling nothing but lavender—or lavender-based products. Oh, and some orchids.

As Sabina threaded her way through the crowd—past people pushing strollers, walking dogs, talking on cellphones—it occurred to her that with a few winks of a digital camera's aperture the NSA or any halfway decent computer programmer could have full access to the private lives of everyone around her. Take a picture of that guy selling ostrich eggs and in fifteen minutes (according to Démerder) you could know all about him: his credit rating, birth certificate, social security number, criminal record, sexual preferences—the full dossier.

Most people were in denial about it, but there was no such thing as anonymity anymore. Anything you did on the Internet these days was the digital equivalent of taking off your pants and dropping a payload in the middle of Times Square. If you were only as sick as your secrets, like those former boozehounds and sex addicts were always claiming, then the Snowden Avalanche was forcing everyone to get healthy. Except for the American Deep State, of course. Those guys were the sickest crew ever.

Maybe Shitbirds.com could change that by revealing the whole sick crew for what they really were—so that no one, not even the Deep State, could keep their crimes and character flaws hidden. But that seemed like a poor alternative to reclaiming the civil liberties that the Fourth Amendment and the rest of the Constitution used to guarantee everyone in the US.

Only a week ago, Sabina had gotten into a minor squabble over the issue of online privacy, or the lack thereof, when she'd taken a short break from MacDuff to go out to dinner with her good friends Ned and Bernice. Bernice had been Sabina's boss at Fordham and Ned was a bridge engineer—the lead technical supervisor, in fact, for the restoration of the Brooklyn Bridge after the truck-bombing incident blamed on ISIS in 2016. They were both upstanding American citizens, the kind of people who made this country great. But Ned—rendered mildly obtuse by his third glass of sangria, perhaps—had sent Sabina off on a rant by saying to her: "I don't see the problem with the NSA collecting all this data on us. The way I look at it is: I haven't done anything wrong, so I've got nothing to hide."

"It's not so much about you hiding your digital shit, Ned," Sabina had told him. "It's about what a really strong and aggressive military-industrial-intelligence kleptocracy might choose to do with that information, once they have it. The mass surveillance system they're building is the most powerful weapon for oppression the world has ever seen. Right now, there's not much stopping them from reaching into your life and taking whatever they want."

She explained to Ned and Bernice that their retirement accounts, the title to their co-op, and even their young daughter's college savings fund were all vulnerable to cybertheft, corporate seizure, or civil forfeiture. Their lives could be ruined with just a few keystrokes.

"And not just by using your own data against you," she warned them. "They can push fake data on you, too. Once they've opened a back door on your computer, they won't have any problem leaving a digital slime trail of creepy illegal porn on your hard drive if they decide they don't like your politics."

"But this is America. They'd never do that," Bernice argued.

"Sure they would," said Sabina. "So far, the government's capacity for mass surveillance seems unmatched by its will to abuse it, but that could all change with one bum spin of the congressional roulette wheel—or one more bad President. Think McCarthyism on steroids. We already know that most of our elected officials put the interests of corporate lobbyists way ahead of what's best for the American people. With all the Super PACs and dark-money controlling elections these days, you can't rule out that the next Leader of the so-called Free World won't be a crypto-fascist dictator disguised in a navy blue suit with a tiny little American flag pinned to his lapel."

Sabina cited examples of paranoid political leaders who'd destroyed the lives of millions of their own countrymen without having access to a mass surveillance system anywhere near so potent as what the world was facing now. Hitler, Stalin, Mao, Pol Pot…. Maybe she'd been radicalized by her late-night talks with MacDuff. Even to her own ears, she was sounding kind of strident.

"Bottom line:" she summed up, "the NSA's rampant domestic spying program is incompatible with a free society. Orwell's *1984* should've taught us that much, at least. As the American Deep State becomes more intrusive and oppressive, which is all but guaranteed, you'll find yourself facing a dilemma: You can either keep pretending to be a USA rah-rah version of the Good German, or your politics *will* be found unpatriotic. And then... *look the fuck out."*

Sabina knew that Ned's German grandparents had lived in Berlin during the ramp up to World War II, and he conceded that she had a point. But still, he thought she was making too much out of the whole NSA deal.

Actually, there was another aspect to it that Sabina hadn't even bothered to discuss with her friends—although she'd talked about it plenty with MacDuff: The NSA might very well be the Orwellian equivalent of Big Brother, but we were all complicit as self-surveilling Little Brothers and Little Sisters, jackassing around with our smartphones, PDAs, and Apple Watches ("handcuffs of the future" Thomas Pynchon called them), putting web-connected activity sensors in our TVs, thermostats, and smoke alarms (and soon, RFID chips in the necks of our pets, kids, and Alzheimer's-afflicted parents...), and then willingly—*unthinkingly*—allowing those nifty devices to track our movements, record our vital signs, store our images, access our bank accounts, compile detailed lists of our friends and associates, and listen in on our conversations.

It was like what Pogo said: "We have met the enemy and he is us."

So was that platinum Asian bombshell walking ahead of Sabina a He somewhere along the path toward becoming a She? Zero in on her from one of the street's many surveillance cameras and you could find out—and then, as an added bonus, if she'd been clueless enough to make her own private sex tapes, you might be able to download some porny hi-def digital videos of her making it with the hot Nigerian boyfriend.

Which reminded Sabina... it was time to call Frank.

She looked down at her feet as she got out her burner phone. She found herself standing in the center of a white chalk circle drawn on the hexagonal concrete pavers by a graffiti artist. Within that circle, the artist had outlined two cartoon footprints and written:

YOU ARE HERE

FOR BAD LUCK
EBOLA CANCER
& George W. Bush

Bush hasn't been in office since 2009, Sabina thought. *Way to hold a grudge, dude....*

Although she wasn't superstitious enough to believe in things like sigils, summoning grids, and interdimensional energy portals, Sabina stepped outside the circle, anyway, before placing the call to Frank.

Why chance it?

Frank answered on the second ring. "Hey! It's my favorite defrosted Norwegian ice princess! What's shakin' babes?"

Some hypersensitive feminists might interpret Frank's banter as misogynistic, but Sabina just found it friendly and fun, coming as it did from a scrawny geriatric white guy who sounded like Curly Howard (from The Three Stooges) with his sinuses packed full of New Jersey crystal meth.

"Hey, you sexist old douchebag, I'm calling about the Bronx Zoo," she said, getting right to the point.

"Already taken care of," said Frank.

"Really?"

"Yeah. MacDuff phoned me earlier this morning. I know all about the helicopter to Manitoba. You didn't think you could just stash that thing on his deck when it gets here tomorrow, did you?"

"I wasn't planning that far ahead, I guess."

"Well, lucky for you, the Bronx Zoo owed me a favor. I did them a solid when that snow leopard escaped a few years ago and threatened those kids at P.S. 57."

"I'm pretty sure that was a red panda. And those school kids were caught feeding it a slice of pizza on Arthur Avenue."

"Yeah, well... that pizza place still could've sued the zoo's ass off. But I stepped in and negotiated a truce."

"Way to go, Frank."

"I know, right? Whenever our cherished public institutions are in crisis I'm always there, swooping in to save the day."

"Just like Mighty Mouse."

"I was thinking more like Zorro—or Captain America. But I guess you're not quite up to the task of stroking my ego today."

"Your ego gets plenty of stroking when you're all by yourself."

"Hey, Maleeka strokes it too, I'll have you know...."

"That's called play-acting, Frank. Don't be delusional."

"It may be play-acting, but when she puts on that black bodystocking and shakes her big rump at me, my joy is true. I still owe you for that, big-time."

"Yes you do," Sabina agreed.

"So to square things up a bit, I talked the zoo into setting up a press conference for you. They're reserving a big room in some place called… wait a sec, I wrote it down…." Frank could be heard rustling some papers in the background. "Here it is! *The LaMattina Wildlife Ambassador Center.* It's scheduled for one o'clock, this Saturday afternoon."

"Shit! That's only three days away!"

"Well, I didn't think you'd wanna drag this one out. You might lose the element of surprise."

"Yeah, but that means I'll have to write press releases, contact the media, book James on a flight out here from San Francisco and get him prepped—all in, like, record time. And on top of that, I still have the Shitbirds launch to get through next week, which has its own long list of things I have to do."

"Then you'd best get on it, Rodeo Girl. I won't keep you."

So that was how Sabina and James came to be standing at a podium three days later in front of two local television news crews, a half-dozen freelance videographers trolling for the cable channels, a troop of sullen-looking print journalists (from the *Post*, the *Times*, the *Village Voice*, *AM New York*, *Gay City News*, and the *Brooklyn Eagle*…), and what appeared to be the entire New York contingent of Greenpeace International—all crammed together inside a stuffy room smelling like wild animal piss and old sneakers under the roof of the Bronx Zoo's LaMattina Wildlife Ambassador Center.

Fetchingly attired in teal flip-flops and his customary, hideous-to-gaze-upon Hawaiian shirt, James leaned across the podium and grazed his gray whiskers against Sabina's ear. "I'm getting a hostile vibe from these people," he whispered. "How 'bout you?"

"Don't worry. They'll love you once we get to the photo op," Sabina tried to assure him. Her gut, however, was telling her to bolt. Public speaking always made her anxious. She gulped down some water from a Poland Springs bottle to wet her dry mouth and then she stepped up to the microphone.

"Okay, let's get started…" she said, cringing at the sound of her amplified voice. "Thank you all for coming out today. We're here to welcome the newest addition to the Bronx Zoo's menagerie—a very special animal whose origins are… well, just a little unusual. In fact, this animal wouldn't even be alive if it hadn't been for the brave and valiant efforts of one man—the man who's standing right here beside me. He can tell you the story much better than I can. So let's let him talk, shall we? Ladies and gentlemen, I present to you James Marrsden, the acclaimed author of fifteen *New York Times* bestselling novels—and perhaps more importantly, for our purposes, the world's most notorious polar bear fellatist. Let's give it up for James!"

Tepid applause. Even some boos from the Greenpeace contingent. *"Polar bear molester!"* someone shouted. James was facing a tough crowd, but he gamely stepped up to the mic and started riffing on the speech he and Sabina had prepared earlier:

"Hi there, kids. I know, I know… I shouldn't have sucked off that polar bear. It was sick and wrong. *Unnatural.* Gross. But what if I told you I did it in the interest of science? Or to save an endangered species? Because, believe it or not, both of those things are true."

"It wasn't just because you wanted to take a walk on the wild side?" one of the journalists piped up.

"Hey, I'm as big a fan of Lou Reed as anyone. But no, I didn't storm the polar bear pit just because I'm a feckless fellatio artist. Although didn't Joseph Beuys do something like that with a coyote in a New York City art gallery once? Any of you guys know?"

There was a universal shaking of heads. But then some art history major in a free Shitbirds.com T-shirt raised her hand at the back of the room and said in a loud voice: "It was in Soho, back in the seventies… but I don't think he had sex with the coyote. They just lived together."

MacDuff and Ron were standing against the back wall behind a long folding table where they'd been giving away T-shirts beneath a **Shitbirds.com** banner. They smiled and waved at Sabina as she stepped away from the podium and moved around the perimeter of the crowd to join them.

"That's good to know," James said, acknowledging the art history girl. "I've got a few facts I wanted to bring up as well. For instance, did you guys know that we've lost over half the earth's wildlife population in the last forty years? Or that the level of carbon in our atmosphere has risen to levels the world hasn't seen in more than a million years? In 2008, the Endangered Species Act listed polar bears as the first mammals ever threatened with extinction due to global warming.

That's huge! I mean, sure, we kill off other species all the time, but that's on purpose—like how we blasted all those tasty passenger pigeons out of the sky because they were so good to eat. But we've never, to the best of our knowledge, ever made a species go extinct just by heating up the planet like an Easy-Bake Oven. Where's the fun in that? It seems more like an accident, something we should try to put the brakes on, before it's too late. And these are cute, cuddly polar bears we're talking about, folks—like on the Pepsi commercials—not some stupid salamander or some butt-ugly, half-poodle-half-crocodile monstrosity down in Puerto Rico that mangles goats for a living. Saving the polar bears is something we can all get behind, right?"

"Not if we have to turn around and suck their cocks," grumbled a silver-bearded fake Hemingway guy with sloping ape-like shoulders—a discontented print journalist, Sabina guessed.

"Well, obviously, I didn't feel as strongly about that as you," James retorted. "You guys know I was on drugs, right? Some hippie kids dosed me in a Starbucks. Put hallucinogenic tryptamines in my Mocha Frappuccino. Probably some Viagra, too. I've posted the emergency room records on my website, in case you don't believe me. But that's almost beside the point. The idea for getting some polar bear DNA was planted in me long before I actually went out and did the deed."

"Hold on…" said the fake Hemingway Guy, "you're telling us you risked your life, going into that polar bear pit, because you were after their DNA?"

James just nodded his head, a humble servant of science.

"There had to be an easier way," Hemingway Guy said. "Couldn't you just sample some polar bear hair, or get DNA from their shit?"

"My friends out in Bushwick said they needed the actual sperm for their biogenomics project."

That was a total lie, Sabina knew. This was the point at which their prepared speech departed from reality into pure science fiction.

"A biogenomics project?" asked a glossy brunette woman with a microphone from one of the local TV news stations. "Are we talking about genetic engineering here? Like what Monsanto does, when they cross bananas with bioluminescent plankton so they'll glow at night and the fruit bats won't eat them?"

"I tried those bananas once," said James. "They were delicious. But then I got arrested for public urination when I tried to write my name on the side of the Transamerica Pyramid in the dark."

The Greenpeace crew was looking dangerously restless, like a troop of mountain gorillas sensing an unseen threat among the Seussian senecio trees in the Democratic Republic of Congo. They didn't like the idea of bioluminescent bananas—or genetically engineered polar bears.

"You jerks tweaked the genes in a polar bear?" one of them asked James with a chest-thumping huff.

"No." James raised his hands, palms out, like a traffic cop. "It was nothing like that, I swear. This is natural selection we're talking about—stuff that happens out in the wild all the time. My Bushwick pals just sequenced the genomes of half-a-dozen in vitro fertilized eggs so they could see what they'd be getting once they knocked-up a she-bear."

"Wait, what?" said the glossy woman with the microphone. "I think you lost us."

"Yeah, well, I skipped ahead a little because it looked like the Greenpeace crew was about ready to tear off my head and shit down my throat."

"We won't tolerate genetically-modified polar bears," a gray-haired hippie lady in a Greenpeace T-shirt said. She raised a bony fist and shouted: "Hell no to polar bear GMOs!"

Others took up the chant: "Hell no to polar bear GMOs! Hell no to pol—"

"Hey, hey, hey!" James shouted into the microphone. "Just listen, okay? You guys need to chill the fuck out! No polar bear genes were modified during this project. It was just selective breeding and a little IVF procedure."

"There are no IVF procedures 'out in the wild'!" the old hippie lady shouted back at him.

"Don't get your organic cotton adult diapers in a twist. *Sheesh*. The point is that we didn't put Fresno Layshaft's genes in a blender. All we did was select among the fertilized eggs for traits that would make the best bear. It's no different than what any Park Avenue trophy wife does to get pregnant after she hits forty."

"Did you just call your frankenbear Fresno Layshaft?" the woman with the microphone asked James, incredulous. She was starting to rile him. Sabina could tell.

"That's his name. What? You don't like it?"

"It sounds ridiculous."

"Which part? The Fresno, or the Layshaft?"

"Both!"

"Just wait until you see him. He looks like a Fresno." Speaking directly into the microphone, James said, "Bring him out, LaFonda...."

A beautiful black girl in a short-sleeved Bronx Zoo uniform emerged from a doorway somewhat behind and to the left of James. She was carrying the most adorable polar bear cub anyone had ever seen. He was round and fluffy and perfectly white, except for a honey-colored splotch of fur around his left eye that made him look like the polar bear equivalent of Spuds MacKenzie—the partying bull terrier that danced in conga lines with beautiful babes in the old Budweiser commercials.

A collective *"Awwww..."* went up among the crowd.

LaFonda passed the bear cub to James. He cradled young Fresno as if he'd been doing it since the cub had been born, although they'd met for the first time only a few hours earlier. James leaned over and tickled Fresno's chin, cooing, "Who's my little polar bear friend? Fresno, right?" As if in answer, the cub stuck out his dainty pink tongue and licked James right under his nose (where a dab of sardine-infused peanut butter had been secreted in his mustache just prior to the show). A flurry of camera flashes went off as another spontaneous *"Awwww..."* swept through the room.

Sabina started to breathe easier. The crowd, she knew, had been won over.

"So Fresno here is a little over four months old," James told his audience—another bold-faced lie. Fresno was actually eight or nine months old, but he was small for his age because he'd been an undernourished orphan for at least a few months before the Inuk had found him. (Canadian Inuits had the right to collect—or hunt and kill—a limited number of polar bears each year, which was why Sabina had contacted the Inuk in the first place.) The average eight-month-old polar bear weighs around 100 pounds, but Fresno weighed less than half that—which was fortunate, in a way, for Sabina and James, because polar bear gestation lasts eight months and, doing the math, that meant that Fresno couldn't be much older than four months if he was supposed to have resulted from James' encounter in the polar bear pit a year ago. And their whole PR stunt hinged on that, of course.

"Augustus, from the Central Park Zoo, is Fresno's polar bear daddy," James said, just to be clear, even though that bit of misdirection had already been laid. "When my biogenomics buddies heard about what I'd done, they sent an extraction team to liaise with me in the hospital and bag my T-shirt, which still had viable polar bear sperm on it. Mission accomplished—even though I was high as fuck and had absolutely no idea what was going on. They told me about it later, after they'd already used the T-shirt jizz to fertilize a bunch of grizzly bear ovums they had in deep-freeze."

There was a mad scientist ring to the story that didn't sit well with the Greenpeace hippie lady. "Grizzly bear ovums! What the hell?" she sniped at James. "Where did those come from?"

"My Bushwick bros harvested the ovums from the she-grizzly star of *Brooklyn Grizzly Adams*—a soon-to-be released original YouTube series featuring Zach Galifianakis as the owner of a failing artisanal cannoli bakery who can't go anywhere in public without being accompanied by his registered emotional-support bear, Ursula Undressed—who happens to be Fresno's mom."

That was utter bullshit. A simple DNA test would blow the whole story out of the water. But Frank had already persuaded Ursula's trainer and the Bronx Zoo to sign nondisclosure agreements in exchange for the massive amount of free publicity that Fresno and James would be sending their way. As an added incentive, Fresno would be making guest appearances on *Brooklyn Grizzly Adams* in the near future. It was a win-win for all parties involved.

"Grizzlies and polar bears have been interbreeding in the wild since, like, forever," James explained. "They only really separated as two distinct species around 600,000 years ago. But climate change is pushing them back together again. The melting of polar ice is forcing the polar bears to spend more time on dry land, while mining and construction crews in southern Canada are persuading the grizzlies to pack their bags and move further north. So the two species are getting together and doing the bear-back horizontal hula. Hybrids are on the rise. And my guys thought: *'Hey! Maybe this is a way to save the polar bears…'* by mixing in some grizzly genes that'll help 'em survive in warmer weather."

"But aren't the hybrids sterile, like donkeys?" asked the hippie lady.

"Nope. That's the beauty of it," said James. "When little Fresno here grows up, he won't be shooting blanks. He's called a *pizzly*, by the way, just so you know… or *Nanulak*, if you're Inuit."

"He's super-cute," the glossy woman with the microphone admitted.

"So are you," said James, trying to make a new media friend. "If you're single, maybe the three of us should go out for lunch sometime."

She yawned like a lioness and said, "I don't think so."

"Fresno really digs sushi," James continued, undeterred. "And seal pup guts. But when he's all grown up he'll be able to eat just about anything. That's one of the advantages of having grizzly genes: grizzlies aren't restricted to a polar bear diet, so they don't have to starve during the summer months when all the sea ice melts and the hunting for ringed seals sucks. But my buds made sure to select for white fur, because you don't want to lose that. That's the polar bear essence. That, and fuzzy-wuzzy feet."

James waved one of Fresno's furry white paws at the audience and said, "I think I'll open the floor for questions now...." He made a show of surveying the crowd. "Yo, angry hippie lady, you look like you have something else you need to yell at me about."

Somewhat taken aback, the contentious hippie lady said in a modulated voice: "When you say you selected for white fur, how did you do that without gene-splicing?"

"Like I said, my buddies just sequenced the genomes to see what was in the DNA, and then they picked the fertilized egg they liked best. Back in 2001, the cost of sequencing a full human genome ran about a hundred million dollars, but these days—if you know the right people—you can analyze a half-dozen polar bear genomes on the Illumina HiSeq 3000 at the Bushwick Biogenomics Lab for, like, two hundred bucks plus a gift card for a free tune-up from Zukkîes Bike Shop."

Fake Hemingway Guy raised his hand. "Was this a one-time deal," he asked, "or will you be trying to increase the pizzly population by sucking off more polar bears in the future?"

James didn't miss a beat. "No, I think with Fresno here, my work is done. Now we can start cloning him." Before the Greenpeace crew could erupt into full-blown eco-hysteria, he added: "Just kidding. But seriously, I'm pretty sure I'm done. Like Voltaire always said about his one and only visit to a gay brothel: 'Once a philosopher, twice a pervert.' Now it's up to others to continue this fight to save a species, blow-by-blow."

James handled the rest of the questions with equal aplomb. Forty-five minutes later he was in the backseat of a gleaming black Maybach with Sabina, Ron, and MacDuff headed downtown.

"Welp, that went off purty durned great. Nice goin', James," said MacDuff.

James wasn't quite so exultant. "I can already see the headline in the *Post:* Polar Bear Knob-Gobbler Spits Out Bushwick Baby."

"That's a little wordy for the *Post*," Sabina said, grinning, "but if it's a slow news day and the photos are cute enough, we might get the front cover."

"I just hope they don't turn me into the Monsanto of polar bear gene hackers," James said glumly. "Jeez, did you hear those guys? They really had the knives out for me."

"I think you won everyone over by the end," said Ron. "Except for that irate hippie lady."

"Can't please 'em all," said MacDuff, patting James on the knee, "but I thought you put on one helluva show. We should be celebratin'. How 'bout we all fly out t' my place in Montauk fer the weekend?"

Sabina still hadn't seen MacDuff's beach house, but from what she'd heard it was supposed to be fabulous. Andy Warhol used to own it… or Peter Beard. She was a little unclear on the property's provenance, actually. MacDuff had only told her about it once, while they were in bed watching Julian Schnabel's movie about Jean-Michel Basquiat.

"Thanks, but I can't," said James. "I'm supposed to have dinner with my agent tonight and then we have some meetings with editors and publishers set up for tomorrow."

"Ron, how 'bout you?" MacDuff asked. "You up for some sand 'n' surf?"

"Emma and the kids are doing an overnight with my in-laws in Darien this weekend."

"Tell you what: we'll send you in the chopper to pick 'em up—the in-laws, too. There's a helipad near the Southport marina you can use. Then you can head back t' JRA and pick up me and Sabina, and we'll all fly out together."

"Let me call Emma and ask her." Ron got on his cellphone.

"James, you got somewhere you want us t' drop you off?"

"Sabina booked me into the Library Hotel on Forty-First and Madison. Thanks for that, by the way," James said to her. "The room's great, with lots of cool books to read when I'm not watching pay-per-view porn."

Later, when the Maybach turned onto Forty-Second Street and drove past Bryant Park, Sabina spotted a familiar-looking white dog on the sidewalk up ahead. She told the driver to pull up alongside him.

"Hey, Guy!" Sabina shouted, rolling down the window. Guy de Bored turned and went sidewalk-scratching toward the Maybach as Démerder/Gordon tried to hold him back on his taut leather leash. "Gordon!" Sabina said with what she hoped was a guileless smile. "These are the guys I was telling you about, Ron and MacDuff."

"What a coincidence!" said Gordon with an expression that told Sabina that he thought she was stalking him again. But he leaned sideways from a safe distance to peer into the Maybach and say hello, explaining, "I can't let Guy get too close or he'll scratch your paint. He's decided Sabina is his new best friend."

MacDuff waved a cheery hello as James stuck his head out the window right next to Sabina and said, "Gordon?"

"James!"

"What's it been, like ten or fifteen years?"

"More like twenty-five."

"You guys know each other?" Sabina asked them.

"We used to share a house together in California," James answered. "Shit, dude, what've you been up to?"

Somewhere in the back of her mind, Sabina could hear Frank laughing. Ron, MacDuff, James, and now Gordon… Frank had set her up with each of them without ever letting on about how they were all connected.

James got out of the car. MacDuff got out, too, and went around to shake Gordon's hand. Sabina was about to follow them when Ron placed a hand on her knee to stay her. "We should let those guys hash it out," he said with a warm smile.

But then Sabina heard Guy yip and saw him looking up at her with a big doggy grin—his whole body wriggling with affection, begging for some pats—so she said to Ron: "I'm just going out to pet the dog. I won't butt in on their conversation."

She got out on the sidewalk and crouched down to Guy's level to give him a hug. He practically leapt into her arms, throwing Gordon off-balance. As he recovered, Sabina overheard MacDuff inviting him out to lunch:

"…they got a restaurant out on the pier by the heliport that serves some durned good crab cakes. We could sit there and I could fill you in on this new network we're gettin' ready t' launch."

"Thanks, but I think James and I have some catching up to do first," Gordon said, looking uncomfortable.

Sabina was torn between eavesdropping on their conversation and giving Guy the attention he craved. She turned back to the big friendly dog, speaking to him in a goofy voice that she usually reserved for kids and pets: "Hi, Stinkyface! Are you being a good doggie today? Did you go poo-poo already?"

Guy just flopped out his long pink tongue and squinted his eyes in bliss as Sabina briskly rubbed behind his ears with both hands, then up and down his back and sides. He had no intention of giving her a definitive answer about the poo-poo.

The three men talked for a while longer. Then they shook hands and said their goodbyes. Before he left, Gordon walked over to Sabina and gave her a hug and a peck on the cheek, which surprised the hell out of her.

"Thanks," he said.

"For *what?*" she asked him.

"For being Guy's friend. And mine."

Before Sabina could get her wits about her, Gordon and James were heading off into the park with Guy in tow.

MacDuff let out a long sigh as he got back into the car with her. "Welp, I tried. Least I got t' meet him face-t'-face. But he still ain't budgin'."

"He might warm up later, now that he's met you," Sabina said. "I'll email him over the weekend to see what he's thinking."

Addressing their chauffeur, MacDuff said, "Let's head on over t' the West Thirtieth heliport." Turning to Ron, he asked, "What'd the wife say?"

"She said okay. They're getting packed."

"Great! You'll like Ron's kids," MacDuff said to Sabina. "He's got about ten of 'em."

"Six," Ron corrected him.

"I'm bettin' it'll be ten soon enough. Let's see if you can get Numero Seven started this weekend."

"I'm not sure we're ready for more just yet," Ron said with a blush.

MacDuff playfully punched him on the shoulder and said: "I know some guys with a lab out in Bushwick if you ain't willin' t' get the job done yerself."

When the Maybach pulled into the heliport's parking lot off the West Side Highway, Sabina saw MacDuff's helicopter parked on the other side of the matte black chain-link fence. It was much bigger than she'd anticipated: glossy white and twice the length and height of a city bus. It sat on the tarmac like a mechanical Moby-Dick that had beached itself from the sloshing grey-green waters of the Hudson just a few yards behind it.

"Holy shit, that's big!" Sabina blurted out

"Some o' the places we been buildin' server farms ain't exactly easy t' get to," said MacDuff, "but the Sikorsky can deliver a 17-ton payload durned near anywhere we want."

"It comes in handy," Ron chimed in.

"That thing must burn a lot of gas," was all Sabina could think to say.

"Yeah, but that ain't nothing compared to the amount o' rocket fuel we burned t' send up our own satellite. Ain't that right, Ron?"

"That one was a budget-buster," he confirmed. "But it was the only way to keep our server farms free of governmental interference. It gave us our own network."

"So Shitbirds.com is out in space?" Sabina asked.

"It will be in a few days," MacDuff answered with a nod of his Stetson. "Nine-Eleven, remember?"

He and Ron got out of the Maybach as Sabina followed them. MacDuff took her hand and led her through a tall chain-link gate with a No Smoking sign on it that had faded into near-illegibility. The Sikorsky's rotors started to turn with an unholy air-sucking whine from the turbines. MacDuff shouted to her above the noise: "You wanna take a quick peek inside before she goes up?"

Sabina nodded. She followed Ron as he ducked into a doorway just behind the helicopter's blunt windowed nose. Two lantern-jawed guys wearing full helmets and amber-tinted aviator shades waved to them from the bucket seats facing the complicated-looking cockpit panel. Ron leaned between them, placing a hand on each of their shoulders, and told them they'd be taking him on a quick side-trip to Connecticut.

MacDuff came up behind Sabina and wrapped his arm around her waist, leading her deeper into the helicopter's interior. It was all rosewood and black leather back there, with expensive recessed lighting and plush wool carpeting, like some Danish-Modern-obsessed interior designer had been told to go crazy with an unlimited budget. Further back, there was a tall rosewood door. Maybe it led to a bedroom, maybe just to empty cargo storage space. MacDuff apparently wasn't going to open it for her. He turned her around and they got out of the helicopter as the rotors whipped up a ferocious juddering thunder that made her frightened. She knew it couldn't happen, but she worried that one of the rotor blades might swing down and slice off the top of her skull. She'd watched far too many horror movies for her own good.

She and MacDuff jogged back out through the gate to stand beside the Maybach as the chopper lifted off. It sort of backed up into the air like a clumsy hummingbird, did a slow lazy spin, and then, with a slight tilt, headed out over the Hudson.

Fleetingly and out of the corner of an eye, Sabina saw a silver-winged flying fish streaking across the sky toward the Sikorsky's tail rotor. She was certain it was a military drone or, as they call it on *Citizen Radio*, a flying death robot. An instant later there was a brilliant flash, followed by the sound and heat of an explosion. The helicopter bloomed into a gigantic fireball, spewing black smoke and metal shrapnel. Sabina cried out as the force of the blast knocked her to the ground.

Another explosion rocked the car beside them. When Sabina scrambled back up, she saw—as if in a dream, or a premonition—that one of the helicopter's spinning rotor blades had peeled off the top of the Maybach like a sardine tin. She could see the driver's torso still sitting behind the steering wheel, his head and shoulders completely gone—just a mess of bloody pulp and bone. His hacked off arm was in the passenger seat, still clutching an iPhone.

Had the driver called in an airstrike? she wondered.

Hacked. The phone had been hacked… she suddenly knew. The NSA could use smartphones to listen in on people's conversations and track them by GPS, even when the phones had been turned off.

MacDuff had taught her that.

Sabina tasted sour bile on the back of her tongue, but she didn't throw up. A bolus of rage and horror swelled in her throat and she screamed instead.

Then MacDuff had her in his arms, blocking her view of the headless driver with his body. He picked her up and ran with her to a tin building that looked like a doublewide mobile home. A dark blue door in its side flew open and two bulging fat men in white shirts scurried out carrying fire extinguishers.

MacDuff sat Sabina down on the steps leading to the door's front porch and told her to go inside. Her hearing was fuzzed by an eerie ringing—his voice sounded cottony and distant. She asked him to stay with her, but he was already running back toward the gate behind the two hustling fat men.

Sabina didn't go inside. She wanted to stay out where she could see MacDuff. She stood up and watched through the chain-link fence as he ran to the edge of the helipad tarmac, kicking off his boots, flinging off his hat. Then he dove into the turbid river, swimming out to the flaming, floating wreckage with long, powerful strokes.

Sabina felt useless. She looked around for something she could do to help MacDuff. She saw three vending machines alongside the building, next to the porch she was standing on. She wondered if she should buy him a candy bar. He might be cold and hungry when he got out of the water.

She was sure cold, even though it was a sunny day.

Things happened very quickly after that. Sirens sounded. Several large black Chevy Suburbans skidded to a halt in the parking lot. Men in black suits with wired earpieces flew out the doors. They weren't New York City cops. They looked more like Secret Service agents. Or CIA. Although one of the spooky-looking men wore a black nylon windbreaker with blocky white letters on the back that said **DHS**—so maybe they were from the Department of Homeland Security.

Two of the men ran up on the porch and grabbed Sabina. They started dragging her toward a Suburban. Others went through the gate. Sabina fought to keep her head up, to see MacDuff. He was swimming back to the heliport, towing something behind him in the water. It looked like a charred black log, or maybe the rubber monster suit they used for *Creature from the Black Lagoon*.

Sabina felt a sting in her thigh and looked down to see a dart with a feathery red tip sticking out of her leg.

What the fuck?

She screamed for MacDuff. They were dragging him out of the water now. Her vision was swimming. He was on his knees, dripping, in front of a yellow concrete curb barrier at the heliport's edge. Two men were trying to lift him up, but he wouldn't let go of the thing he was holding—the log or blackened husk of rubber. He kept shaking them off. Finally, the two men got frustrated and whipped out their tasers. Twin mini blue bolts of lightning zapped into MacDuff's neck from both sides. With a helpless epileptic shudder, he dropped the thing in his arms. It rolled over onto the tarmac, staring.

By that point, tunnel vision was narrowing Sabina's perceptual field to a pinhole, but she still saw—*and understood*—what MacDuff had been trying to hold onto:

It was Ron.

THE DEVIL

"Wakey-wakey, little rebel girl…."

The return to consciousness was like coming back from anesthesia: no time seemed to have passed at all, but for all Sabina knew she could have been out for days.

The first thing she saw was a face, old and hideous, framed by wispy white hair. It was looming above her upside-down. Wait… not upside-down, exactly. She was lying on her back on a gritty concrete floor and the old man was standing behind her head, leaning over from a considerable height. His wrinkled, pockmarked, maggoty white face was arranged into an unbecoming leer.

In a flash, Sabina knew she was naked.

Well, not *completely* naked. There were tight steel handcuffs binding her wrists. The handcuffs were fastened to a heavy iron chain that dangled from a big rusty pulley bolted to an equally rusty iron girder. The girder traversed a sooty cinderblock ceiling high above her. A bare, dim light bulb dangled on a cord up there, providing the only illumination. Steel bars formed a cage on all four sides. Beyond that: darkness. Sabina was in some sort of an underground jail cell—

—or a torturer's dungeon.

Maggot Face said to her: "You pissed yourself like a toad in the SUV. We had to remove your clothes."

"You didn't think to cover me up with something?" Sabina asked, feeling numb and woozy. "A blanket maybe?"

"You'll find we're rather short on creature comforts around here," the pitiless old man said. He turned away from her and went out through the jail cell's open door. By tilting her head, Sabina could see him fussing over a big winch with a red wooden handle and industrial gears. When he started turning the handle, she found out that the winch was connected to the chain that connected to the handcuffs on her wrists. Her arms slowly rose above her head. Then she was standing up, whether she wanted to or not.

Being upright made her dizzy. Low blood pressure, maybe. She felt like puking. An avalanche of tiny sparkling pixels fractalized her vision and she passed out.

Sabina woke to a fire hose spraying her down with icy cold water.

After a few minutes, the hose was directed away from her and then shut off. Maggot Face appeared between the cage's bars, saying, "You vomited all down your front, you disgusting child. We had to hose you off."

The adrenaline surge had cleared Sabina's head. At least she didn't feel dizzy anymore. "Why am I here?" she asked.

The old man was inordinately tall—just shy of seven feet. Those pockmarks on his cheeks were really something. They made Sabina think of worm-chewed mushrooms. He must have had one hell of a case of acne when he hit puberty. He was wearing a black undertaker's suit (too short at the sleeves and cuffs), a pristine white dress shirt, and white Nike training shoes.

The Nikes looked ridiculous.

"You're here because you don't know your station in life," the cadaverous old fuck said with a puckered rotten apple scowl. "How dare you even *think* to trespass in our domain?"

"What domain would that be? The one where you're the master?"

Sabina was thinking of that old *Seinfeld* euphemism for refraining from masturbation—becoming the *master of your domain*—but she was pretty sure he wouldn't get it.

He didn't.

"You've angered some very important people… people who are superior to you in every significant way."

"You must mean rich people," Sabina ascertained. "But why should the VIPs care about someone like me? I don't know anything. I'm just a girl who says 'fuck' a lot."

"You know what you've done with your little potty joke—Shitbirds.com." He practically spat out the Shitbirds part.

"Oh, *that.*"

Sabina decided to change the subject. "Hey, you know who you remind me of?" she said brightly. "The Tall Man in that movie, *Phantasm.* Ever see it? You look just like him."

"He must cut quite a dashing figure," said Maggot Face.

"Oh, for sure…" Sabina said with a roll of her eyes. The Tall Man in that movie was about as creepy as a human being could get. "Angus Scrimm… I'm pretty sure that's his name. I knew one of the other actors in that movie when I was growing up: Bill Thornbury. His brother, Skip, taught me how to play the ukulele."

"That's irrelevant." Maggot Face wasn't up for idle chitchat, apparently.

"Well, I'm just hanging out here with nothing much to do. So I thought we could at least play some Trivial Pursuit."

"Don't worry… we can think of lots of things for you to do," the old man said with a shrewish tone of menace. "You can start by telling us where Limelight's server farms are located. And if you refuse, the next thing you'll be doing is begging for your life."

"It's my life. I'm not going to beg you for it, asshole," Sabina said. She found, to her own surprise, that she really meant that. "If you're so pathetically screwed up that you think you need to kill me, then go ahead and kill me. Obviously, I can't stop you."

"That's not how we do things here. First, we inflict the maximum amount of pain. Then we leave you to suffer and rot."

"Great. Is it fun being a sadist?"

"We might be more lenient if you tell us what we need to know."

"A kinder, gentler form of torture? I don't think so."

"Try us. Where are the servers?"

"I don't fucking know."

That wasn't entirely true. MacDuff had told Sabina he had server farms in Iceland, Ecuador, Venezuela, Nunavut, and an underground bunker deep inside a mountain somewhere in Vermont. But she assumed (or pretended to herself) that he was building other server farms that had gone unmentioned. So she wasn't exactly lying in that case, was she?

"We know you're lying," said Maggot Face.

Okay, so maybe she *was* lying. But so what? *All kidnapped people should lie to their captors,* she thought to herself.

"Who's this *we*, anyway?" Sabina asked him.

"*We* don't have to tell you anything, but we can assure you, we're the ones in charge. Not you. Not your troublemaking buckaroo boyfriend. You don't get to make the decisions that matter. We do.

"As one of our kind so eloquently put it in 2004: 'We're an empire now, and when we act, we create our own reality. And while you're studying that reality—judiciously, as you will—we'll act again, creating other new realities, which you can study, too, and that's how things will sort out. We're history's actors… and you, all of you, will be left to just study what we do.'"

"Then fuck every last one of you," said Sabina. "Where do you smug bastards get the arrogance to think you can run the world?"

"It's simple, really," Maggot Face said, as if addressing a petulant child. "Technology runs the world and we control the technology."

"It figures that a self-deluded jerk like you would be into machines instead of people."

There was a web of blue veins or arteries running across Maggot Face's forehead. It distended and pulsed like a shovel blade full of angry worms as he said to her:

"The vast majority of human beings are malignantly useless. We want to see the global population level ease down to somewhere around half a billion people. That's all the earth's ecosystem can comfortably support."

Sabina felt better, now that she'd riled him. "And I assume," she said, "that you don't mind using wars, genocide, and an occasional manufactured plague to 'ease down' the numbers."

"You have assumed correctly."

"Ebola—was that you guys?"

"Ebola *might* have been released into the kaffir population from a certain bioweapons lab in West Africa." He said that evilly, eyes aglint. "But we can't speak with any authority on that subject. It's not our department."

Was he South African? He had a slight accent that Sabina couldn't place, but his use of the derogatory term *kaffir* seemed like a solid clue.

"So what's *your* department all about?" she asked him.

"Enhanced interrogation techniques."

"Just my fucking luck."

"Would you like to watch some television?" Maggot Face asked her as he slithered away into the shadows.

"No, but could you get me some coffee?" Sabina called after him. "Or a Mocha Frappuccino?"

Moments later, Maggot Face returned from the darkness lugging a small cathode ray tube TV set—an old Sony. He set it down on top of a spindly wooden chair just outside the jail cell and hooked it up to a couple of cables. When he turned it on the screen was facing Sabina. After it warmed up, a grainy video feed appeared. It showed MacDuff, naked and dangling, in an underground cage just like her own. His head hung limp, his face bruised and bleeding.

"Is he here?" Sabina asked, flaring with anger. *"MAACDUFFF!"* she shouted. But there was no reply—and no indication on the video feed that he'd heard her.

"Why should it matter if he's here," Maggot Face asked her, positioning a wireless security camera on top of the television set, "when you don't even know where *here* is?"

Up until that moment, it hadn't even occurred to Sabina that she and MacDuff could have been abducted by an extraordinary rendition team and spirited away to a CIA black site. She wasn't necessarily in the US anymore. For all she knew, she could be in some human-rights-denying shithole like Abu Ghraib or Guantánamo.

"Your cowboy friend there has a television just like yours. The only difference is that his shows him what's happening to you. And what's about to happen to you will be exceedingly unpleasant unless you tell me exactly where those server farms are located."

Her situation was getting more fucked by the moment.

"I think there's one in Greenland…" Sabina said just to see if she could get away with lying to him.

"Where in Greenland?"

"Beats the fuck out of me. Do you even know the names of any towns in Greenland? I sure as hell don't. It's not like I've ever been there."

Sabina's stomach gurgled, loud enough for Maggot Face to hear it. She was experiencing some gas pains. Probably stress related. "I think I need to use the ladies' room," she said, feigning daintiness.

"That's what the drain in the center of the floor is for."

"While I'm just standing here? What if I have really bad diarrhea?"

"That's what the fire hose is for."

"You enhanced interrogators are so considerate. You think of everything."

Maggot Face entered the jail cell and stood behind Sabina, peering over her shoulder to watch the video feed. MacDuff's head jerked upright on the screen, staring straight into the unseen camera, as the old man's grotesquely smooth and flaccid hands snaked around and cupped her breasts.

Yuck!

Sabina reflexively pushed off the concrete floor and snapped her right leg up and back, ankle-kicking Maggot Face in the groin. Unfortunately, the old man's legs were so tall that she barely grazed him. But it was enough to get his hands off her tits and make him back up a few steps.

"So there's still some fight left in you," Maggot Face said, obviously unhurt. "Splendid! That will make for much better drama when we molest you in front of your lover."

Did molest mean rape? Oh fucking hell....

So far, Sabina had managed to get through life without being raped. She felt no need to add that particular subcategory of the human experience to her personal Top Forty list of horrors and humiliations now—especially not with old Lurch there.

"If you try to rape me, then you damn well better kill me," Sabina said, "because if you don't, I'll come back and kill *you*, for sure."

"We said molest, not rape," said Maggot Face, "although it's often difficult to distinguish between the two. Let's see if you can spot the difference. Your man there is about to be molested by your coeval, Marzanna."

Talk about Abu Ghraib… on the television screen outside the bars a female bodybuilder entered MacDuff's cell wearing one of those pointy Abu Ghraib hoods that had covered the heads of the Iraqi prisoners while they were being tortured by sickos in the US Army and the CIA—only this hood was sunflower yellow and it had two tiny eye slits cut into it. The only other items of clothing on her were a studded leather G-string and a pair of black lace-up Army boots.

The bodybuilder's grotesque musculature was oiled and bulbous. Her tits looked like a man's pecs and her crotch was shaven bare around the skinny, spiky G-string. There was nothing even remotely sexy about her. She just looked scary.

"Is that Marzanna?" Sabina asked.

"In the flesh," Maggot Face confirmed.

Marzanna flexed, struck a pose, and then lunged for MacDuff's cock like a fencer. She grabbed him by his big balls and yanked. MacDuff's body swung in a pendulum arc across the cell as he loosed a silent howl. Marzanna let him swing that way until his bare, bloody feet dragged him to a stop. Then she stepped in close again and brutally slammed her fist into his abdomen.

Sabina clenched her own abdomen in sympathy as the air was knocked out of MacDuff's lungs.

"You fucking cunt…" she heard herself saying. Profanity was her default mode—she didn't even have to think to use it.

"You can stop his torment if you tell us what we need to know," Maggot Face said behind her.

"I'll tell you whatever you want," Sabina said through gritted teeth. "Just make that bitch stop."

Maggot Face stepped around her and waved at the television set. Marzanna peered over her shoulder and seemed to acknowledge him. She left MacDuff's cell. But then she returned a few moments later with a spiked leather collar and a dog leash made of shiny chrome chain. She belted the collar around MacDuff's neck and attached the leash. Then she dragged him toward the camera lens, as someone offscreen put some slack into the heavy iron chain holding his arms above his head.

The slack allowed Marzanna to force MacDuff to his knees in front of the bars of his jail cell. His face filled the screen of the little television set as Sabina watched. Marzanna's hands worked quickly at the edges of the frame, wrapping the chrome dog chain tightly around the horizontal bar directly in front of MacDuff's chin. Then she roughly grabbed his jaws and forced him to bite down on it.

Sabina felt sick to her stomach again as Marzanna looped the chain around MacDuff's neck and then pulled it tight, effectively locking him into place with his open mouth crushed against the chrome-wrapped bar.

"Tell us where the server farms are located," Maggot Face said while MacDuff's pleading eyes blinked at Sabina from the television screen.

"Iceland, Ecuador, Venezuela, Nunavut, and Vermont."

Sabina knew she didn't have any bargaining power. She and MacDuff would probably be killed, no matter what. But if the truth could alleviate MacDuff's suffering, even just a little, then she thought it might be worth spilling her guts.

"Thank you," Maggot Face said. "We already knew that, but it helps to know you're willing to be honest with us. Now, on to the next question—and this one's important: Has Shitbirds.com been uploaded to any of those server farms yet?"

If I lie and say yes, would it make any difference? Sabina couldn't see how the answer mattered either way. So she went with the truth:

"Nothing's been uploaded outside of Limelight's downtown office yet," she said. "The plan was to launch on the Eleventh. But I thought you already knew that. Weren't you listening in to our conversation in the car on the way to the heliport?"

"Parts of that conversation were indecipherable."

"So I guess the NSA isn't such hot shit, after all."

"The NSA is just one tool among many at our disposal."

"What are you then? CIA? Mossad?"

"We're your archontic masters."

"Don't make me laugh," Sabina said. But then a tiny voice in the back of her mind whispered: *The Dark Brotherhood*—the term MacDuff had used to refer to evil fucks as a collective in the documents he'd written under his Wes Bramley pseudonym.

"Our minions are those you intended to expose with your little afterschool project," said Maggot Face, puckering his withered lips into a chimp-like moue. "We can't have that. We need those assets in place. They function as superior slaves directing lesser slaves in accordance with our wishes."

It occurred to Sabina that Maggot Face might be psychotic in addition to his other batshit personality traits. Or maybe demonically possessed.

"Does your wife buy this Master of the Universe routine? Because I sure as hell don't."

"I never married."

"Somehow, I'm not surprised."

"Human relations make you vulnerable to emotional manipulation. Take your friend there…" Maggot Face pointed at the video feed. "So far, he's chosen self-harm over answering our questions. But here's the beauty of relationships: He might be persuaded to answer our queries if we torture you instead of him."

"That sounds like a really bad idea…" Sabina said.

"We could waterboard you," Maggot Face mused, fingers stroking his pasty hairless chin like some histrionic Bond villain, "but that wouldn't have the visual impact we're looking for."

"Right," Sabina agreed with him. "I already waterboard myself with a neti pot whenever I get a cold. That's just lame."

"So perhaps we should use this instead…." With a vampire-like flourish, Maggot Face whipped opened his undertaker's coat. Its black silk inner lining was embroidered with all kinds of weird occult symbols stitched in blood red thread, like something from the sale rack in Aleister Crowley's thrift shop. He withdrew something from one of the inner pockets that looked like a thick platinum and gold wizard's wand—or a streamlined dildo. When Maggot Face brandished the blunt instrument at her like a police baton, Sabina asked him:

"What are you gonna do, orgasm a confession out of me?"

"It's a cattle prod, not a vibrator," he said, insulted.

"*Slick*. Is Apple designing those now?"

The blue veins in Maggot Face's forehead twitched again like a skein of angry worms. He sneered: "You won't be acting so smug after we shove this up your round little bottom and turn on the juice."

"Since when did the US government declare anal jihad on its own citizens?" Sabina asked, tensing.

"Welcome to the New American Century…" Maggot Face said as he stepped behind her and rammed the prod home.

When the voltage hit her from the inside out, Sabina lost all muscle control. Piss and shit poured out of her in torrents. It was the worst pain she'd ever experienced. Somewhere in there, during her electrocuted spasming, she clenched her jaw so tight that she cracked a few molars.

When it was over, she was sure her heart had stopped beating. But then with a horrible inner lurch she felt it start back up again—a thready inner thumping that felt dangerously fast and out-of-control.

If she got hit with that fucking cattle prod one more time, she was sure that would be the end of her. But Maggot Face had already left the jail cell. He was fussing with the fire hose over by the television set, washing her liquefied shit off his hands like a fastidious raccoon. When he looked up at her from his crouch, he scowled and turned the fire hose on full blast to go after her with it.

Sabina found the icy, stinging water almost a relief compared to the searing pain of all that horrible voltage, but when the water was finally turned off, she was shivering and couldn't stop the chattering of her painfully cracked teeth.

MacDuff's face was still on the television screen in front of her, biting the chrome dog chain wrapped around the bars of his prison cell. His eyes were projecting a murderous rage. He'd seen the whole thing on the video feed at his end.

Now it was Sabina's turn to be horrified on behalf of her lover. She watched, helpless, as Marzanna's black boot entered the screen's frame and crashed down on the back of MacDuff's skull.

The boot's impact shattered his lower jaw. MacDuff gagged on bits of broken teeth and blood. But the diabolical horror show wasn't finished. Somehow, the scene immediately looped, and the boot came back down again... *over and over and over.*

Later, when Sabina had time to think about it, she realized that she and MacDuff were trapped in not just one kind of prison, but two. And that other prison could be by far the worst, even though it was a universal human condition that almost everyone took for granted.

We're all serving a life sentence inside a sack of meat, prisoners in our own bodies.

THE MOON

Sabina needed to get warm. The lunar coolness of her prison cell was sapping her body heat. It didn't help, of course, that she was still naked, wet, and chained. The endless video loop of MacDuff's jaw getting smashed wasn't helping her, either. She was still shivering, but she wasn't sure if it was from the cold or fear of her imminent death.

Maggot Face had disappeared after spraying her down with the fire hose the second time. That came as a relief. It gave her time to think—although her thoughts were uniformly grim. Sabina wondered how much pain she would endure before she died. She wondered if MacDuff was already dead. It didn't seem like there was any chance they'd be getting out alive.

Her arms were going numb from being held above her head for so long. She needed to do something about that before she lost all feeling and the handcuffs started cutting into her wrists. So with the last bit of strength she had left, Sabina stood on her tiptoes and grabbed the thick chain dangling between her palms. Then, using her yoga-toned abs, she jackknifed her body upward and latched onto the chain with her ankles.

She could feel her arm muscles on the verge of failing. By sheer force of will, she clenched the chain and pulled herself up one more time. As she did so, she straightened her back, upside-down, looping the chain around her ankles and calves. She found she could support most of her weight that way, taking the pressure off her shaking arms. She just hung like that for a while—like a gutted carcass in a slaughterhouse—feeling the blood coursing back down into her hands.

After some time had passed, she detected a tiny amount of heat radiating from the 25-watt bulb hanging from the ceiling. She could feel it on her feet. An atavistic urge to get closer to that feeble warmth inspired her to push herself higher, re-looping her ankles in the chain as she went, until she was as far up as she could go, hunched in a ball right near the ceiling.

Her face felt fat and flushed from all the exertion. She had gone from shivering cold to just uncomfortably cool as the water evaporated on her skin.

"Get down from there right this minute, or we'll shock you again," Maggot Face said, emerging from the shadows outside the cage's perimeter. He sounded like a parent scolding a child for climbing too high on the monkey bars—more annoyed than genuinely pissed.

Sabina didn't want to get shocked. The fall would be unpleasant. At the very least, it would break her wrists, if not yank her cuffed hands right off. So she unhooked her legs and swung toward the floor, making sure to moon her captor on the way down.

Maggot Face entered the cage carrying a spare set of handcuffs, which he attached to Sabina's wrists just behind the handcuffs she was already wearing. Then he unlocked the original handcuffs and freed her from the chain. Sabina was so surprised that she didn't think to make a dash for freedom until Maggot Face slammed the door to her cage and started cranking the winch, raising the heavy chain with its silver handcuffs to the top of the rusty pulley, beyond her reach.

"No more climbing," Maggot Face said. "We don't want you to hurt yourself."

"That sounds a little hypocritical coming from a torturer," Sabina said in a chirpy tone, feeling much better. "Do you think I could get my clothes back now?"

"We prefer to see you naked."

"Yeah, that's what all the guys say...." Over the years, Sabina had gotten so used to guys sneaking peeks at her breasts that she almost felt insulted whenever a new male acquaintance didn't try it.

Maggot Face just scowled and faded into the darkness again, but he soon returned lugging two large black boom boxes. He set them down outside the cage.

Music! How thoughtful! thought Sabina.

But of course Maggot Face's stereophonic intentions turned out to be nothing like MacDuff's gift of the Bose speakers and all those Nick Cave albums. Maggot Face had sonic malice on his mind. His music was intended to drive Sabina insane.

She figured that out right after he pushed the PLAY buttons and disappeared into the shadows again. The two loud but shitty-sounding boom boxes started blasting out loops of two songs—simultaneously and continuously—at an ear-splitting volume: "Crazy" by Gnarls Barkley and a charming little ditty by John Frusciante called "Your Pussy's Glued to a Building On Fire."

Despite all the distortion, Sabina recognized both tunes. She knew that Gnarls Barkley was the stage name for the musical collaboration between CeeLo Green and Danger Mouse, and that John Frusciante was a former guitarist for the Red Hot Chili Peppers who'd quit the band to go off by himself and do a shit-ton of drugs while recording a series of trippy albums. It just so happened that Sabina had both of those songs stored on her Apple iCloud service. Maggot Face could have hacked into her account and downloaded the songs from there.

Oh, the fucking irony….

Couldn't he have picked something more soothing? Like Stars of the Lid, or maybe that beautiful song by The Antlers ("Refuge") that MacDuff had turned her on to a few weeks ago? But she knew that would have defeated the purpose. Maggot Face wanted to break her down… and those two particular songs, combined, were just the sort of mind-shredding earworm to do it:

> *I remember when [Your pussy's glued] I remember [to a building on fire] I remember when [I paid my mind] I lost my mind [just cuz I'm alive]… Well, I think you're crazy [The smile on my face] I think you're crazy [isn't always real] I think you're crazy [But the way you make me feel] Just like me [is all that's really real]….*

For the longest time, Sabina couldn't even think. John Frusciante's druggy, lo-fi sincerity scratched like fingernails on a blackboard against the slick production values of Gnarls Barkley. But at least she actually *liked* those two songs when they weren't combined. Metallica overlaid with Barney the Dinosaur's theme song would have been worse. She'd read somewhere that the CIA had been putting suspected al-Qaeda operatives in metal shipping containers out in the hot sun and forcing them to listen to that shit for days.

Harsh.

As the hours passed, Sabina was able to regain enough mental focus to tune out the music, in much the same way that an impoverished college student living above a rowdy bar becomes accustomed to the noise and stench, and then forgets about it.

It became invisible to her.

Tuning out the video loop of MacDuff's jaw getting broken took a while longer, but eventually that, too, was reduced to invisibility—something she could look at without being disturbed by it.

Was she desensitizing herself to noise and violence, or just shutting out the things that were meant to do her harm? She didn't know the answer to that. She suspected it was a little of both.

It reminded her of what Ron had said to her in the gallery that day (*Poor Ron! And all those kids of his, now without a father...*), something about how the art of Lars von Loon and Javier Pendejos de Amores and Démerder showed the world its own shame. It was the kind of art that made most people want to look away.

When you really thought about it, instead of just taking everything for granted, the world could be a strange and horrific place. Little girls forced into prostitution, teenage boys killing each other at the behest of drug lords, first-world governments perpetrating acts of false flag terrorism against their own citizens to justify spending their tax dollars on a ravenous military-industrial-intelligence complex. And we were almost all culpable, participants in great chains of self-centered actions that resulted in worldwide suffering. Downloading free Internet porn, snorting a line of coke, acquiescing to the lies our government officials told us... all those seemingly harmless acts led to horrors.

At the most basic level, most of us were carnivores, causing millions of innocent creatures to die in agony each day for our collective suppers. Sabina was as guilty as anyone on the carnivore front. She'd tried to go vegan, but she couldn't bring herself to give up cheese and bacon. At least she wasn't drinking powdered tiger penis tea, like *some* people... but still, she was probably responsible for killing scores of animals each week with her heedless, blundering existence. Sometimes she felt like an appalled spectator at the samsaric crime scene of her life.

Maybe the material universe was a hellish rehab clinic we incarnated into so we could work through our addictions while safely isolated from the more spiritually advanced inhabitants of the multiverse. That was the kind of airy-fairy thinking Sabina usually scorned, but it made a certain amount of sense from her vantage point in an underground jail cell. It seemed the Earth was a place where you could indulge your worst impulses and sample almost any vice, but only within limits *(unless you were Keith Richards...)*. Ultimately, the pursuit of earthly pleasures led to frustration. Crave anything too much in this world and it would eventually harm you, whether it was drugs, butter, sex, sugar, money, fame, drama—even sunlight and love.

She was really missing those last two at the moment.

So was the material universe a prison for souls, like the Gnostics said? Spiritual flypaper, maybe? Sabina didn't know. But it sure seemed like a lot more people were ending up in *physical* prison than ever before, especially in the US. She'd seen the statistics. Even though the

US had only five percent of the world's population, it had twenty-five percent of the world's prisoners. She knew from reading Matt Taibbi that there were now more people in jail or on parole in the US than had populated Stalin's gulags; more black men in prison now than had been slaves back in Lincoln's day. And the vast majority of those prisoners—six or seven million total, most of them poor and nonwhite—were being locked away for nonviolent crimes. Thanks to the inefficient and idiotic War on Drugs, over two million US citizens were arrested on drug charges every year and about $20 billion was being spent annually to keep them imprisoned. And that trend was only getting worse. Now that prisons were being privatized and run by corporations like CCA and The GEO Group, with avaricious shareholders to coddle, locking up people had become a big business—with expectations of big profits.

If she ever got out of her current predicament, Sabina thought she should make a serious effort to produce and host a Kafkaesque TV talent show called *Amerika's Prisons Got Talent*. She could become the Simon Cowell of the disenfranchised. Each week, she and her crew would travel to a new prison where the most talented inmates would audition in front of a panel of celebrity judges. Singers, dancers, comedians, magicians… whoever made it to the final round would compete for a prize of one million dollars and a suspended sentence.

Imagine the ratings if someone on death row turned out to be the next Miley Cyrus!

Prison reform, marijuana legalization, and saner drug control laws could become a political possibility if American TV viewers made the show a success. But Sabina could just as easily envisage her idealistic notions being crushed and perverted by market forces. Seeing a chance to cash in on the caged bird singing fad, the for-profit prisons might decide to partner with one of the big on-demand streaming media companies that produced their own content these days, like Netflix, Amazon, or YouTube. Then they could start creating their own in-house shows using the cheapest talent available—incarcerated actors.

It would devolve into mostly porn, of course—that bedrock of American Internet culture. Louche boudoir sets watched over by an array of hidden cameras would be constructed inside every prison. Sex-starved male prisoners would be offered unlimited conjugal visits after they signed consent forms allowing their dalliances to be broadcast in any way the corporations saw fit. Female prisoners would be coaxed into participating with offers of reduced sentences. Corrupt police officers would be paid bonuses for arresting particularly lewd-looking women on trumped-up drug charges and then offering them the choice of spending years in a penitentiary or a single day getting reamed on a jailhouse porn set.

Sabina had to wonder if that was part of what was going on with her own situation. Was she being digitally recorded for some torture porn enthusiast's future viewing pleasure? With Maggot Face in charge, she saw that as a distinct possibility.

She decided to make things as dull as possible for her nameless watchers. Lying on her side near the drain at the center of the jail cell, she curled into a ball and went to sleep.

After an interlude of darkness, Sabina dreamed she was walking along a wintery city sidewalk. The snow pelting her was hard as hail. Her cheeks were stinging from the cold. Snowdrifts were piled as high as the parked cars. She was passing a big department store with elaborate window displays—Saks or Bergdorf Goodman, or maybe Lord & Taylor. Men hurried past her from the opposite direction, wearing cashmere overcoats and felt hats, but they didn't seem to notice her, even though—she realized only then—she was still naked and her skin was covered in goosebumps.

Suddenly, one of the snow banks exploded behind her. A gigantic albino crocodile came thrashing out of it. The thirty-foot-long monster scrabbled after her on its stubby but powerful and fast little legs. Sabina ran for her life. When she felt like she'd put enough distance between them, she looked back over her shoulder and saw Démerder's dog, Guy, romping alongside the crocodile, barking at it while wagging his fluffy white tail. Miraculously, the crocodile's jaws had been bound with a strong rope. Sabina slowed to a jog, knowing the crocodile couldn't harm her anymore—and that's where the dream ended.

She woke to a rat's whiskers brushing against her cheek.

Sabina sat up, her heart still thudding from the dream. Two rats were looking up at her from the concrete floor with curious, beady black rat eyes. Their fur was coarse and brown—and their nude tails were a grotesque, scabby pink—but she didn't sense any hostility coming from them. In fact, they seemed friendly, like the working-class Norwegian cousins of the pet shop rats that kids took home when their parents wouldn't let them have a puppy or a kitten.

"Hi, guys…" Sabina said to the rats. "You're not gonna bite me, are you?"

The rats put on grave expressions and twitched their whiskers to the left and right as if to say: "Absolutely not! Such a barbarous act would be unthinkable!"

That was good enough for her.

Sabina noticed that someone, probably Maggot Face, had placed a white paper plate inside the cell near the drain. A shiny red apple sat in the middle of the plate, surrounded by wedges of cheese. That's what had attracted the rats, no doubt. But they were polite rats, waiting for Sabina to feed them, rather than gnawing on the snacks without her consent. Charmed by their good manners, she picked up a hunk of cheese, broke it in half, and gave each of the rats a piece.

She moved slowly, so she wouldn't scare them. One of the rats actually got close enough to nibble on the cheese before it left her fingers. She enjoyed watching them eat. They chewed with lots of rat gusto. When the first two chunks of cheese were gone, Sabina went back to the tray and got them some more.

"Did you guys ever read *1984?*" she asked the rats, in jest. "There was this scene, toward the end of that book, where this guy named Winston Smith was being tortured. At least I *think* that was his name. It's been a while.... Anyway, the guy who was torturing poor Winston brought out a cage full of rats. Not nice rats, like you guys, but mean, wild, totally starving and crazed rats. And the torturer guy was all like 'I'm gonna strap this cage to your face, Winston, and then when I lift up this little latch a door will open inside the cage and the rats will all dive in and eat your fucking eyeballs out.'

"But you guys would never do that. No way, right?"

Again, the earnest-looking rats twitched their whiskers as if to say "What an appalling idea! We could never do such a thing! We'd commit rat *hari-kari* first."

Sabina was starting to love those two big-ass rats. She fed them some more cheese.

"You guys wanna try the apple?" she asked them.

The rats seemed interested.

Digging her thumbs into the indentation where the stem went in, Sabina pulled the apple apart into two roughly similar halves. She gave one to each of the rats to gnaw on, thinking they might appreciate the juice if they were thirsty.

As for herself, she'd seen *Snow White* when she was a little girl and she was wary of biting into apples given to her by weird-looking strangers. The rats, however, seemed to enjoy tearing into the apple's firm white flesh, so maybe she was just being paranoid.

Or not.

A few seconds later, the rats went into mini-convulsions and died with bitter-smelling green foam leaking out all over their tiny rat chins.

"Oh shit!" Sabina exclaimed. "Guys… I'm so sorry!" She felt really bad about being an inadvertent rat murderer.

So Maggot Face had resorted to the old cyanide-in-the-apple trick. Wasn't that how Alan Turing went out? The father of the modern computer, the guy who shaved a few years off the Second World War by cracking the code on the Nazi's Enigma machine… and how did the Brits repay him? They hounded him for being homosexual, told him he could either go to jail or submit to chemical castration, and then—after he chose castration and started growing boobs—he got the poison apple as an early retirement gift.

What a fucking world….

It reminded Sabina of what Edward Snowden had said about GCHQ—the British equivalent of the NSA: GCHQ was actually far worse than the NSA when it came to spying on their own people. Orwell was definitely onto something when he wrote *1984*. That novel looked cozy and nostalgic compared to what we were facing now. The moral order was inverted. The criminal class was in control. The fate of our whistleblowers was as good an illustration of that as any. In a just society, Chelsea Manning would have been a prosecution witness against war criminals. Instead, she'd been locked away for thirty-five years without a fair trail. Edward Snowden would have faced a similar fate if he hadn't escaped to Russia. But now Snowden was being forced to rely on the kindness of Vladimir Putin for his freedom—Putin, with his well-documented anger management issues and his roots in one of the most savage intelligence agencies on the planet. That was an ugly, Sword-of-Damocles situation if there ever was one.

Sabina picked up the two dead rats by their tails and flung them outside the cage at the boom boxes, which were still blaring "Crazy" and "Your Pussy's Glued to a Building on Fire." She was hoping to hit the STOP buttons with the rat's bodies, but no such luck. The music kept playing.

It occurred to Sabina that she might have some stray cyanide on her fingers from cracking the apple in half. She didn't want to risk poisoning herself by wiping her nose or rubbing an eye. She had no idea how much cyanide it took to kill a person. But she knew that just a microdot of LSD on your tongue could warp your whole world for eight hours straight. Just to be safe, she squatted and pissed on her palms, hoping her urine would wash all the cyanide away. It felt undignified—especially when she remembered that Maggot Face was recording her every move. Then again, dignity had been in short supply ever since MacDuff's helicopter exploded... *so screw it.*

There was no need to be modest when she'd be a corpse soon, anyway. Eating and drinking were definitely out. She could fast. That didn't scare her. She'd done it many times before. But fasting meant that she didn't have long to live—a month or two, at the most. Without fluids, she'd probably die sooner. Maybe she could open her mouth and gulp down some water the next time Maggot Face blasted her with the fire hose, if that ever happened again.

It was a terrible situation to be in—*over the moon terrible*—but she didn't have any choice in the matter. In a way, that felt liberating. It was like her grudging resignation to the long, cold months when winter set in. Sabina suffered from Seasonal Affective Disorder. She hated winter in New York City. The cold and the lack of sunlight made her feel depressed—especially around Christmas, when she tended to gorge on sugar cookies and self-pity because she didn't have a family. Every November, after the clocks had been reset and the days started going dark by 5 PM, Sabina had to constantly remind herself that if she could just get through the next few months—by drinking a lot of coffee, reading some good books, doing her yoga—the sun would eventually return and make everything warm again. Over the last several years, however, she'd noticed that during those frigid winter months her normally spiky daily anxiety level completely flatlined. She didn't stress about anything. She was cutting herself all kinds of slack because she felt like Persephone during her annual descent to the underworld.

If you're in hell already, why worry?

At the moment, strong coffee and good books weren't an option, but she could still do some yoga to de-stress. It was either that or eat the rest of the apple.

She went with the yoga.

Some poses couldn't be done in handcuffs, but others could. Downward Facing Dog? Yes. Cobra Pose? Sure. Twisting Dragon? No fucking way.... Sabina worked through the poses that were possible.

Maggot Face and his torture porn cronies were probably getting an eyeful, but to hell with them. It felt good to stretch. The yoga was making her feel better about things in general.

She was right in the middle of a One-Legged King Pigeon Pose when the police broke in.

THE SUN

Sabina had never been so glad to see the sun. It almost washed out her vision at first—so bright after all those days in the dungeon—but the way it made the world shimmer and dance, almost at a cellular level, filled her heart with gladness. The warm September rays on her face felt like a benevolent deity's all-encompassing love.

Some chivalrous SWAT team guy in a riot helmet and black Kevlar body armor had taken off his shirt and lent it to Sabina so she could cover up before the rest of the team converged on her. The keys to her jail cell couldn't be found, so she'd had to stand around for a while, draped in the big policeman's shirt, while the burly guys from the NYPD went about their business. Finally, they sawed through the lock and escorted her upstairs to some vulgarian's marble reception gallery, where she saw a pricey-looking indoor fountain *(fat-bellied little boys pissing on sea dragons… what else?)* and a bronze sculpture of a skinny stick figure standing on a platform between two proportionally huge spoked wheels. Then they went outside through the double doors into all that beautiful sunshine.

Frank was waiting for her out there, his frizz of silver hair glowing like an angel's halo amid the police vans and ambulances with their frantic flashing lights.

"Frank! How did you find me?" Sabina tried to hug him, but she was still in handcuffs, so Frank hugged her instead.

"It wasn't me," said Frank, kissing her filthy cheek. "I just brought the cavalry. Your friend Démerder found you."

"You mean Gordon?"

"Right. The guy with the art project—the big black cube. It has a computer inside it… with GPS. Did you know that?"

"I did," said Sabina, "but I'm not quite sure how that's relevant."

"It's here. The cube is right inside that asshole's den."

Sabina turned and looked up at the massive stone house behind her. It was like some hedge fund billionaire's tacky update on the Palace of Versailles.

"Where are we?" she asked.

"Long Island," said Frank with a New Jerseyan's scorn for the hoity-toity. "Kings Point, to be specific. *Gatsby* territory."

With a lurching heart, Sabina asked, "Did they find MacDuff?"

"He was here, too—in another part of the building." Frank gave Sabina a look that told her everything she didn't want to know. "He's already in an ambulance on the way to the hospital. He wasn't conscious. It looks bad, but they're not sure *how bad* yet. At least he's still alive."

"Oh Frank...." Sabina leaned into her old friend's arms. She couldn't stop herself from sobbing. "I saw it happen. They made me watch it on TV."

"They're both dead now, if that gives you any satisfaction."

"What?"

Frank placed his palms on Sabina's cheeks and peered into her teary eyes. "They won't ever harm you again," he said, as if addressing her inner child. "My friends in the NYPD said the tall guy and his bodybuilder freak girlfriend had guns. Big mistake. Now they have about a hundred bullet holes in them. Each."

"They didn't seem like the type to use guns."

"Yeah, well, maybe it was something else... but whatever it was, it must've looked like guns from a distance."

"They shot them after they found MacDuff and me, didn't they?"

"Blew their fucking lights out. They were trying to get away."

"I'm glad, I guess..." Sabina said. But was she really? She just felt numb.

"I had some time to do a little Internet search on your abductor on the way over. He's quite the guy," said Frank. "Or *was*. He would've been untouchable in court."

"Some rich, whacked-out old geezer gets caught red-handed—kidnapping and torturing poor, innocent me—and you can't put the bastard away?"

"Not this guy. The court case would've dragged out until we both died of natural causes."

"Who was he?"

"It's not so much who he was, but what. He's definitely one of the bad guys. Everything you see here was paid for by American tax dollars."

"Even that sculpture of the skinny guy on giant rollerblades?" Sabina asked, pointing back at the foyer she'd just passed through.

"That's a Giacometti," Frank informed her. "The last time Sotheby's put it up for auction, it went for just over a hundred million to Big Stevie Cohen. I'm assuming he must've traded it for something equally valuable—like insider information."

There was a lot of stuff to get through at the police station. It was all kind of a blur. Statements had to be made, bodies identified. Frank helped Sabina every step of the way. He seemed to have a lot of friends in the NYPD. They were all treating him like some kind of hero. Going by everything she heard, it sounded like Frank had helped them nail plenty of criminal scumbags in the past, but this latest one was the biggest and by far the most loathed.

Maggot Face's name turned out to be Heindrik DeFoggi. He was a contemporary of the first George Bush—maybe ten years younger. It was hard to get an exact fix on his age or place of birth because he was one of those guys who ghosted through life on multiple passports with different aliases, all backstopped by full documentation and credit cards linked to bank accounts in tax havens and secrecy jurisdictions like Switzerland, Luxembourg, Singapore, Brunei, Vanuatu, Labuan, and the Cayman Islands. He owned shell companies within shell companies. The NYPD had a thick dossier on him and two dozen cartons of discovery material—someone had made DeFoggi a personal hobby—but Frank was right: the old man had never seen the inside of a courtroom, even though he'd been implicated in hundreds of crimes throughout his long life.

The logical explanation was that DeFoggi had enjoyed the full backing and protection of the CIA, but the Agency claimed to have no knowledge of him. It was just a coincidence, apparently, that he'd tended to pop up in the same far-flung countries in which major CIA covert ops were taking place at the time.

He first blipped onto the radar during the late-sixties, in Vietnam, where he was one of the bright young assassins in the Green Berets tasked with implementing the Phoenix Program. Going by the name Heinrich "Hank" Defoggi in those days, he was an Eastern European Lodge Act enlistee who rose to the rank of Master Sergeant in US Army Special Forces before the end of his ninth (and final) tour of duty.

He took the name Hendrick during the seventies, when he became a traveling stage magician known as Hendrick the Mystifier. The act was a weird combo of faked psychokinesis demonstrations and very real feats of masochism. He bent spoons and hammered railroad spikes up his nose; he made wristwatches run backwards and stuck knitting needles through his cheeks (which explained all those deep pockmarks Sabina had seen...). A muscular, leggy female in a sparkly blue bikini and stiletto heels usually assisted him during his performances. Some of the tricks, like the spoon bending, required manipulating objects with sheer brute force via sleight-of-hand—hence DeFoggi's enduring sexual penchant for female bodybuilders like the bullet-riddled Marzanna.

Hendrick the Mystifier also, somewhat tellingly, performed as an escape artist. In 1971, he was in Bolivia getting strapped into a straightjacket, wrapped in chains, and locked inside a iron box that was then dumped from a boat into the deepest part of Lake Titicaca a week before the coup that brought dictator Hugo Banzer Suárez to power. In 1972, around the time of the Watergate burglaries, he barely escaped electrocution from the Electrified Mummy Lid Torture Board at a promotional event performed free to the public in front of the Washington Monument. In 1973, he spent 43 minutes encased in a block of ice in Santiago, Chile, just two days before the September 11th coup d'état that overthrew the socialist government of President Salvador Allende. He was seen defying death in Angola in 1975, in Afghanistan and Iran in 1979, and in El Salvador in 1980.

Then, when Reagan and Bush took office in 1981, DeFoggi got into the savings and loan business, operating under the *nom de guerre* Loyal Blankfien. (Sabina couldn't stop herself from mentally adding a *d* to the end of that surname every time she saw it.) Somehow, he raised enough money to buy a controlling stake in a failing savings and loan—the Ohio Federal Union Community Thrift—where he soon appointed himself president and CEO. The thrift had been offering interest-bearing checking accounts and modest fixed-rate financing to low-wealth individuals in Cleveland and Cincinnati. Blankfien got in there and rallied the troops, ordering them to offer adjustable-rate mortgages to anyone with a pulse, while doing whatever it took to get them approved—falsifying credit scores, revising income statements upward, losing the paperwork from past bankruptcies… *anything.* Manicurists in Cincinnati started making six-figure incomes. "Landscape architects" who mowed lawns for a living could suddenly afford McMansions overlooking Lake Erie in the tony suburbs of Cleveland. With an assist from a major Wall Street firm, Blankfien immediately turned around and sold those subprime loans to Ginnie Mae, Freddie Mac, and Fannie Mae. The default rate on those loans verged on the spectacular, but since the US government owned the paper by the time they went sour, that really wasn't Blankfien's concern.

Where Blankfien tripped up was with his self-dealing commercial real estate loans. He approved a $100 million loan to two of his business partners for a real estate development project that went bust and then—as if to underscore his lapses into control fraud and the breaching of his fiduciary duties as CEO—he gave *himself* a loan for a cool $30 million to cover his supposed losses. He also kept a slew of construction loans on the thrift's books that all went into default. By 1985, the Ohio Federal Union Community Thrift was so hopelessly overextended that it collapsed. Claims by Ohio depositors drained the state's deposit insurance funds and cost taxpayers $1.3 billion dollars. (The Savings and Loan Crisis would eventually cost American taxpayers around $130 billion dollars—making DeFoggi/Blankfien responsible for a mere one percent of that total.) Loyal Blankfien was fined $50,000 *in absentia* for his role in the thrift's collapse. The $130 million that he lent to himself and his friends went missing, never to be recovered.

A few months later, Hendrick the Mystifier was playing to packed houses in Nicaragua, where he was so popular that he had to fly back by private jet for return engagements from his new home in Arkansas every few weeks. He and Ollie North were seen on numerous occasions shooting pool and eating boa constrictor tacos in a strip club named *Luna Chicas* in Managua. ("The same place where Lars von Loon found the prostitutes for his pictures?" Sabina wondered aloud.) In 1987, Hendrick the Mystifier was summoned to testify against North during the televised hearings of a joint congressional committee looking into the Iran-Contra Affair, but he starred in his own disappearing act when the day arrived, failing to show up.

The next three decades held more of the same, but on a much grander scale.

Using the creepy alias Buster Fuldbottom, Deffogi created a shell corporation in Grenada called Donkey Prong Industries that went on an acquisition binge, buying up abandoned storefronts in economically disadvantaged areas of the US and turning them into a nationwide chain of check-cashing stores that specialized in payday lending. Donkey Prong's payday loans, with annual interest rates averaging 730 percent, skirted state and federal laws that applied only to banking. The profits from those loans, stripped from the poor and the desperate, piled up in an obscene way during the Clinton years. DeFoggi then redeployed those profits to create an online lending company, QuickFixLoans.com (registered to his transgender alter ego, Celeste Greengrass, as a limited liability company in Delaware called Loosh Online LLC), which got into home mortgages in a big way right around the time that Bush the Younger took office.

Working with the same major Wall Street firm that had assisted Loyal Blankfien during his years with the Ohio Federal Union Community Thrift, QuickFixLoans.com did a rinse and repeat of OFUCT's history: ramping up a slew of no down payment / interest-only loans with impossible balloon payments due in five years to unqualified home buyers during the early noughties; selling those subprime loans to Freddie Mac and Fannie Mae before they went into default (while also bundling the worst of those loans into mortgage-backed securities and selling them to gullible managers of municipal pension funds); bleeding the company dry with bogus construction loans to a pool of business associates with their own offshore shell corporations; and watching the whole venture collapse into a sea of red ink along with the rest of the big banks in 2008. The major difference between the two swindles was that QuickFixLoans.com was one of the hot IPOs of 2006, a publicly traded company (QFIX – Nasdaq) with thousands of shareholders to defraud.

DeFoggi really knew what he was doing by then. Not only did he perfectly orchestrate the rise and fall of QuickFixLoans.com to coincide with the general market collapse of 2008 (so he wouldn't stand out, or assume too much blame), but he also had the gall to start a hedge fund—the Quantum Event Horizon Fund, managed by the soon-to-be-notorious Heindrik DeFoggi—that built up a huge short position against QFIX (his own company, unbeknownst to the SEC) in late-2007, just prior to the collapse of Bear Stearns and the global financial meltdown that followed. DeFoggi closed his short positions in October 2008, becoming a billionaire in the process.

In the years since, DeFoggi's slimy tentacles had been seen dipping into all kinds of deep, dark money pools in which there was something very nasty circling underneath: money laundering for the Iranians and the Sinaloa Cartel, profiteering from the Libor-rate fixing coming out of London, trafficking opium and rare earth minerals out of Afghanistan via a fleet of aircraft based in West Africa, and so on.

One detail in the dossier stood out: DeFoggi had fathered a child with one of his magic act assistants in the mid-seventies, a mildly autistic boy named Nicholai, who was currently the acting director of cybersecurity at the US Department of Health and Human Services. Under a slightly different name, Nicholai also happened to be a convicted child-porn peddler. Sabina remembered reading about that while she was revamping the Shitbirds.com site. So had old Maggot Face kidnapped and tortured them as an act of filial devotion? Had he done it to halt the launch of Shitbirds.com in a twisted bid to defend the privacy of his pedophile son?

That was certainly one plausible theory, but DeFoggi had plenty of other good reasons to want Shitbirds.com preemptively shut down—him and all the other rich white-collar criminals out there, thinking they were above the law. And that was what Sabina and Frank would soon discover:

Heindrik DeFoggi hadn't acted alone.

MacDuff was still in surgery when they finished up at the police station. A receptionist at Mount Sinai said his condition had been upgraded to stable—*whatever that meant*—but a decision had been made to keep him in an induced coma for a few days to reduce the intracranial pressure from his head injuries. Sabina decided to go home and check in on him at the hospital first thing in the morning. She didn't feel right about staying in MacDuff's penthouse without him, but she needed some of her things—like her laptop and her iPhone—so she asked Frank to go with her to pick up her stuff. She didn't want to do it alone. They both knew that DeFoggi had gotten into MacDuff's place to steal Démerder's cube, and they didn't know what they'd find when they got there.

To be safe, Frank had a couple of friendly NYPD detectives accompany them—Kunstler and Palast—two big, brave veterans of the force who would have no problem pointing their guns at any bad guys that needed to be taken down.

When they got to MacDuff's building, the usual security guard at the front desk, Ernesto, told them that the Department of Homeland Security had been there all morning, carting stuff out of MacDuff's penthouse and Limelight Research Capital's corporate headquarters. The security guards had tried to stop them, but the DHS team had warrants—and machine guns.

"They pointed their *pinche* guns at our heads right when they came in," Ernesto said. "We didn't have no choice, so we gave 'em the keys. I tried calling Mister Everton and Mister Geng, but no one picked up."

"No. They wouldn't have…." Sabina explained that MacDuff had been abducted and tortured and was now lying in a coma at Mount Sinai Hospital—and Ron Geng was dead.

"*Shit!*" said Ernesto, slapping the desk with his open palm. "I *knew* those DHS guys weren't acting straight! I should've called the cops."

"That could've turned into a citywide clusterfuck," said Detective Kunstler. "We're supposed to cooperate with those guys—and we didn't know about the kidnapping until this afternoon."

"Besides," said Frank, "if they hadn't stolen the cube from MacDuff, we might not've found him… or Sabina here."

"If only they'd stolen it sooner," Sabina sighed. "I might not've gotten the anal probe."

"Wait, this was an alien abduction?" Ernesto asked with a sincerity born of watching too many *X-Files* episodes. "Are the Grays tied in with the Department of Homeland Security?"

"We're not at liberty to say," Detective Palast deadpanned. "Can you show us where they went?"

"Just let me get the keys…."

"Grab my iPhone while you're at it," Sabina called after him. She was assuming it was still in the Faraday-caged locker behind the front desk.

It was. She had about five hundred text and email messages to scroll through.

The first stop on Ernesto's tour was Limelight's corporate offices, which had been gutted. Every last server and desktop computer was gone. Ditto for the laptops and phones. Even the wiring had been ripped from the walls. All the employees had already left the building. Ernesto said a few, like Sergei, had been led away in handcuffs, but most had walked out on their own.

"You guys have to find Sergei," Sabina told the detectives. "He knows as much about what Limelight was doing as me or MacDuff. They'll kill him."

"We'll talk to our liaisons at DHS," said Detective Palast. "In the meantime, does anyone have his address?"

Sabina shrugged and looked to Ernesto, who said: "He lives right here. On the forty-third floor."

"Let's go up there," said Frank.

"I don't have his key. I'll have to go back down and get it."

"Then we'll meet you in the penthouse. Sabina, you still have your keys, right?"

"I was naked. Remember, Frank? I don't have anything."

Sabina was still wearing the baggy green jumpsuit and neon pink Crocs they'd given her at the police station. She looked like a hospital orderly—or an escapee from a mental institution.

Ernesto handed over the key to the elevator and bid them *adiós* as he jogged toward the stairwell.

When Sabina mentioned to the detectives that the elevator doors opened right into MacDuff's living room, they drew their guns.

It was a long ride up.

MacDuff's place was trashed. No surprise there, after seeing Limelight's headquarters, but still, it was like a punch to Sabina's guts when she saw what they'd done. All the furniture had been overturned, the upholstery knifed open, stuffing vomited everywhere like chewed up clouds. Orchids and bonsai trees lay in muddy ruins on the Turkish rugs with their straggly (and somehow pathetic) roots exposed, their antique vases shattered. Worst of all, someone had taken a can of piss yellow spray paint to the beautiful wooden wall above the fireplace and written:

WHOSE THE SHITBIRD NOW?

The vengeful dickheads couldn't even spell.

Sabina walked straight to the home office—the last place she could remember leaving her laptop. If it had been in there, it was gone now. So was the Kandinsky above MacDuff's burlwood desk. She idly wondered if it had ended up in Maggot Face's mansion, or some other evil art maven's lair. The desk itself had been hacked to kindling, the state-of-the-art computer and monitors from its hidden innards stolen, nowhere to be found. Books were strewn in piles across the floor, covers torn off, pages ripped and flung. Obviously, the DHS crew had no respect for literature. Some of the book piles were even topped with gross coils of human poo.

Could they get any more disgusting? Sabina asked herself as the smell wafted through her sinuses and down her throat, making her gag.

She got the hell out of there.

"I'm heading up to the bedroom," she told the detectives.

"We'll go with you," said Detective Kunstler.

They went up the stairs ahead of her, guns still drawn. The bedroom turned out to be relatively untouched, aside from Sabina's bras and panties, which had been laid out in a snowflake pattern on top of the bed. There was something mega-creepy about that, but Sabina couldn't put her finger on what it was, precisely, until she looked closer and saw the tiny pearlescent blobs of jism.

Ew. Her strangely arranged underthings had been the occasion for a circle jerk. She wouldn't be wearing *those* again.

"Speaking as a US taxpayer, I don't feel like I'm getting a good bang-for-my-buck from the Department of Homeland Security," Sabina complained.

"Oh, we're getting banged, all right… they spend over a hundred million a year on undercover ops alone," Detective Kunstler informed her. "But I can't see how jerking off on a lady's undies helps them find terrorists."

"I'm not so sure these guys are DHS," said Detective Palast.

"They seem more like Satan worshippers," Frank observed. "Or Iggy Pop during his formative years."

"Let's get out of here," Sabina said. "I can't take this. I don't even want my clothes now."

"They're not clothes anymore," Detective Palast told her. "They're evidence. I'll get a forensic team in here to collect the DNA. Then we'll see if we can get a match to anyone on the DHS payroll."

"Why would they be that stupid?" Frank asked him.

"Maybe they're not stupid," he answered. "Maybe they just think that no matter what they do, they won't have to face justice."

Looking at her soiled underwear, Sabina said, "I vote for stupid."

So Shitbirds.com was gone. Every computer it had been on had been stolen. There wasn't a trace of it left anywhere. On the way back to her apartment with Frank and the detectives, Sabina mentally berated herself for not insisting that MacDuff launch the website before they started advertising it. The site would have been safe if they'd beamed it up to Limelight's private satellite. No wonder Maggot Face wanted to know if Shitbirds.com had been uploaded to the server farms. If it had, sending the DHS team to break into MacDuff's penthouse and Limelight's headquarters would have been beside the point.

Sergei hadn't been home, of course. His apartment had been ransacked just like MacDuff's (minus the sticky panty collage). Even if they were pretenders, those DHS guys were certainly thorough. Like old Maggot Face, they knew exactly what they were after.

So just how big did this anti-Shitbirds conspiracy go? Sabina wondered. *And what had they done with poor Sergei?*

Poor, painfully shy little Sergei, with his bristly buzzcut, his bowel-troubled eagle's face, and his bitten fingernails. Sabina couldn't help thinking that he wouldn't last very long under torture—although he was Russian, so maybe he'd already had some practice.

"Will you guys be looking at the surveillance tapes of whoever took Sergei?" Sabina asked the detectives from the backseat of their unmarked police car.

"Already on it," Detective Kunstler told her.

"Because I know a guy with really good biometric surveillance software, if you need some help."

"Démerder?" Frank asked Sabina.

"Yeah. Gordon. He can identify anyone in, like, fifteen minutes."

"We've got that, too," Detective Kunstler told her. "The NYPD's still cruisin' along on the big budgets from the Bloomberg and Giuliani years. And Weiner knows better than to make any cuts."

"Your department's gotten fat off a manufactured climate of fear and hysteria. You know that, right?" Frank said to them.

"It's either that or all those burritos from Chipotle," Detective Palast said agreeably, patting his big stomach.

"So when you guys find Sergei, will you call me?" Sabina made a point of saying *when*, not *if*, as if she could make it happen just by using the proper semantics.

"We'll call Frank. How about that?"

Frank nodded at her, indicating that she might be overstepping some invisible boundaries if she didn't back down.

"Okay. That works. Thanks, you guys…" she said. "I know I must be sounding a little hyper right now, but I just got butt-raped with a cattle prod not too long ago, and I'm thinking that if the same thing happens to Sergei, it's Game Over."

"We'll do our best to find him," Detective Palast assured her. "We don't want anyone getting butt-raped, ma'am."

Frank started sniggering.

"Oh, you think it's funny…. Just wait until it happens to you!"

"What makes you think Maleeka hasn't done it already?" Frank asked her. "Without the high-voltage, of course."

Sabina slapped Frank's veiny old hand, saying, "You're an even bigger perv than I thought!"

"My joy is true…" he sang through a crooked little grin.

The detectives dropped them off at the curb in front of Sabina's apartment building. They stayed out in the car while the doorman let Frank in to check things out. He came back a few minutes later and gave them the all clear. As the detectives drove away, Sabina breathed out a sigh of relief. At least her apartment hadn't been violated. But someone had her keys. She'd have to get the locks changed right away.

Frank asked her if she wanted to spend the night in Montclair. "You might feel safer at our house," he volunteered. "We have plenty of room."

"Thanks. That's really sweet of you," said Sabina, "but I'll feel safe enough if I can just get a locksmith over here tonight."

Frank waited with her while she made the call. A locksmith's shop on Broadway was open late. The guy on the phone said he could send someone right over. Manhattan could still be convenient like that at odd hours. Frank insisted on staying until the locksmith showed up and the work was done.

"You're the most chivalrous old perv I know," Sabina told him on his way out the rekeyed office door. *($765 for half an hour's work. Goddam Medeco locks... FUCK!)* She kind of hated to see him go. Frank was good company. Sabina's eyes welled with tears—despite her natural inclination not to appear sentimental. Her voice even cracked a little when she said:

"Thanks, Frank. You literally saved my ass today."

"You should be thanking your friend, Gordon, not me," said Frank, giving her a hug. "But I did what I could. People like us have to look after each other. We're confronting some sinister forces out there in the world."

"Y'think?"

"I *know*... but we don't have to give in to them." Frank was looking a little red-eyed and blue himself. "Now go get some sleep." He kissed Sabina on the forehead. "And no bad dreams, okay?"

Even though she was mentally prepared for it, seeing MacDuff lying comatose in a hospital bed still tore at Sabina's heart. He looked so pathetic and damaged, more like a mishandled corpse than a living, breathing human being. The lower part of his face was covered by an oxygen mask, the left side of his head had been shaved and stitched up with ugly black thread, and his eyes were so bruised and swollen that it didn't seem like they'd ever open again.

She kissed his forehead the same way Frank had kissed hers the night before. "Hey, it's me..." she said, but there was no response. The MacDuff she knew was somewhere else. His confidence and strength and cowboy charm were entirely absent.

MacDuff's left arm was immobilized, taped to a gauze-covered board with an IV cannula dripping fluid into a vein in his wrist. His right arm was free, however, so Sabina pulled up a chair and sat holding his hand, trying not to cry as she talked to him in a quiet voice:

"I don't know if you heard," she said, "but the police got our kidnappers. Shot 'em dead. I'm not sure how you feel about that, but it came as a relief to me. Although I think it might've been too easy a way out for the bitch that did this to you. I would've liked it better if she'd been skull-fucked by polar bears.

"Speaking of which, James made the cover of the *New York Post* the other day. So that worked out. They had a really cute shot of Fresno licking his face. His books are all in the Top 50 on Amazon today. I thought I might read a few to you while you're here—to help pass the time—so I brought along my Kindle. Although I have some other books on there about Gordon that I thought we might read first. I mean, according to Frank, Gordon saved our lives—so it might be nice to get to know him better.

"His brother, Derek, has written two big fat novels about him. But you knew that, right? You've already read those, I'll bet. But I haven't, and I'm the one making the decisions around here until you wake up, so if you don't want to read them again, well... *tough*. Wake the hell up, if you don't like it.

"Sorry. That sounded mean. It's just that I love you and I'm pissed off that this happened. And I know you probably don't want to hear this, but in a way, it's your fault. If you would've uploaded the Shitbirds site before we started advertising it, like I told you to, then this might not've happened. But no... you wanted to go for 'Shock and Awe' you said. I should've reminded you how fucking useless 'Shock and Awe' ended up being in Iraq. Now we've got ISIS and a whole lot of other problems coming out of the Middle East, thanks to 'Shock and Awe'—which was really just terrorism under another name. Maybe from here on out, whenever you're unsure about something, you should ask yourself: 'What would George W. Bush do?' And then do the exact fucking opposite.

"Okay, I'll start reading now. No more editorializing. But just remember... I love you, okay? I'm here for you. And I'm not going anywhere until you wake up."

The first book in the series was *Crash Gordon and the Mysteries of Kingsburg*. It started out with a quote from Aldous Huxley:

Maybe this world is some other planet's hell.

"Picture six-year-old Gordon Swansson skulking along a shag carpeted hallway in the predawn stillness of a suburban ranch house..." Sabina read aloud. She kept right on reading for the next few hours, until her voice started to give out. She took a break at that point—got something to eat, watched the TV up near the ceiling across from MacDuff's bed, sucked on a Thayer's Slippery Elm Throat Lozenge until it dissolved to a razor-edged oval thin enough to be chomped between her molars—and then she read some more. She maintained that pattern for the next three days, until both *Crash Gordon* books had been read to the end.

What a fucking head-trip....

If Gordon's little brother was to be believed, Gordon had grown up in a CIA mind control program known as Project MONARCH. It was designed to shatter a child's psyche into multiple personalities—or *alters*—by using drugs and torture to get the young subject into a disassociated state. The compartmentalized alters could then be hypnotically programmed for superhuman tasks like assassinations or remote viewing or, in Gordon's case, *remote influencing*, which was something like telekinesis and mind reading combined. It sounded like pure science fiction, but both books backed everything up with historical facts—from news stories about the CIA's MKULTRA program and Freedom of Information Act documents and so forth... so who knew, really?

Sabina still thought it was all pretty far-fetched. According to the second book, *Crash Gordon and the Revelations from Big Sur*, Gordon had stopped a Project MONARCH girl from assassinating Mikhail Gorbachev by giving her a remote orgasm. It was like something Terry Southern might have written: *Deep Throat* meets *Dr. Strangelove.*

The next time she saw Gordon she planned to ask him to remote-orgasm her right there in Bryant Park, just to see how he'd handle it.

Another weird thing was that James Marrsden was a major character in both *Crash Gordon* books. Apparently, James and Gordon had been buddies from childhood on up through their twenties.

Who said truth was stranger than fiction? In this case, fiction was plenty strange enough.

She wondered if Gordon was also a character in the books written by James. She'd find out soon enough. She did a Kindle search on Amazon and downloaded James' first book, *Vampirism Made Easy*. As the story was told in *Crash Gordon and the Revelations from Big Sur*, Gordon and James had shared a house in Cambria while James was writing that book; his agent later sold the film rights to Disney for the tidy demonic sum of $666,000.

MacDuff didn't seem to be in any immediate need of a bedtime story involving vampires, so Sabina decided to watch TV for a while instead. She clicked through the channels with the hospital bed remote until she landed on *Real Time with Bill Maher*. Maher had a panel of guests on his show that included Sabina's favorite journalists, Matt Taibbi and Glenn Greenwald. They were talking about the latest NSA whistleblower, a guy named Milton Anton Newcombe (now bunking at the Ecuadorian Embassy in London with Julian Assange), who had supplied the independent journalists at First Look Media with classified documents revealing that the Snowden Avalanche had been a covert operation undertaken by the US government to demoralize and financially exploit its primary enemy—its own citizenry.

Holy Fuckeroo! A lot had happened since she'd been abducted.

There was a woman sitting between Taibbi and Greenwald that Sabina didn't recognize. (*Laura Poitras, maybe?* She wasn't sure.) The woman was saying: "What's astounding to me is that there's only one crime in post-9/11 Washington that has been prosecuted to the full extent of the law. And it's not for committing perjury while testifying before Congress, as we now know ex-NSA chief Keith B. Alexander did while testifying to the Senate Intelligence Committee. And it's not for kidnapping, torture, or being responsible for the deaths of prisoners in an extralegal prison system. We're the world's only superpower now... why should we abide by the outmoded rules of the Geneva Conventions, right? And it's certainly not for destroying evidence of a crime, which those on the inside of our national security state, and the jolly cannibals on Wall Street, seem to do with impunity. No, the only crime that is prosecuted by our government, in a terrifyingly relentless way, is whistleblowing. If you dare to tell the American people something true about what their government is doing to them, you can expect to be hounded to the ends of the earth."

The studio audience erupted into applause. Then the other panelists chimed in with some pithy comments. Following that, Bill Maher showed a clip, for ironic effect, of Michael Hayden—the former director of the NSA and the CIA—giving a speech on cybersecurity to the Bipartisan Policy Center in Washington:

"If and when our government grabs Edward Snowden, and brings him back here to the United States for trial, what does this group do?" Hayden asked rhetorically. "Nihilists, anarchists, activists, Lulzsec, Anonymous, and all the twenty-somethings who haven't talked to the opposite sex in five or six years... they may want to come after the US government, but frankly, you know, the dot-mil stuff is about the hardest target in the United States. So if they can't create great harm to dot-mil, who are they going after? Who for them are the World Trade Centers? The World Trade Centers, as they were for al-Qaeda."

Sabina was so focused on the television that she almost missed MacDuff squeezing her hand.

"Hey! Are you awake?" she asked him.

MacDuff's eyelids clenched and then opened slowly. He tried to speak, but he could only huff.

"You can't talk," Sabina told him. "Your jaw's broken. They wired it shut. But it's so good to see you! I can't believe this!"

MacDuff seemed to be making a great effort just to stay awake. He made a scribbling motion with his free hand.

"What? You want something to write on?" Sabina guessed. She looked around the room. "I don't think we have any paper. *Oh, wait!*" She picked up her Kindle and tapped her finger on the Search box. A keypad appeared on the screen. She held it up in front of him.

"Here," she said brightly, "you can type."

MacDuff grasped the right side of the Kindle and started typing with his thumb. The letters appeared slowly because his hand was shaky and he was trying to hit the right keys. Eventually, Sabina was able to read:

less talk more action

Then:

have serge launch shitbrds

And finally:

i love you s

After the s, MacDuff's hand dropped from the Kindle and he closed his eyes again. Thrilled that he didn't seem to be brain-damaged, Sabina pushed the button to call a nurse. Then she lowered MacDuff's oxygen mask so she could kiss him. He smiled at that. The smile grew wider when she told him that everything was going to be all right.

Was it wrong of her not to mention that Sergei had been kidnapped, along with all their computer files for Shitbirds.com? She felt a little guilty about that, but y'know... *fuck it.*

The man had suffered enough.

The text message from Gordon came encrypted via something called Red Phone, an app that Sabina didn't even know she had. When her iPhone decrypted it, the text read:

Can you meet me today at the usual spot?
One o'clock. Revelations to come...

Sabina didn't like the idea of leaving MacDuff's side, but when he woke up in his hospital bed an hour later and she told him about the message, he waggled his fingers bye-bye and made a shooing gesture—his way of telling her to go.

Gordon and Guy were waiting for her at a round green table in a sunlit patch of Bryant Park. Guy perked up and started wagging his tail as soon as he saw her coming around the carousel. Gordon waved to her and stood up.

"I promised myself that the next time I saw you, I'd ask you to give me a remote orgasm right here in front of everybody," Sabina said in lieu of a more traditional greeting. "But now I'm feeling a little shy about that."

"I take it you read my brother's books," Gordon said, giving her a hug.

"Ooob!" said Sabina, fake-shivering. "I'm feeling a tingle already."

"I can't help it. I have that effect on most women," Gordon joked. He seemed to know that his doomy urban Viking look was never going to be a big hit with the ladies.

Guy let out a bark, as if to mock his master's suave pretending. Then he made a funny bunnyish leap into Sabina's arms. She caught him around his ribcage and gave his furry neck a hug.

"Guy-guy! How've you been?"

The big white dog wriggled in a way that told her he was feeling frisky and fine. Gordon commanded Guy to sit in a stern voice.

Guy sat.

"He was on the verge of humping your leg," Gordon explained. And indeed, Sabina saw that Guy was rather cheerfully *in flagrante*. He looked over his shoulder at Gordon with his pink tongue lolling, as sweet and innocent as any child movie starlet who would grow up to snort mounds of coke, star in an X-rated music video directed by Terry Richardson, and convert to Scientology on her eighteenth birthday so she could marry Tom Cruise.

"I guess we're both feeling pretty horned up today," Sabina said. She sat down in one of the park's green metal chairs and rubbed the scruff of Guy's neck. A spontaneous boner was no cause for offense between friends.

Gordon sat across the table from her, saying, "Thanks for coming today. How's MacDuff?"

"He'll live. He's pretty messed up at the moment, but the doctors say he'll be good as new in a few months."

"That's great to hear."

"I guess we both owe you a big Thank You. You saved our lives, according to Frank."

"I just told him where you were. He did the rest."

"That was pretty crucial, though… telling him where we were."

"You're just lucky that idiot was greedy enough to steal the cube. It has a Tesla lithium-ion battery pack inside it, so the GPS system stayed active while it was being transported. Plus, I saw his face, so I was able to identify him with my surveillance software."

"How'd you see his face?"

"Surveillance cameras inside the cube, on all six sides. If you'd looked closely you would've seen them. They look like little obsidian chips embedded in the meteorite's metal."

"Oh shit…" Sabina said. And then she said it again: "*Oh shit!* Does that mean you see everything the cube sees?"

"Pretty much. Remember when I told you that I make it my business to learn about my so-called patrons? Well, that's how I do it. The cube always has to have access to the Internet so it can sell itself on eBay and communicate with me. It's in the contract."

"Did you see us on the couch that one time, having sex?"

"Nearly scorched my eyeballs," Gordon joked. "But don't worry… I've already erased that. You guys won't be showing up as the latest celebrity sex scandal on TMZ."

"Now I'm really embarrassed."

"Don't be. I had no intention of spying on you, personally, Sabina. It's just the way the cube was built."

She said, "Well, I guess I was doing a little spying on you, too, so it's only fair. By the way, how much of the stuff about you in those *Crash Gordon* books is true? Some of it? All of it? None of it?"

"How about 'All of the above'?"

"Meaning what?"

"Meaning it's all fiction, but someone—I forget who—once said that fiction is the lie that tells the truth. So it's all true, but some parts are more true than others."

"Are you always this evasive?" she asked him.

"Would it help if I told you my brother isn't a writer? He's an architect out in San Diego. He has hobbies—he builds furniture, he brews his own beer, and he's very proud of his homemade kegerator—but he doesn't write books."

"Wait… so does that mean *you* wrote the books?"

"Why would I? I already go around feeling like a fictional character in a fraudulent universe. Writing a book about myself would make that feeling ten times worse. So no. All I'm saying is that my brother the author is just as fictional as all the other characters in the *Crash Gordon* series."

"So I'm confused… who wrote those books then?"

"*I don't know.* I've been trying to figure that out for the last dozen years. It's someone who knows me, obviously. They have way too many details about my life down right for them *not* to know me. On the other hand, I have no memory at all of Project MONARCH."

"You wouldn't, according to the books. Your mind has been split off into compartmentalized alter personalities, remember? Maybe one of your *alters* wrote the books."

"That's a scary thought…." Gordon smiled at Sabina's ingenuity. "My theory is that this world is a *holomovement*—a three-dimensional holographic projection progressing in linear time—that we all subconsciously co-create from our innermost thoughts, making each of us the unwitting author of our own destiny. And in some cases, like mine, that unwitting author idea might apply on more than one level."

"Really? So this is what you wanted to talk to me about? Your California hippie PhD in 'Blowing Smoke Up the Collective Ass of Humanity'?" Sabina was quoting directly from one of the books.

"Good memory," said Gordon. "But no, that wasn't my plan at all. I have something I want to show you—only we can't talk about it here. There's a good chance we're being spied on."

"No shit. So where can we go?"

"Would you mind coming up to my apartment?"

"Sure," said Sabina, "but I'm not up for any bong hits, just so you know…."

JUDGEMENT

Sabina recognized the sinuously jangling music coming from inside Gordon's apartment even before he opened the front door. It was The Brian Jonestown Massacre. Most people only knew them by their song "Straight Up and Down"—which had been the opening theme music for the long-running HBO series, *Boardwalk Empire*—but Sabina liked almost everything the band put out. The song currently playing—"Memory Camp"—was from their *Revelation* album, one of her favorites. She ranked it right up there with their *Tepid Peppermint Wonderland* retrospective.

"The music interferes with electronic eavesdropping," Gordon explained, sliding his key into the lock. "Besides," he said as the door swung open, "Sergei likes it loud."

"Limelight's Sergei?" Sabina asked. And then there he was, in all his bristly buzzcut glory: sitting in an Aeron chair in front of a wall loaded with computers and monitors and other electronic devices that Sabina couldn't immediately identify—all of them artfully arranged on bird's eye maple desks and shelving at the far end of the loft-like apartment.

Sergei spun around in the chair and waved a cheery hello. He seemed uncharacteristically relaxed and animated. Maybe Sergei and Gordon had bonded. Sabina ran right over to him with Guy, off his leash, chasing at her heels.

"Sergei! God, I'm so glad you're okay!"

"Yes! No torture for Sergei. I was—how you say?—*lucky ducky*."

"Did Gordon find you?"

"Yes! Gordon, he very smart guy. He call lawyers and say, 'Listen, bitches, you give me Sergei or shit come down on all your faces.'"

"Well, that's not exactly how it happened…" Gordon said, coming up behind them.

"You scare piss in all their pants," Sergei elaborated.

"I just made them aware of what had happened to Heindrik DeFoggi—and then we cut a deal."

"I'm not following…" said Sabina. She could barely hear Sergei and Gordon above the music, but she was pretty sure they weren't making much sense, anyway. "It sounds like you got set free *after* us," she said to Sergei. "So why didn't you get tortured, like me and MacDuff?"

"They want to torture. They say, 'Sergei, we spit on your balls and put in lamp socket if you don't tell us about Shitbirds.com.' But I say, 'Look guys, what is this Shitbirds? I don't know it. But now you have super-fast Limelight computers. I show you how Sergei trade stocks with super-cool algorithms. Don't you want to be rich, like MacDuff?'"

"And they went for that?" Sabina asked.

"Oh, for sure! They say, 'Okay, Sergei, you hook us up and we won't fry your balls.' First day, I make two-hundred-forty-three thousands of dollars. Is good day in market, so no torture; Sergei can still make sex with American MILFs without electric sperm shocking their big wet vaginas. But next day, Gordon call and lawyers start freaking out. They take Sergei to library steps and say, 'You stay here, between two lions—"

"—Patience and Fortitude—" Gordon fills in.

"—then they run away like scared little bitches. Then Gordon come and say, 'Hey, Sergei, I'm friend of Sabina.' Then I come here."

Sabina said to Gordon, "I still don't get how you found him."

"Let's go into that room over there, where it's quieter, and I'll explain everything." Gordon pointed to a copper-colored door with rounded edges and a spoked wheel for a handle, like the door on an old submarine. It was set into a curving, copper-covered wall reminiscent of Frank Gehry's museum project in Bilbao. Sergei turned back to his monitors and started typing away on a computer keyboard.

"Sergei, aren't you coming?" Sabina asked him. She didn't want him to feel excluded.

"No guys, you go talk. Sergei has to install new Python flup so Django can use FastCGI. Right now, is fucking up."

Sabina took a good look at her surroundings as she followed Gordon to the copper door. His apartment had a friendly, funky vibe to it that she really liked. A wall of tall windows overlooked Bryant Park. All the windowsills were lined with lush green houseplants in beautiful hand-glazed ceramic pots: cobalt blue shading into aubergine, jade spiderwebbed with crooked little veins of verdigris, crimson blushing through summer peach. The plants had shed a few leaves onto the pumpkin-colored pine plank floor, which was littered with colorful rubber chew toys. The planks were old and scuffed (mostly by dog claws), but they somehow looked better that way. Near the foyer, there was a tidy open kitchen with rust-colored marble countertops and stainless steel appliances. A wide hallway, lined with bookshelves, probably led to the back bedrooms. And on a concrete pedestal right beside the copper door, she saw a huge black cube—either an exact replica of *A Black Box for Humanity's Redacted History* or the real deal, returned from Maggot Face's mansion.

"Did you get the cube back?" Sabina asked Gordon as he opened the copper door and ushered her into a dimly lit windowless room.

"I did," said Gordon. "Frank helped with that." He closed the door behind them. Everything suddenly got much, much quieter—eerily quiet.

"Wow..." Sabina barely whispered.

Gordon picked up on her unease. "Sorry, I know... it's like the bottom of the ocean in here," he said. "But you get used to it. This whole room is a giant Faraday cage, shielded from electromagnetic radiation. Plus, the floor and the ceiling are suspended and baffled, so no vibrations pass through. We can talk freely in here. No one's listening."

"Not even the cube?"

"I guess you can never be too sure about the cube," he joked. "The police wanted to keep it as evidence, but Frank told them it was my property—even though, contractually, it still belongs to MacDuff. But I don't think he'll mind that I'm taking care of it for him right now. Do you?"

"Not at all," said Sabina. "So tell me how you found Sergei."

"While MacDuff's apartment was being robbed, the cube's surveillance cameras captured images of every person there. I was watching it all happen in real-time. When I fed the images into my surveillance software, names started popping up on my screen almost right away. None of them had criminal records, but almost every one of them had a LinkedIn profile."

"So who were they?"

Sabina's eyes were adjusting to the subdued lighting in the room. She saw a queen-sized bed in one corner with lots of throw pillows and a quilted duvet cover. Just beyond it was an open closet lined with bookshelves. A few feet to the right of the bed, there was a big desk pushed up against the wall with another Aeron chair in front of it. The only thing on the desktop was a silver rectangle with rounded corners and a stylized, upside-down Apple logo in the center: a MacBook of some sort.

"They weren't working for the Department of Homeland Security," Gordon told her, "even though that's what they wanted everyone to believe. They were actually corporate attorneys."

"That's what I thought Sergei said… fucking lawyers!"

"They all work for a big corporate law firm called Bassie, Wouter, Cromwell and Loosh."

"Never heard of 'em."

"Yeah, they like to keep a low profile, but they've done work for some very high-profile clients. Names like SAIC, Booz Allen Hamilton, Palantir Technologies, i2, Raytheon, Oracle, and Northrup Grumman. Are you noticing a pattern there?"

"They're all private defense contractors for the US government?"

"Right. Roughly 70 percent of the US intelligence budget goes to private sector corporations now—well over $50 billion dollars a year—all of it funded by US taxpayers who are, in effect, paying those corporations to spy on them."

"That's incredibly fucked up," Sabina said. "And we're probably paying the tab for those lawyers at Bassie, Hooters and Whatever when those companies get sued for invading our privacy, aren't we?"

"Of course."

"So they're the ones who nabbed Sergei. But why?"

"They were trying to protect their clients from Shitbirds.com. Sergei told me you guys had dirt on every one of those corporations I just mentioned. I've read some of the articles. It's damning stuff."

"What do you mean, you read some of the articles? Shitbirds.com is gone. They stole every computer it was on."

"Not mine. While you and your team were at MacDuff's, revising the Shitbirds website, the cube was wirelessly scooping up everything you guys were doing. According to Sergei, I got about ninety percent of the website intact. He's out there rebuilding the other ten percent right now."

"*Omigod!* That's totally awesome!" Sabina spontaneously gave Gordon a hug. "Your cube fucking rocks!"

"That's what Sergei thought. I guess I named it *A Black Box For Humanity's Redacted History* for a reason."

"I think you just gave me a remote orgasm, after all. Wait 'til MacDuff hears about this!"

"I don't think he'll be too happy if you tell him I've been giving you orgasms."

"You know what I mean…. When can we upload to the satellite?"

"Like I said, we're working on it. But there's a problem. Right now, it's almost a sure bet that we're all under the most intense surveillance that the US government can muster. You, me, Sergei, MacDuff… anything we try to send out is going to be immediately intercepted. Internet, wireless, satellite—it doesn't matter which route we go—if it's a communication from any one of us, they'll scoop it right up and it'll never get to its intended destination. And that's a major problem with Shitbirds.com because we have at least a terabyte's worth of data to upload to the satellite before it can start sending all that data back down to the server farms."

"How long will that take?" Sabina asked.

"The rates fluctuate depending on the satellite's distance from the Earth. And it has to be overhead, so there's only a window of a few hours to send the signal every night. If we do it using the standard satellite radio frequencies, it'll be measured in megabytes per second. It could take days."

"Can't you make it go any faster?"

"Sergei told me that Limelight's satellite uses laser-frequency wavelengths to communicate with the server farms, so the download will be much quicker—a matter of minutes. But they'll be watching for that, so we both decided it's too risky to use a laser communications relay for the upload. We think the best way to go is a slow and stealthy radio frequency upload from somewhere outside the United States. Someplace where, even if it's detected, they might not be able to do anything about it right away."

Sabina said, "The way they've been acting lately, I'm surprised they haven't just blown the satellite right out of the sky."

"They still might get around to it," said Gordon. "But remember, for all the surveillance powers of the US intelligence agencies, they're still bureaucracies. And bureaucracies are inefficient and slow to react. We, on the other hand, can move fast—that's how Edward Snowden got away, and that's how we can get this done. It's our only advantage, really, now that they're onto us."

"So how do we get the Shitbirds website out of the country when everyone's watching us?"

"*We* can't. Everyone directly associated with Limelight is on the No Fly List now. If any of us tried to leave the country, we'd probably be detained without recourse to counsel under US anti-terrorism laws."

"*Great…*" said Sabina, "so now I'm a terrorist."

"You look like one," Gordon kidded her. "But the good news is that we don't have to go anywhere. See that laptop?" He pointed to the MacBook sitting on his desk. "It's a brand new, air gapped MacBook Pro with a ten terabyte solid-state drive. It's never been connected to the Internet and Sergei has already combed through the firmware to make sure there isn't a backdoor already programmed into it from the factory. I paid for it in cash. It's perfectly clean and untraceable. When Sergei finishes the Shitbirds rebuild sometime later tonight, he'll load the whole website onto that laptop disguised as digital photographs."

"Why disguised as photographs?"

"It's an old spy agency trick. They send their data encrypted in porn images, so that if someone intercepts it, all they see are old stills from Ron Jeremy movies—usually from the seventies, when everyone was hairier."

"Yuck," said Sabina.

"Exactly. No one wants to spend any serious time looking at that, so the encrypted data usually goes unnoticed. I have a bunch of images that I retouched for Lars von Loon years ago, when I was at Pier 69—you saw some of them in Laylon's gallery—so we'll be using those. They'll provide the perfect cover, since Lars still has a photo studio in Amsterdam—and that's where the laptop's heading."

"Why Amsterdam?"

"I have an ex-girlfriend there with a satellite dish on top of her, um, coffeeshop." Gordon almost imperceptibly cringed at the association.

Sabina was immediately suspicious. "Is that a euphemism for one of those places that sells marijuana cupcakes?" she asked.

Gordon nodded. "We've stayed in touch, using PGP encryption—which, like the name says, is pretty good privacy—so we can use her PGP public key to encrypt all the data for the satellite access. That way, only she'll be able to decrypt it. I know we can trust her and I'm pretty sure she'll agree to do it for us."

Sabina didn't like hearing that, for some unfathomable reason. "What's her name?" she asked, envisioning some gorgeous nomad.

"Why should that matter?" Gordon asked her back.

"I don't know. Maybe I'm just a little jealous. I know it's irrational, but humor me."

"Her name's Kayleigh. Kayleigh Fuller, from West Virginia. She's a practicing white witch and Buckminster Fuller's niece, among other strange distinctions."

Now Sabina knew what was bugging her: *she* wanted to be the heroine of this story. She didn't want to share it with strangers. *She should be the one launching Shitbirds.com, not some dumb stoner witch across the Atlantic who probably speaks Dutch with an Appalachian accent.*

"And who's taking the laptop to her?" Sabina asked, feeling snippy. *Maybe I can go in disguise,* she thought, although that seemed unlikely. "I'm assuming we can't just FedEx it."

"You're right," said Gordon. "Sending a computer through the mail would be far too risky. We need a courier. Someone we know and trust who travels to Europe so often that she won't be suspected."

They both said the name simultaneously:

"Dominique."

Great. Now they were bringing her glamorous, jet-setting, pseudo-lesbian best friend into the mix.

But then Sabina thought about it and decided it was okay. The world's problems were way too big for any one person to solve: global warming, deforestation, mass extinction, the pervasive corruption of governments, the creation of a global surveillance state that was tilting toward totalitarian ends....

Truly, it takes a village to save the world—

—at the very fucking least.

THE WORLD

Are you here to change the world? Or is the world here to wreak its changes on you?

If you have a choice in the matter, which world will you choose? The one where the caterpillar gets her wings? Or the one where the moth hits the burning candle and goes down in spattered paraffin and flames?

Who will you be? The kinky district attorney who leads his friends to love and world-transforming work? Or the abstaining Mormon whose need to be seen as a good family man leads to an encounter with a flying death machine above the Hudson River? Will your high-frequency trading firm turn you into a folksy cowboy billionaire? Or will your insatiable thirst for Starbucks Mocha Frappuccinos turn you into the world's most beloved fellator of polar bears?

When you're not called upon to be the hero in your own life story, can you play a supporting role? Can you be the gleefully foul-mouthed blonde who puts on a silk camisole with a secret kangaroo pouch designed to hide a MacBook as it rests upright beneath your shoulder blades? And can you then slip into a loose-fitting black cashmere sweater and walk that hidden MacBook across town to an old friend, who will then take it in her carry-on luggage on a flight to Amsterdam's Schiphol International Airport, where she will hand it over to the former girlfriend of an aging Swedish-Norwegian neo-conceptual artist, who will greet the courier with free hash brownies and a pot of strong coffee for her trouble? And can you really trust that neo-conceptual artist's stoner witch ex-girlfriend to do the right thing when she connects the MacBook to her satellite dish and uses a PGP key to decrypt a rather elegantly coded satellite communication program?

(A program, by the way, that was created by an exiled Russian physicist whose balls did not fry, despite his abduction by a cabal of sociopathic corporate lawyers whose law firm was taken to the brink of insolvency two weeks later because they continued to deploy the physicist's proprietary stock trading algorithms to grow the firm's pension fund, algorithms in which the physicist had purposefully hidden a virus that gradually slowed the velocity of the trades so that competing high-frequency trading firms could detect the pattern and start manipulating the other side as the lawyers' stolen computers bought ever-increasing amounts of stock on margin until, in a single catastrophic day, the margin calls grew so huge that the total sum of the assets in the law firm's pension fund was not enough to cover the losses.)

Will your heart be filled with gladness—even if you didn't get to play every role—when the smuggled MacBook does its job over the course of several days, undetected by US intelligence agencies, and the satellite it was communicating with begins firing bursts of laser-encoded data down to various server farms hidden throughout the world, launching a soon-to-be-globally-famous website that exposes the predations of white-collar criminals, everywhere and always, until the end of the Internet as we know it? Or will you still pout and complain that the sucky parts of the world aren't changing fast enough?

Changing the world is a slow and incremental process, requiring the help and goodwill of billions. But if you take a public stand for the public good and follow through with patience and fortitude, you just might win the day.

The world can change for the better.

So can you.

Milton Keynes UK
Ingram Content Group UK Ltd.
UKHW012252040923
428045UK00003B/32/J